THE RIPPER OF MONKSHOOD MANOR

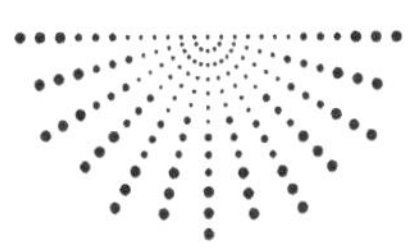

MARY GRAY

Copyright © 2019 by Mary Gray

All rights reserved.

No part of this book may be reproduced in any form or by any electronic or mechanical means, including information storage and retrieval systems, without written permission from the author, except for the use of brief quotations in a book review.

Cover image from Shutterstock.com

Cover design by Cammie Larsen

For Cammie, the person who I knew would get this book.

CHAPTER ONE

WHY, yes, I am cold . . .

But I'm sure I've been colder!

Plus, this floor's not even that hard. I might even go so far as to say it's cushy—what with its pillowy soft spots and water-damaged warps and curves. True, it's dark as a coffin in here, but I'm *sure* tons of light will be coming through that torn, lace curtain covering the window soon . . .

Cough.

Hack.

Cough.

Guess I got a little tickle in my throat.

Sore throats are the worst.

And that squeaking sound? It's *definitely* not a rat feasting on a long forgotten hand bone . . .

Mom always says the Monkshood Manor is very grand—with its arrow-tipped, wrought-iron fencing and mile-long front stairs. The sandstone might be crumbling, and there might be a crazy amount of moss growing on that copper roof, but I'm sure Luther's family will get around to sprucing things up soon.

There sure are a lot of cracks in that stained glass window . . .

And I gotta say, I never expected bright red . . . salsa to be artfully splashed pretty much everywhere.

Maybe it wasn't a good time for me to come?

But Luther *himself* invited me over.

Though, I must admit, this isn't how I expected our first date to go. I was envisioning more of a movie night—with handholding, root beer, and popcorn . . .

Aw, dang, my eyes are growing heavy.

But I *can't* allow myself to nod off now. Must be awake when the boy returns.

I pull the scratchy blanket around my shoulders even tighter. Do my best to ignore its mildewy smell and how the fabric sorta reminds me of sandpaper.

Drip.

Drip.

Sounds like a leaky roof.

DRIP, DRIP, DRIP.

Somewhere in this house, a healthy little puddle grows.

I wonder how long it will take Luther to return.

Wonder if he'll bring hot cocoa.

I'd be lying if I said my butt wasn't sore. Heck, I'd sit in that wingback chair over by the door, but the seat cushion's been taken out.

Found out the hard way earlier.

Maybe Luther's pretending he caught me in an Escape Room. He's been waiting for me to find a way out all on my own.

Hey, I like games; I'll search for clues!

A fine layer of hair coats the floor . . .

Not an electric light anywhere.

I suppose there's that ancient-looking lamp on the other

side of the wall, but I'm pretty sure a family of spiders came and took up residence in that decades ago.

Maybe the light switch is outside?

Near the gargoyles!

I *knew* I should have looked at those cute, unfathomable creatures a little bit longer.

All I know is, Monkshood has gone through several different remodels. So that light switch? It could be anywhere.

I have to check on something, Luther had mysteriously said when he opened the front door. I stepped inside, just grateful to be out of the storm. Umbrella broke during a particularly nasty wind gust, and while I know I should have tried to follow Luther to the rest of the house, the second he left, the foyer door locked closed.

This sure is one sticky floor.

Almost like the time Rosalyn spilled honey all over . . .

Something hard and metallic scrapes from inside the wall.

A key, a key!

I tense with excitement, becoming uber still.

Hinges shriek—they sing a Hallow's Eve song of spooks and gnomes—and with a heavy, malignant sigh, something opens the door.

A figure raises a candelabra high above his head. The silhouette stares down at me like I'm the hunchback of Notre Dame on the floor. The same red and cream scarf haphazardly drapes over Luther's shoulders, though, and the leather patches? On his jacket's elbows? They are to die for.

When a lock of dark hair falls into his eyes, Luther shoves it out of the way, and mmm, mmm. If I were a library book, he could check me out three times in a row.

"Boy, am I sure glad to see you." I raise to my knees, mindful of the fact that I probably look like a bag lady as I rise from the floor. Not in the mood to give up the blanket yet, I add, "Where'd ya go?"

Luther hovers in the doorway four—five—seconds longer.

My stomach rumbles, I age about three years, and he looks both ways before crossing the threshold into the foyer.

When he watches the torn, lace curtain rustling over the window, his face becomes super impassive and smooth. "I am sorry I had to disappear . . ."

"No problemo!"

With a heavy thud, he pulls the mahogany door closed, and when he examines my face, it gives me ample time to study his in return.

Sharp cheekbones and slanted eyes say that his roots are from Europe or Asia somewhere. He's got a little facial hair, but not enough to need a razor, and, aye yai yai, Luther Dvorak's goin' to be the death of me, with his bohemian outfits and missing smile.

He looks at me and *clank!* He drops his candelabra, and his sharp gasp has me rethinking my decision to get a perm two hours ago.

Swiftly stomping out the embers, Luther scoops up his array of candles and stares at my blanket, which has fallen, a little shawl-like, round my arms.

Maybe it's a sacred family heirloom. Maybe it's stitched together with nothing but rib bones and horse hair, so I shrug it off. Not like it's been real comfortable.

Avoiding eye contact, Luther runs a shaky hand through his jet-black hair. "Maybe you should return home . . ."

Well, now, I would be offended if I were a different girl.

But, despite what one would think, I've learned how to defy the odds and stay the course. I lift my chin and throw back my shoulders.

"I am sure your mother will be looking for you soon . . ."

It's like he's gone and forgotten the chemistry between our text convos.

But when his dark, melancholy eyes wander back to me —*all* the way down to my boots—I cross, then re-cross them to give him a little show.

Rubbing a restless hand over his jaw, he looks away real fast. "I am sorry I left you for so long."

"You can make it up to me." I wink. See if he can get what I throw down.

"Dog escaped."

Guess not . . .

Wait . . . "You have a dog?!" I drop the blanket to the floor. "Why didn't you *tell* me? Did you get him home?"

Luther ogles the blanket like it's got razor-sharp teeth and deathly-poisonous tentacles. I've no clue what that's about, but no need for anyone to feel uncomfortable, so I bend down, wad up the whole messy ordeal, and toss the entire thing straight through the chair's hole.

Clink!

Score!

Though Luther's shoulders go so stiff, he has me cringing, too.

He pulls a long skeleton key from his pants pocket, and my heart goes *whumack-whumack*. 'Cause he's *really* going to show me the rest of his home.

Casting a weary glance over his shoulder, Luther murmurs, "Stay close." Ooh, his breath is like black licorice from one of those gourmet candy stores.

It's obvious the boy's pretty down and out, and I'm not real sure why he's so unusually quiet and somber.

So, I take one for the team and give him a quick peck on the cheek.

'Cause I happen to know what it's like to have a weird phobia or two.

CHAPTER TWO

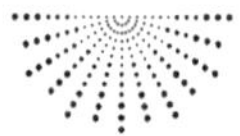

I LIKE A LITTLE "MYSTERY" in a home.

Left, right. Left, left, right.

All these wonky halls make a pretty legit corn maze pattern.

Curtains and beads hang like mighty fine jewelry on the walls, and I gotta say, these candle sconces with the bat skeleton bases kinda remind me of a medieval torture chamber.

Dreamcatchers sashay like they're on the dance floor, and I don't exactly know where the breeze is coming from, but I do get the sense that this is the sort of place where one's quiet in reverence—and whispers.

Truth is, Mom and Rosalyn wouldn't believe me if I described what I saw. Mom's always had these grand illusions that Monkshood's all perfectly decked out, Downton Abbey style, and Rosalyn's too young to form any real opinions of her own.

By the time Luther and I amble through what feels like our seventeenth hall, my ankle bootie catches on a fallen scarf. I almost trip—almost trip!—but, miraculously, I stop myself by grabbing one of those bat sconces on the wall.

Fingers come away a little sticky, but . . .

This sage-y, tobacco-y scent lures me into the nearest room and makes me cough about three times over. 'Til it settles in and smells real nice. The walls bloom out, and we stumble into a gourmet kitchen, the likes of which should be in a historic parade of homes.

Scroll-edged espresso cabinets, a metal rack with pots and pans—enough kitchen space to cook for a ball.

Ooh, and is that a bell system? Guess this place is way more "Downton Abbey" than I originally supposed.

A butler's pantry juts to the right, and fun leaf patterns are carved into the floors.

Mom would *definitely* die for a tour.

White sheets cover just about every counter, and between those and all the garage sale stuff goin' on in the halls, *I* know what the Dvoraks are up to. "You're renovating!"

Pale, turnip-like roots dangle from the rafters, though, as Luther mutely absorbs my words.

I'm not exactly sure "renovating" is the right word.

Vials of murky liquid line one of the counters; fancy wainscoting crisscrosses the length of the walls. And when I catch a whiff of nutmeg, I smile real wide, 'cause I *knew* Luther would know how to treat a girl.

"You're baking!" I smile from ear to ear.

Luther moves aside one of the dangling roots. His cautious movements are reflected by a set of long, vertical mirrors. The mirrors hang over a fireplace in the next room, and the front of the fireplace has these pretty little green tiles.

Never seen such murky mirrors hanging in a front room before . . .

A bejeweled kaleidoscope sits smack-center on a random

table, and a card deck, gramophone, and top hat, of all things, rest a little ostentatiously on the mantle.

It's the mass of ropes hanging in the corner, though, that confuddles me the most.

Is Luther's family renovating . . . or no?

Straightening one of the off-white sheets covering the counter, Luther sends up a plume of dust that would cause anybody to need another lung.

"Sorry." I hack three more times. Luther winces at my smoker's tone. I pound my chest. "Sorry! Dust and I don't exactly get along."

He frowns down at me, as if knowing what I'm going through. "I feel the same way," he says forlornly, and I just love that we've already established this common ground.

Reaching out, Luther delicately lifts a sterling silver tray —all decked out with pretty black swirls and flowers.

Yep, another item my mom would die for.

Looking down at a trio of burnt-looking muffins, Luther shyly murmurs, "Pumpernickel?"

Not exactly your most popular flavor . . . but I'm sure they're good. Maybe a little crispy on the outside, but I secure the least burnt-looking one and pop it into my mouth.

Ooo, bitter.

Actually, my stomach might have alotta issues, but I'm sure I can make up for it by taking a few extra enzyme pills later . . .

A shrill noise suddenly bursts from the kitchen to the living room, and a kettle—just a kettle—is making that shrieking noise from the stove.

Luther tromps over to rescue it, then seizes a white, crinkled packet from the counter. Tearing it open, he dutifully shakes out what appears to be brown cocoa powder into a hefty mug he probably got from an antique store.

Everything about this place looks like it belongs in an antique store.

Shooting him a grin, I say, "Luther Dvorak, are you making me hot cocoa?"

His handsome cheeks flush as he averts his gaze to the counter. Reaching for a drawer, I presume for a spoon, he says, "I promised I would feed you."

Another blast of wind shrieks, and I scamper toward the living room. Must get away from all these spooky sounds.

Oh, hello!

Time to make friends with old mirrors.

The couch has a nice, puffy upholstery to it. Only a few tears to boot.

Something clanks from the far side of the room, and when I turn, I don't know what I expect, but it certainly isn't a bag of bones.

Bones.

Hanging all innocent-like in a green, silky rope bag from the rafters.

Neatly arranged—probably a wind chime for cannibals.

Not really in the mood to sit directly beneath this giant pile of bones, I *very strategically* make my way to the other side of the room. Whew, don't know about these Dvoraks and their avant-guard style of decor.

Dead plants fill out the entire window-filled wall, and they're these brown, crusted-over things, sprouting *directly* from the plaster.

No small amount of mildew grows over the plaster, too, and if Mom saw this little detail, she'd be wrapping me up, stat, and sending me home in a hazmat suit.

Slowly, I swallow what's left of the pumpernickel. Luther sets his tray back down on the counter.

"You're a fan of baked goods," he says with a little more pomp and circumstance than the occasion allows.

I don't have the heart to say otherwise, so I tell him, "Mmmm! *So* good."

"I am a sucker for comfort food." Luther wanders toward me from the far side of the room. His silky vest ripples as he walks, and his hair falls almost cleverly in his eyes. "I was going to try my hand at some soup, but Bastian . . ."

The biggest, sleekest dog I have ever seen suddenly saunters down the stairs. I hadn't even noticed the stairs before, 'cause I was too busy looking at the plants, bag o' bones, and mirrors . . . but *behind* the bones is this fancy, swoopy staircase that looks like it belongs in an opera house.

And the dog, well . . . he's *beautiful*. Practically moves like a panther, and those tall, cropped ears and that docked tail tells me he couldn't be anything but a Doberman Pinscher.

Gorgeous. Deadly. Beautiful.

Proudly wagging his nubby tail, he looks like he belongs in a dog show, and his muscles ripple like meaty strings on a bass guitar.

"Wow . . ." I'm unable to tear my eyes from the pretty shine of his onyx coat, loving the caramel coloring of his toes, chest, and snout. "We used to have a Doberman." Though we left Autumn's ears and tail alone. Mom says it's barbaric to do the surgery, and I gotta say, I kinda agree. I hold my hand out for the dog. "They sure do make great service dogs."

Luther murmurs something too low for me to hear while Bastian—I believe that's his name?—wanders close enough to nuzzle my leg with his damp snout.

I give him a little scratchy-scratch behind the ears and . . . what the—? Scratch marks line one side of his jaw.

I hate to see a hurt animal.

"Did he get into a fight, Luther?"

"Fighting is his love language," Luther grumbles while

marching his way back to the kitchen to secure a pair of floral potholders.

Well, huh. No need for no negative Nancys here. . . . I pick my way around the creatively placed kaleidoscope table and kneel down next to Mr. Bastian. "What happened to you, boy?"

Bastian licks my fingers. Part of me thinks Luther will elaborate on what he said before, but the boy's too busy glowering into the mugs as he stirs the hot cocoa.

"I think you're jealous," I say as Bastian flops into my lap, and ooh, my, it's a good thing I'm already somewhat sitting down. Otherwise, I'd be fallin' over.

"Well, aren't you an affectionate boy?" I ask as he nuzzles my arms, his nubby tail wagging all the while.

"We really should do something about these scratches." I survey the red, two-inch slices along Bastian's jaw. "What did you say scratched him again?"

"He has all the care he needs in this home." Luther wanders toward me with steam drifting from our mugs, and *hot dang,* I am parched. I accept mine without a word, and while the mug doesn't have any clever quotes like Mom's, this one certainly has a nice weight to it. Kind of like the sconces, but clean . . . er.

When I take a sip, I am not *too* much disappointed that the cocoa's watered down. But a boy has never made me cocoa before, so I shoot him the first honest compliment I can think of at the moment. "Smoother than mushroom juice."

Luther's eyes crinkle at the corners. He's clearly unsure of my choice of words. May not be my best compliment ever.

Setting down his mug, Luther actually uses a stack of old books for a coaster.

Won't his mom or dad rip him a new one?

But, seeing as he's behaving like that's the most natural thing in the world, I good-naturedly follow suit.

"Would you care to play . . . Scrabble?" Luther looks up, a bit of foreboding in his tone.

I grip my hands together in a formality I never knew I could own. "Why, yes, Luther. Yes, I would."

He must fail to catch the sarcasm in my tone—not that I don't want to play, because I do—because he immediately turns to retrieve an old version of the game with faded lettering from the kaleidoscope table.

The floppy lid and worn corners of the box prove the game's been rather loved, and I'm just about to comment on the pretty, scrolled lettering on the side when something that sounds like breaking glass crashes in the other room.

All the color drains from Luther's face.

He grapples for his candelabra that's somehow ended up near the sofa . . .

Leveling skittery eyes on me, he says, "Whatever you do, do *not* leave this room." And he tears past me like he forgot the miniature marshmallows.

Maybe the family's prized antique chandelier fell down.

Maybe that stained glass window up and experienced its last rodeo.

All I know is, Bastian's looking at me with these uber soft eyes, and I can't help reaching out and scratching behind his magnificent ears.

Giving his wiry hair a good, thorough pat-down, I scratch all along his neck, too. "Why does he think I would ever stay put, hmm?"

CHAPTER THREE

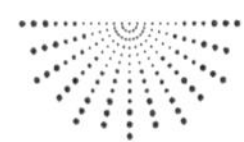

I suppose I did—stay put last time. But that foyer was locked, and heck if I'm going to sit around while Luther's contending with some chandelier-dropping, escaped convict from Wrightsville.

Except, as I try to shove Bastian off of my lap, he nuzzles me like I'm nothing short of his mom.

"Come on, boy." I give him a quick scratch behind the ears before trying, once again, to lift him off. But this puppy's at least a hundred pounds. Something between a growl and a grumble curls from his throat, and he thinks I need to stay? I pat his belly. "Opinions aren't wrong. It's what you *do* with them that counts."

Using arm muscles I didn't know I had, I heave and ho, and, by golly, I actually succeed in nudging him off.

He doesn't seem too happy about it, though. He squints his pretty brown eyes and whimpers, but he's the one who gets to stay close to the fire. Didn't realize the house would be so drafty. Shoulda brought my parka and panty warmers.

Scrambling over the gray and red rug with a silver medallion down the middle, I go right, left, right down the super-long halls.

By the time I knock into a second dead end, though, my enthusiasm's starting to wane. Um, which way did he go?

Too bad Luther didn't leave behind that candelabra.

At least I'm pretty good at rummaging through the dark.

Pointy objects clang like tambourines. Silks and scarves don't drape like snakeskins *at all*, and when the hallway suddenly veers right, I end up standing right in front of a statue that's screaming for his mama.

Wowza, his mouth is *really* wide, and I don't believe I've ever seen somebody with such terrified eyeballs. Beside the statue stands his marble friend, and *this* guy's so freaked out, he's playing peek-a-boo behind some marble covers.

A burst of fire suddenly blazes from one of the sconces on the wall; this whispering, tongue-clicking noise has me knocking into another mirror.

It sways on a hook—back and forth, back and forth—while *another* ear-splitting, glass-breaking sound steals like a thief across the labyrinth.

Luther!

I'm blocked by yet another velvety curtain, so I swoosh that aside, suddenly blinded by a host of lightbulbs.

Not from the ceiling . . . but about five feet from the ground. You'd *think* I'd be all about seeing what's going on, but artificial lights? Remember, I've got weird phobias of my own.

Taking deep, slow, even breaths, I playact like I'm merely going to the dentist for a cleaning on my own.

Freaky, pristine white suits, not at all discomfiting drills—

Gotta scamper past this last curtain and mirror.

Plowing through twin stretches of velvet and argyle, I

stumble into an enormous room filled to the brink with glass boxes.

Not planter boxes, mind you. But rectangular, glass boxes —as in aquariums, y'all.

Black and yellow moths or butterflies flutter about, and the whispering, tongue-clicking sound goes on and on.

Smells like rotten underwear in here, and several aquariums appear to be real broke.

"Olly, olly oxen free!" I warn the hiding imposter.

Luther bolts upright from behind an aquarium, and boy, oh boy, if I'm gonna have a coronary, I pray I'm at least thirty years old.

Deep frown lines take over Luther's brow, and his hair appears taller than usual. "I told you to stay . . ."

I fold my arms. "Well, hello to you, too, stud."

Backing away, Luther bumps into yet another aquarium, and I don't know why *he's* the one who's acting all scared. I've hit a Noah's Ark level of hodgepodge, and those bright yellow moths? They are creating one eerie, buzzing sound.

Casually, I knock on the side of one of the aquariums, which may or may not house a respectable amount of black mold. "How many you got?"

Luther's eyes stretch wide at my question. "Pardon?"

"Aquariums. Lost count?"

Luther's cheeks turn so pink, I have to wonder if *he's* the tongue-clicking trickster. But when he takes a hefty step to the right, he clamps a warm, muscular hand on my arm. "*Go.*"

I can neither affirm nor deny the sultriness of his tone.

Actually . . . I'm not all that accustomed to receiving orders. Mom discovered I'm more of the "suggest-what-you-think-I-should-do" type when I was only four years old.

I ease my arm from his fingers, doing my best not to be rude. "Would you like some help cleaning this up, Luther?"

That's all I say, but despite my best intentions, he seems to be sensing all my other questions, too:

Why are there aquariums in here?

How have they managed to become broken at all?

And, is it just me, or has another button become undone on his shirt?

My seductor averts his gaze to a pair of yellow-spotted moths splayed open-winged on the floor. They remind me of *The Mothman Prophecies*—you know, that horror movie with Richard Gere.

"They're attracted to the plants," Luther says about the moths in a low tone.

I suppose that makes sense. I mean, the plants may not look real alive in the living room, but it's quite possible that I missed a healthy geranium or two.

"You should leave," Luther says again, glancing guiltily at the door.

"First the dog gets out, then your aquariums explode." I hold out my hand in apology. "Looks like you need my help."

Luther lets out an exasperated breath, surveying just how bad things are. From all the broken glass, it appears two massive aquariums went *ka-boom*. If I were the gambling sort, I'd say cleaning this up would take him all night.

So, I square my shoulders and give him my best can-do, Hellstrom woman charm. "Where's the broom?"

His sultry eyes widen.

"*Broom*." I play off his effect on me by doing jazz hands. "If we don't get to work, for all we know, animal control will show."

Luther rubs the middle of his forehead like it's a worry stone.

So, I up the ante. "Take my generosity. It's rarer than you know."

Looking more than a little lost, Luther scans my eyes

before analyzing the floor. Ooh, this room's got cute maple leaves carved into the ebony and oak.

Eventually . . . eventually . . . Luther glances back to the corner, where more than a few unsettling shadows lurk. He turns his gaze to the great, long hallway before murmuring, "A shovel would be better than a broom."

I sure do like a man who knows what he wants. After all our work, maybe he'll confess why the aquariums blew.

CHAPTER FOUR

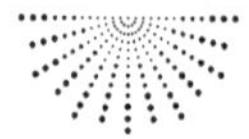

NEVER KNEW SHOVELING BROKEN glass could be so fun.

Luther's scooping it up like he was born to do it, and I've dumped sixteen or so shovelfuls. My back is working on the mother of all cramps, but I'm not about to complain as Luther continues his work.

Scoop, dump.

Scoop. Dump.

When the bin gets full, I accept it without a word and begin to wheel it out when Luther catches my arm. "I will take it."

I was hoping to explore and learn a new thing or two about this house, but the square-mouthed shovel's like an Optimus Prime weapon extension on Luther's arm. Dude could have a future as a gravedigger.

Though there sure is a lot more "salsa" stained on that handle.

Maybe a bunny died. Wolves made a meal of it, and Luther buried the poor creature with love in his heart.

When the boy turns to drop the last shovel-full of glass into the waste bin, I kick it out of the way, 'cause I don't exactly want our bonding time to be over. I know it makes me selfish, but what if he sends me home?

Glass has successfully spilled everywhere, and Luther shoots me a look of such deep loathing that I can't help cackling, a big ol' pile of nerves. Not sure what to do with my hands, I grab hold of a nearby curtain and cast it over my shoulder. "Please, sir," I say with my starving orphan voice. "Won't you tell me how the aquariums broke?"

Scrrrape, goes the shovel as Luther wordlessly resumes his gravedigger job.

Hmm. I cough a little, adding to my melodrama.

Appears he's not a softy for orphans. So, I tuck the thick, argyle fabric beneath my chin and switch to my favorite octogenarian character. "Come on, laddy. Granny here's *dyin'* to know what's goin' on."

Luther stomps around me to scoop up yet another piece of broken glass. I'm not a fan of being ignored, so I nudge his shovel handle out of the way with my foot.

"You are being ridiculous," he grumbles.

Granny's voice trills, "Anythin' a girl's gotta do to be noticed!"

After he scoops up the final shard of glass, I make sure we're locking eyes—before reaching down, grabbing the lip of the bin, and thoroughly dumping out the contents.

The resulting silence that spills over the . . . conservatory? . . . is enough to spook Dracula himself. I know I shouldn't have done that, but we're not gettin' anywhere.

Scattering the bits and pieces of broken glass with my boot, I feel pretty darn Cruella de Vil. With any luck, Luther will find my actions endearing. Of course, I can't rightfully say what's going on in his head, but I'm sure I'm not the only one who's noticing the heat, like a Jacuzzi bubbling between us. The edge of his jacket grazes my arm, and his legs are planted a mile apart.

The skin on his knuckles flares white as he grips the shovel hard. Flipping it around, he sticks the handle into the side of my knee and grouses, "Shoo!"

Not the reaction I expected, but I'll roll with it.

A muscle feathers along his jaw, and the shovel *clunks* as Luther sets it down. "I notice you. But I . . . do not trust you."

"Oh?" Why might that be? This, I gotta figure out!

Luther scratches the side of his arm like he *knows* the answer, but he's not about to show his cards.

Maybe it would be helpful if we played Twenty Questions. Rosalyn begs me to play all the time. But, the Mountain Dew I drank earlier is definitely wearing off, and my energy's zapping for real. While I glance around the weird, half-smashed, aquarium-filled room, I can honestly say that I've gotten to the point where I just want to know *why* he invited me over in the first place. I know we got along real well when we first met at the library, but it's been three whole weeks, an, ever since that morning, the boy's been ever so formal. He has a classic look about him, sure, but *why*? Is he into cosplaying old historical dramas?

Feeling the tired lines round my eyes, I lift my dark hair from the nape of my neck. I'm gonna wear myself out and need a ton of medicine if I'm not careful. "How did the aquariums break?"

He simply stares at me, his sharp cheekbones the perfect cut-outs for a historical sheriff character.

Seems as though he's not goin' to answer, so I pull the shovel from his hands and begin scooping up glass like it's something I was born to do.

Shouldn't have dumped it all out. That was rude.

Luther prowls toward me with his stoic face and flowing scarf.

He stops just six inches away from me, and he's about six inches taller than my five foot four stature.

Peeling off his jacket and scarf, he places his hands together and absently twists the fatty black ring on his right ring finger.

My mouth about runs dry as I say, "Don't tell me a baseball broke the glass, 'cause I don't see any broken windows. And for baseballs to come sailin' in, windows would be broke."

"What do *you* think broke the aquariums?" Luther doesn't bother to break eye contact, nope, not at all.

I . . . have to scratch my nose.

"Solar . . . arctic. . . heat flares?"

Sage and heat dance between us like a mariachi band on tour, and as Luther takes another small step, glass crunches and crackles beneath his boot.

He's four inches away.

Four.

What if he's going to kiss me?

Eee, truth is, I've never *been* kissed.

His licorice breath puffs on my nose as he takes another step. There becomes three teeny-tiny inches between us.

I swallow a string of phlegm in my throat. What Luther *doesn't* bring up is the fact that someone else *has* to be in this house.

Aquariums don't suddenly explode on their own. Solar arctic heat flares? Not sure if you could tell, but I up and made that up.

Luther stares at my chin. The lights are kinda bright near his eyes, so I stare at his ears.

A heady wind whistles through the walls—that's not odd at all—as Luther's eyes dart toward the nearest one.

I have to tell him what I'm thinking. "We're not alone."

"No," he says in a low tone.

Gosh, after putting that curtain over my shoulder, I probably smell like mothballs. That doesn't make me feel self-conscious at all.

Scouring my cheeks, my nose—the bright lights are cooperating, y'all—Luther patiently says with a lilt, "I do not understand you."

He doesn't understand *me?* "Imma Rubik's Cube with hidden compartments . . ."

"You do not run when you should fear to be in this house."

Ah. "I *like* blood stains and bone bags."

"I haven't treated you properly from the moment you arrived."

The fact that he knows that he's been lacking in the hospitality department works wonders in warming my nerves. Problem is, hot flashes from my condition are spillin' over me, full kilter.

Grasping the bottom hem of my blouse, I begin to pull off my sweater.

Oh . . . whoops!

Totally forgot to put on a T-shirt under there.

Giving my sweater a patty-pat, I pretend all I meant to do was straighten it all along.

Luther reaches over and slides his fingers through a tendril of my hair, and that one movement steels my nerves.

But he doesn't do anything other than that, and now the moment's grown all awkward. So I set to rearranging my favorite curtain's argyle pattern. "I just love this fabric . . . I'll have to have my mom ask yours where she found it. Mom's always lookin' for a smokin' deal."

Eventually, I find the nerve to look up, and the boy's staring at me with the most inexplicable expression—lips pressed tightly together, brows furrowed . . . before turning and wheeling the garbage bin out of the room.

So much for chemistry and answers!

Scrrrape goes something round abouts that shadowy back corner.

BOOM!

BANG!

More aquariums burst with this awful, fantastical sound, and Luther spins a hundred and eighty degrees. Seizing his jacket, he gallantly leaps to cover me as glass flies from here to Saturn.

CHAPTER FIVE

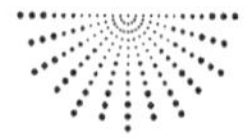

I'm livin' the dream.

More like nightmare . . . all right, I'll admit it.

But Luther, after all the glass stops flying, lets me crawl out from under his rather manly form. My hair's definitely full of static as he pulls me along.

Still don't know what's making those aquariums burst, but the boy's first instinct was to protect me. For real.

While Luther pulls me through these raspy halls, I am *certain* somebody has to be hiding in the likes of a secret passage. Maybe whoever it is really is a serial killer—who's forced Luther to bring a girl home.

But serial killers don't work in teams.

They tend to work alone.

When Luther and I pass the screaming statue and his claustrophobic BFF, my toes curl, because I can't help thinking about the time I disappeared around a *different* corner.

Mom put me in charge of the house and assumed I would stay home, but I most definitely did not.

"You need to leave while you can." Luther grabs my

shoulders and not-so-gently turns me toward what I assume is the front of his home.

The boy sure is giving me mixed signals.

Also, my breathing really needs to even out.

Heave.

Ho.

I'll calm myself in front of this here wicker basket.

"Why are you trying to get rid of me?" I accidentally breathe all deep and cough. "Someone's obviously trying to harm you. Let me help you out."

Luther rubs the back of his neck, which is the color of sea salt caramel. "Why are you wheezing like that?"

"Not everyone's breathing can be soundless."

"Yes, but why do you cough?"

Feeling a little bit derided, I plant my hands on my hips. "I already tried to play Twenty Questions with you." And now it's getting even harder to breathe—especially in such close quarters.

Leaning against the curtain, I try to catch my breath, only for the curtain to give way, and I pull it straight from the wall.

'Tis a nice, silky fabric.

"Do you have the asthma?" Luther lifts the curtain from my arms.

"The *asthma*?!" Cough, cough. "Who are you, my grandpa?"

With what I assume to be a great deal of effort, Luther ever so patiently sets down the fabric and steeples his fingers. Raising his eyebrows with emphasis, he awaits my answer. But, see, my question was last.

He just stares at me with those piercing, beautiful gray eyes.

"Tell me . . ." I casually take his arm. "What is going on?"

Luther sits me down on a stool next to a ginormous silver

pot. At first, I think the pot's a throne of some sort, but then I see the vase-like shape, porcelain exterior, and I can tell it's an urn.

Watching me, Luther waits for my breathing to even out. But all this lollygagging won't keep us one step ahead of whoever's in those walls.

A swatch of beads dangling from the ceiling jangle a little, and now it sounds like someone's upstairs, moving around.

Luther swallows. His Adam's apple bobs up and down, and I have *no clue* what's really happening, but he's holding his hand out to me, so I accept it without a word.

Letting him lead me past the dreamcatchers, beads, and feathers, we pass a black and white portrait leaning up against a fatty urn.

When we get past all that, Luther casts a wary glance in my direction. "She's even more temperamental as of late."

"Who?" Hope it's not his girlfriend.

My mind always goes to the worst possible answer.

Rubbing the ring on his middle finger, Luther says, "What I don't understand is why you haven't left for home."

My breathing still hasn't evened out, so I steady myself by grabbing hold of a nearby beaded scarf. Feels like baby teeth tied to yarn.

You know, I *could* talk to him. *Really* talk to him, like a normal girl, but this girl didn't come to Monkshood Manor for a heart-to-heart. She came for love and distraction with a really cute boy who has as many secrets as herself.

Clearing my throat, I take up my most poignant therapist voice: "What are we but lone humans, blindly traversing through the errors of our past?"

"That is an awfully bleak outlook for a girl who so clearly enjoys her jests." Luther narrows his eyes. "I cannot leave, I'll have you know."

Yowza, not sure why the boy would lie about that . . . I

mean, I met him at the library, for one. Though I am oh so good at playing gullible. "And why is that?"

The boy disappears like a phantom around the corner, and I'm not real sure if he's purposely avoiding the question or if he *likes* making me all hot and bothered by playacting a retro James Bond.

What I'd like to know is . . . who, between us, has more bottled up secrets?

Or maybe this *is* some elaborate Halloween prank.

Luther's got a friend lurking in the shadows, and he or she is waiting to see how long it takes before I run for my mama.

What Luther doesn't know is, I specialize in the weird and unexpected.

I couldn't have survived thirty-nine trips to the hospital without being the warrior of tough luck.

Take a lickin', you keep on tickin'. Yup.

Scrambling after him, I add, "Hey, I'm here for the long haul." I pause to lean against a tall, spindly thing that feels like a hanging cadaver.

Taking Luther's hand, I show him my newfound desire to stay here despite any answers, and thread my fingers between his.

Luckily, Luther doesn't let go or pull back.

Sparks of electricity shoot through our clasped hands, and as he casts a look over his shoulder, he says, "The living room will be the safest place for us."

CHAPTER SIX

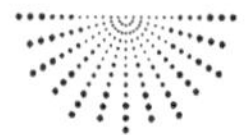

PARANOIA JUST MIGHT BE my middle name.

Also *Actor*, with a capital *A*.

I just need to trust him and roll with anything that happens. He wouldn't seriously murder me. I'm sure the boy has my back.

And besides, these old stone houses are infamous for making people go nuts. I could maybe, quite possibly be crazy and not even know it.

Except, I *did* see those aquariums explode.

Maybe Luther's mysterious friend has remote control glass bombs?

Eh, I sincerely hope not.

Truth is, it's probably only four in the morning, so I have *plenty* of time before Mom and Rosalyn wake up. They'll catch a few cartoons, eat fried ham and apple pancakes before doing a few chores and wondering where I am.

By the time Luther and I settle on the living room's fancy, tufted couch, I have to say, I'm pretty darn tuckered out. If it were up to me, we'd just sit back and watch a movie, but nowhere on these ginormous, leaf-patterned walls is there a television.

Below the mirrors is the gramophone, sure, its horned metal flower looking pretty alongside that old, rickety book shelf blocked by dark, leaded glass. . . . Hey, where's the dining room? I thought dining rooms were all the rage back in the Victorian era. Mom would certainly say that, since she prattles on about old homes all the time.

Out of nowhere, Bastian comes struttin' across the medallion carpet. Behaving like the Queen of Sheba, he collapses at my feet on the floor.

His cuts look significantly better!

Did Luther put some medicine on him when I wasn't looking earlier?

Sneaky Luther.

Wonder if the boy's still offended that Bastian and I get along, though I don't think now's the time to ask since Luther's gone on to arranging the fireplace logs.

So I set to scratching behind Bastian's super tall ears. Such a pretty puppy. I sure wish Rosalyn were here to pet the dog.

Suddenly rolling over, Bastian sticks his paws in the air, and his eyes flutter closed as his fatty, pink tongue lolls out.

"Wow . . ." I murmur, quasi-loud. "Is he always this trusting?"

Luther offers me a second mug of cocoa I don't remember asking for . . . or seeing him make, truth be told. "Having you here is unusual for us all."

I accept the mug, feeling a new cotton-y layer of phlegm in my throat.

Who exactly does he mean by "us all?" I know he referred to a "she," but . . .

Ah, the warm porcelain of the mug is a balm to my

freezing fingers. The cocoa tastes pretty watery, but cocoa is cocoa, y'all.

"So . . ." I raise my eyebrows toward the mess of dangling ropes. "*She* can't get us when we're in here?" Surreptitiously, I take another sip, pretending to know who *she* is.

Luther's shoulders immediately slump. "I don't know why . . ."

I sincerely hope we're not talking about his girlfriend. "I'm sure I'm *way* hotter in a swimsuit."

Luther sputters on his cocoa.

"But I lost mine, so I'd have wear my little sister's, which would be *super* tight."

Luther chokes so hard, his cocoa splashes from his mug to his vest. Pulling a handkerchief from his pants pocket, he dabs extra fast at the amber spots.

I make him an offer just to make him feel uncomfortable. "I can lick up the cocoa if you want . . ."

Luther springs from the couch so fast, you'd think he was a superhero.

"WHAT IS WRONG WITH YOU?"

This he whisper-shouts.

"Sorry! I'm sorry." I hold up my hand. "I believe it runs in the family. I get this way when I've been cooped up."

Luther firmly sets his mug down on the old stack of books with the moisture ring on top—only to pluck it up again. After a few attempts, he ultimately clears his throat. "Have you ever read John Keats?"

Didn't exactly hit the turn signal before landing on that segue. "I haven't ever *not* read John Keats. Have you ever read *Horton Hatches the Egg*?"

With his pointer finger, Luther *tap-taps* his mug. Not sure where we're going with this, but I sure do know Seuss' work. Got a few of his books memorized ever since Rosalyn made me read three of them every night before heading to bed.

Setting down his mug with finality, Luther says, "I could read you some poetry. If you want . . ."

Well, huh. It's not every day a girl receives such a tempting offer. And while I'm not exactly sure I'll be able to *understand* said poetry, I could give it a whirl. Look up Spark-Notes if I really end up lost.

Gripping my hands together, I pretend I'm the newfound belle of the ball. Ever so slightly, I bow my head. "I would be ever so delighted."

Luther's eyes bore into my skull, and I've no idea what he's thinking. But he's not the only one whose intentions are catawampus.

Lifting the tattered book from the top of the stack, he opens to what must be his favorite passage. It's dog-eared and practically falls apart.

Clearing his throat, he very studiously reads, "My heart aches, and a drowsy numbness pains. My sense, as though of hemlock I had drunk, or emptied some dull opiate to the drains . . ."

I hold up a heavy hand while Luther raises his luscious eyebrows.

"Those can't honestly be the first lines!" I cry.

Luther says nothing, primarily or secondarily at all, so I tug the Revolutionary-era book from his hands.

"A girl's gotta warm up to the idea of a boy." I pretend to skim the passage. "A boy should hold his cards close to his chest until he knows *exactly* how she's feeling!"

Luther gazes at me as I hand the book back. Prolly 'cause we both know I'm the biggest hypocrite ever when it comes to following my own advice.

"I'll let John Keats know . . ." he eventually murmurs.

I laugh, 'cause this boy is a riot. "How about we get on with our game of Scrabble?"

His chest visibly falls.

"Or, you can keep reading!"

All too fast, he relinquishes the tome to the pile of books. "Not if you detest it."

"Are you kidding?" I scramble for a way to mend my mishap. "I *love* melodrama!"

Luther's eyes flare with hurt, and I sputter for a sounder explanation. But the only thing I can think to do is offer to do the Macarena, so I stay put.

Between his downcast shoulders and drooping head, it is truly clear that I have insulted the boy, so I retrieve the Scrabble game from the coffee table to cheer him up—only to end up coughing up a vengeful storm.

Eyebrow cocked, Luther tugs the Scrabble box from my hands. "Are you unwell?"

"Smoker." I use my fist to pound my lungs.

Luther presses his lips together, and, ooh, he's got a cute, little, white scar underneath his mouth.

How very Indiana Jones.

"Why does your place attract so many moths?" I decide to play a little Nancy Drew.

Luther lays out the game board.

"Why didn't you get something cuter? Like gerbils?" I drain my cup.

"So, you are fond of rodents?" He looks up.

I think of that rat skeleton thing beneath the floorboards. "No. Definitely not."

Lifting the mug to take another drink, I find it's empty— oh yeah—so I watch as Luther's long, graceful fingers gently arrange the game's tiles. I haven't even drawn mine, so I grab a handful of wooden squares and stuff them on a stand that's gone a little soft with humidity but is still good.

I stick the tiles in ABC order. Er, how does the game go again?

When Luther extends a gallant hand for me to go first, I pretend to know what I'm doing.

Look down and try to spell what I can.

T, U, L, R . . .

Hmm . . .

I pluck up and rearrange a tile.

Pluck up and move another.

When I very nearly spill all the tiles, I feign a deep concentration that's prevented me from dealing with such mundane matters as "order," completely keeping my eyes on the stand.

And that's when I see it.

The "U" and "A" and "T" and, by golly, I'm a virtuoso.

Swooping up all the letters, I slam them on the board and proudly say, "TARANTULA."

Luther stares down at the board with not exactly the enthusiasm I would have hoped for. His graceful neck bends forward while he casts an uneasy glance at me. "You . . . were only supposed to take seven tiles."

Ah, I knew I forgot a part of the rules. With another great flourish, I take off the "T" and "A" and proudly say, "RANUT-LA," whilst rolling the "r."

Luther's eyebrows raise again, and I'm pretty sure that if I supply a definition, I'll dig myself outta this here hole. "Rantula," I enunciate again, rolling the "r." "Cousin to Dracula and prone to ranting at gerbils."

Luther gazes at the letters so long, I'm pretty sure he's gonna offer me some custom ranting of his own. We can't have any of that, so I kick off my boots, lift my legs, and very vixen-like lay them across his lap.

Good thing I'm wearing my cute leopard socks, but they might as well be old sponges for all the notice Luther gives them.

I lower my voice to a sultry purr. "What kind of girls have you dated in the past?"

Luther dutifully plucks up his tiles and rearranges them, one by one.

"Ugly ones?" I tap my forehead. "With only one eye?"

He plucks up another tile. "There's actually a plant that causes that. *Veratrum californicum.*"

I shove him on the arm. "Well, aren't you a bona fide bilingual. Wait . . . there's a plant that causes you to be a cyclops?"

Luther nods, and this little nugget o' truth appears to be something he's known for a great, long while. "It happens to a fetus when its mother ingests some when it's in the womb."

"Huh." I let that horrific little fact sink in. "And they say reality ain't special."

Luther absentmindedly runs his thumb along the seam of my pants, causing little crackles of heat to erupt all the way from my knee to my ankle.

Definitely feeling the moment, I reach out to take his hand, but he flinches back, hard.

"You should probably go." He flexes his jaw, and is he kidding me? We've already been over this.

Maybe he still has feelings for his elusive "she?"

Maybe I really *am* a science project . . .

Though, I gotta say, he is turning out to be more of a puzzler than I first expected. My head's starting to spin. It's like I've just gotten off the State Fair's Caterpillar, and *yowza*, there must be a lot of crack-laced caffeine in that cocoa.

Antihistamine?

My head is pounding harder.

Feels like I'm driving, about to cusp a hill . . . and I'm losing control. This ain't good.

Panting, I lean into Luther as he reaches over and pats my back.

"It is a good idea to go to sleep," he says with a mortician's smile.

Hey! That's what I want to be! Either that, or a funeral director . . . but I do believe sleeping wasn't in the plan.

Especially since all I can see is the dangling bag o' bones reflected in Luther's deep, sorrowful pupils.

CHAPTER SEVEN

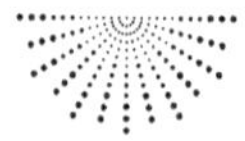

THE SWEET, scintillating scent of sage wakes me up.

Actually, this particular scent reminds me of a vacation I went on.

Mom, being into décor, wanted to see Magnolia Market, and Rosalyn, only seven at the time, opted to run around outside in the lush, green garden. I wasn't really in the mood to shop vases and candle holders, so I hung back with her. We wandered around tulip beds, Swiss chard, and roses. There were cute, little name plates for the plants that told us what they were.

The confederate ivy-covered tepee was Rosalyn's favorite. Those toadstools were adorable.

Rosalyn's favorite part of the day, though, was when we stood in line for one of the fifteen or so food trucks. Pepperoni pizza was her go-to treat, so we waited and waited, listening to the bass-thumping music.

Boom-ba-doom.

Boom-ba-thump, thump, thump.

That isn't bass music.

Someone's rapping on a door or the wall.

They're rapping even harder now. I spring open my eyes to find mahogany bookshelves, an old, fancy fireplace . . . I'm not with Rosalyn.

The coffee table and spiderweb-like plants along the walls tell me I am very much not. I'm at Luther's, sitting near that giant rug with the red and gray medallion.

Truthfully, my head feels like the landing pad for a helicopter, so I hold it as I try to sit up. Dude, living room's as dark as when I first zonked out . . .

"Cate!" A muffled voice comes somewhere in the direction of the hall labyrinth. "Caaate!" The muffled voice is female. Matronly. My mother. Ugh. She's so far away, it's amazing that I can hear anything at all.

My labored breathing comes out pretty darn sketchy, and my throat is parched. I grab my mug to dow—

Empty.

Maybe Luther or his compadre put something in the cocoa? That made me zonk out?

"Open this door right now, Ophelia Cate, or I'm going to call the cops!"

I would pay someone to stop my mother from railing on.

How in the Samhain does she know I'm here at Monkshood at all?

Setting down the huge mug on the stack of books, I can't help feeling more than a little miffed that she's here. Mom never usually cares how I spend my time.

When I roll to my feet, the floor audibly groans, and Mom's knocking sure is getting loud.

Tick, tick.

Hey, where'd that mahogany grandfather clock come from?

Tick.

And where did Luther go?

My head and stomach spin helter-skelter, and I shouldn't have eaten that muffin.

I do my best to stagger down the halls. Duck around the statues and beads and stuff. My boot hits something squishy—prolly just another bone-and-baby-teeth-infused scarf—and did *I* knock over those urns? Eee, check out all the ashes, spread like an extra dark layer of dust everywhere.

Candlelight flickers from the bat skeleton sconces on the walls, and I don't remember knocking over any urns.

There's like six—seven—knocked over.

And it's so cold, my breath comes out in little white clouds.

Goosebumps prick my arms, and I can't tell if that heavy breathing is coming from me . . . or the walls.

By the time I make it back to the foyer, I'm a popsicle. Luther's weird family heirloom blanket isn't exactly my first choice for heating up, but I grab the scratchy thing from beneath the bottomless chair and wrap myself up in it like a taco.

Did Luther drug me? I sincerely hope not.

Mom's wavy curls flutter from the other side of the stained glass window, and I really truly do not want to deal with her right now.

Maybe I can pretend I'm not here?

I pull the blanket across the crown of my head. Make myself look like baby Jesus' mother . . .

"I can *see* you, Ophelia Cate."

So much for my biblical drama.

Mom's so close, she's nearly pressing her nose to the green and purple stained glass. I know she's been wanting to see in this house forever, but that doesn't mean she gets to embarrass me in front of Luther.

Still, she's seen me, so I loosely grab the fancy lion's head door handle, and twist and twist 'til the mechanism finally catches and I'm able to partially open the door.

Mom's crossing her arms, and it's been months since she's been peeved like this, so I don't rightly know how to respond.

"What exactly made you think you could sneak over here, and at this time of the night, hmm?" She is quite terrifying in this coat I've never seen before, and her skin looks unusually pale in the moonlight.

Still, I do sort of expect a hug . . . especially since I have been missing for quite a while.

Mom balls her hands into fists. "You should have told me where you were!"

Is Rosalyn awake?

Mom grits her teeth and roughly grapples for my arm. "A man broke into our house—"

Man?

"—and grabbed your father's hammer—"

"What hammer?!"

"Rosalyn and I have both been *so* scared!" Mom's eyes go from angry to wild. "Just stay here so I can take care of your sister."

My jittery breath turns into confetti in my lungs.

That is not what I expected her to say.

First off . . . she's saying someone broke into our home. Second off, why isn't she freaking out about Monkshood's plausible mold?

All too fast, Mom releases my arm, and part of me wants to tell her that Luther's been trying to get rid of me all along. But I don't *wanna* play the victim card every day of my life!

"Is Rosalyn okay?" This, I have to know.

"Fine!" Mom slathers on a fake smile. "*Just* fine!"

And I do not have *any idea* why she's acting so terrible.

Usually . . . she's an awful lot more reserved.

Usually . . . she only *secretly* thinks of ways to get rid of me when I say I'm comin' home.

"Did you call the cops?" I ask, feeling more than a little lost.

"What do *you* think?" she snaps.

With her hair all sopping wet, part of me thinks I should offer her my umbrella, but now I don't want to offer it. She can be rained on, for all I care.

Oh . . . but . . . truth is, the umbrella broke practically the second I got to the porch. Maybe it would work just a little?

I'll invite her in . . .

But she abruptly turns to go. She's not taking me with her?

She came over only to abandon me even longer?

Normally, Mom feigns mild concern—about my extra curriculars, about any boy or friend drama. She's never told me not to come home before.

And as she stalks down the front steps, she doesn't so much as glance over her shoulder. Rain pings the roof and splatters the cement and grass. Everything smells so mildewy and old.

I never rightfully thought I would long for the days when Mom would overreact and order me home.

Now, though, she's just confirmed the truth.

It's what I've always feared. It's what I've always known.

I don't deserve to be safe.

I do not deserve to be cared for.

CHAPTER EIGHT

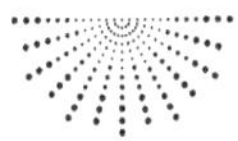

Luther's been gone for over an hour.

I'll wake myself up with some . . . not hot cocoa.

Far as I can tell, there aren't any tea bags in the cupboards, so I grab a handful of the mysterious dried herbs hanging above the sink—wonder what they are?—and grind them up in my hands.

Feeling Irish, I tell myself they'll be "grand."

Sprinkling them in another random mug, I add a little hot water, and *voila!*

I may or may not drink it now.

Mom really hates it when I play Russian Roulette with my health, but what kind of mother tells her daughter not to come home after her family's been attacked and robbed?

We should be regrouping, reporting what happened.

Staying in a hotel.

Is Rosalyn okay? Glad she has Mom . . .

When did Mom have the time to go shopping? Buy a new coat? She told *me* that she didn't even have enough time to go to my last three band concerts.

I play tuba.

First chair!

Of one.

The back door swings open, sending in a few burnt orange maple leaves and a whole lotta raindrops and fog.

Luther, of all things, staggers in, hair so caked with mud, I can barely make out the natural black color of his hair. One of his sleeves has nearly been ripped off.

With a *clank,* I set down my teacup. "What happened?"

A few claw marks slash Luther's face, and, what, do the Dvoraks have wild boars?

"Did Bastian escape?" I have to know.

Ooh, in his hands is a large paper bag.

He went to the store?

Snacks!

He may not want to tell me what happened to his face, so I waddle round the island. What I wouldn't give for a can of Easy Cheese and Reese's peanut butter cups.

"How did you sleep?" Luther asks, clutching the cobwebs that are fastened onto the paper bag.

"As well as Uncle Jimmy did when he threw himself off a twenty-two story building." I shrug.

"Have you eaten anything?"

"Just the tea." I vaguely gesture from the dangling roots to my mug.

Luther's face goes so pale, he could be the sheets' camouflage, and I didn't actually *drink* the tea, so no need to freak out.

Marching across the room, the boy stiffly grabs the mug, dumps its entire contents down the drain, then rounds on me like he's my mom. His eyes are boiling with hot lava. But the thing is, *my* mom doesn't actually care enough to want me back. And as far as I can tell, Luther already drugged me with that cocoa, anyhow.

"*Please* tell me you brought cookies." I can't deal with the drama, so I reach for the bag.

When I grab hold of it, though, Luther pulls it away, causing a masterful rip, and I'm left with a medium-sized piece of the bag.

Blushing, Luther stammers, "I . . . uh . . . brought you some food from outside."

"From the boars?"

". . . From the root cellar."

Well, now, he didn't have to go and do that. Setting my piece of the paper bag on the counter, I wait for him to reveal real motives and such, but all he does is stare at the contents in the bag.

I *tap-tap* my fingers on the counter.

"I didn't want to wake you," Luther begins.

Glass clinks as he sets the bag on the counter, and, ah, man. That most definitely is not an Easy Cheese kind of sound.

"You were in a deep sleep," he adds as the morning light filters through the fogged window.

I could tell him about Mom coming by, but that would involve feelings and such. That could get real dangerous, and fast. Besides, between the mud, scratches, and torn clothing, I would say that Luther's already shouldering a world of hurt on his own.

Bastian prowls into the room, muscles rippling through his fur. I swear, that dog is smiling as he stares at the scratch on Luther's nose . . .

Pausing at the corner of the counter, Bastian actually seems to be expecting a treat from Luther. But Luther just stands there—as massive, brown slugs slink from his eyeballs.

Slugs. From his eyeballs.

I grip the edge of the counter.

What the—?

Absolutely knowing I'm seeing things, I presume that it's from touching and smelling the leaves of the root Luther threw out.

A hallucination—from the residual of the hot cocoa.

And the slugs—they're big. They keep coming.

Big, black bodies drip from Luther's face, and they're leaving a horrific, sticky trail . . .

Honestly, I don't know which scenario is better: that I'm actually seeing things, or that I'm not, and it isn't until twenty or so goobers have slipped from Luther's face that it occurs to me that I should offer to help.

Whoop! They're gone.

"The thing about Monkshood," Luther says with great meaning, "is it can make you see things that aren't really there . . ."

So, there were no slugs?

Sagely, Luther pulls a jar from the bag with something pink and squishy suspended on the inside.

Reminds me of pigs feet . . . in vinegar.

Twisting open the jar, Luther crouches down and dumps the ingredients into a bowl. His clothing may be tattered, his hair might give Rosalyn a fright, but he still looks so good. "I am sorry I have not been as attentive as of late."

Bastian scampers over and devours the fishy-smelling food, though Luther doesn't so much as pat his dog.

"You really don't like him," I say, deciding to forget about the slugs. Bad tea. Must remember.

Gathering up the contents of the bag, Luther marches to the other side of the kitchen like I've up and insulted his lasagna.

"What'd he ever do to you?" I joke. "Threaten to steal your 'history professor' hair?"

Dude, where's his sense of humor?

Clink, clink. Wordlessly, Luther pulls out jar after jar from the bag and sticks them in a cobwebby cupboard.

The grimy shelves look like the last time they were cleaned was . . . about the time those Washington-era books were wrote.

Man, everything about this place is so pretty but neglected and beautifully gross. I don't know why it's taken me so long to notice, but I guess I wanted to be excited about it for Mom. Even the coffered ceiling has water stains and enough cobwebs to trap a horse.

Gathering all my curly hair into a low, messy bun, I have to ask myself: Why does Luther *really* have those scratches on his face and rips in his clothes?

And is he the only person who ever does chores in this house?

"We have a history . . ." Luther answers, and, uh, what's this about?

Bastian devours what looks like an onion that's been pickled for eons, and, ah, yes. I wanted to know why Luther hasn't bothered to bond with his dog.

"I owe you an explanation," he says as he pours hot water from the tea kettle into a mug. "You wanted to know why I said I would never leave. The truth is, I do not wish to." Unhurriedly, he tears open another cocoa packet and shakes the powder into the mug. Sliding open a drawer, he settles for a pretty spoon with half a dozen rust marks and stirs the cocoa.

I gotta say . . . I've a sneaking suspicion that the boy's not being entirely truthful. He told me he couldn't leave before. Now he says he doesn't want to? Feels fishy. Though we've all got our reasons for fibbing every once in a while, so I'll let him spin his web of lies, then I'll enjoy sifting through and untangling them later.

Crossing to the living room, Luther sets to rearranging

the aged books on the coffee table. Both mugs are in one hand—that looks a little precarious—so I scamper over the squeaky floor and slip the closest of the mugs from his fingers.

I take a sizable sip, 'cause I've a short memory . . . and I highly doubt he'd drug me again so soon.

"I wouldn't be comfortable anywhere else," Luther adds, nestling his John Keats poetry book between two other volumes in the center of the table.

"Gosh, I wouldn't, either." I gesture to the "salsa" stains in the carpet.

"I have lived here a very long time."

"Plus" —I nod toward the sketchy, corroded mirrors— "reflections are *way* more interesting when they're blurred."

"This is my home."

"Slugs are *unavoidable* at most!"

Luther freezes, mug halfway to his mouth. "Slugs?" He glances sideways, like I've told the entire neighborhood that he has a termite issue.

"Oh, I thought you . . ." I gesture to my eyes, meaning *his* eyes ". . . figured you knew." I mean, he threw out the tea, so he must have known I'd see a delusion or two.

Or maybe Luther and his invisible girlfriend really are playing some big, giant, elaborate hoax.

"I am sorry." He covers his face with his hand. "It has been a very long last few hours."

"You're tellin' me!" Honestly, all of this is so exhausting, I could use a nap.

Er, another one.

And I know I said I like boys who are hard to get to know, but we're going on five or six hours, and instead of peeling off his layers, I feel like all we're doing is lathering on gorilla glue.

He and I have chemistry. True. And his family may have

really odd choices for décor. But, beyond that, I can't tell if he's the next Jack the Ripper or Mr. Rogers.

Gesturing toward the couch, Luther seems to want to make things right, so I have a seat.

I absorb the high renovation ropes, the sheets on the counters, and all the stuff in the hallways, and oh my heck! I can't believe I didn't see it before. "You're putting your house on the market!"

Here I thought he was a multifaceted human being with really good hair, but he's simply horrifically normal.

"That is madness." Luther grits his teeth. "Do not be absurd."

But is it? Am I?!

The Dvoraks fell behind on their mortgage . . .

After seeing my mom's Volvo, they wrongfully assumed we have alotta dough, and Mom unwittingly played into the charade by buying herself a new coat.

"Listen, it's been a hoot and a half," I say, beginning to set down my mug, "but I better get going. Don't wanna hit traffic!"

Luther reaches out and catches my mug. "I do not expect you to have that kind of wealth."

"*Ooh.*" I relinquish the mug to him and make sure to do overdramatic movements as I zip my ankle booties back on. "Now we're laying the foundation for, 'It only costs X amount!'"

Luther looks up to the coffered ceiling as if I'm *way* more than he bargained for. Sinking his head into his hands, he looks so defeated, my conscience gives a little twang.

Those gashes on his face look to be about two full inches long, and I can't believe I haven't even offered to help clean him up. Maybe we can put on that same medicine he used on his dog?

"What happened to you?" I jut my thumb toward the back windows. "Out there."

Luther digs his fingers into hair and mournfully says, "Just go."

What kills me is that we've been talking for hours but haven't really *communicated* the entire time. Obviously, when he went outside, he got roughed up.

Maybe I was right when I reasoned that whoever's here is forcing him to do whatever he does.

But I've a feeling that he can't say.

Or won't.

I scramble for the first, most obvious, indirect clue that I can. "Where did you get the ring?" Not a great question, but maybe I'll get lucky this time around.

Luther glances down at his fingers, his eyes so full of pain and sorrow. "It belonged to my mother."

Ooh! Not thinking that one's a lie.

"You know . . ." My chest warms with compassion. "When my Uncle Jimmy died, and I had to miss a bunch of tests, I couldn't come up with a convincing fake reason to explain to my teachers why I had to go to the funeral. So I supplied them with all the gory details. And then they thought I was a liar, 'cause it was all so unbelievable. Maybe that's your predicament?"

Tick, tick. That grandfather clock gets extra loud at this moment.

Sinking closer to him on the couch, I go with my gut. "Is your mom still alive . . . ?" Because there's no mimicking that kind of sadness.

Luther rubs the back of his neck. "Not for a very long time."

I'd ask about his dad, but something tells me not to go there. In terms of MIA fathers, I'm in the same boat.

"Would you allow me to play you something?" He nods to the piano that I *swear* hadn't been there until now.

A pi-a-no.

Huge, ginormous, and top dollar.

I could have missed it . . .

"When I'm done" —his eyes soften round the edges— "I will explain anything and everything you wish to know."

CHAPTER NINE

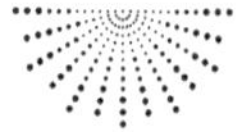

Some people play by striking notes; others faithfully count off measures, priding themselves in not missing a single stroke.

Not Luther.

Luther actually plays several incorrect keys, but that almost adds to the mood.

He's wholly muse-driven.

And I have to say, I like this side of him—this rowdiness. The unexplained misery pouring from his fingers. Before, when we talked, he was so reserved—snobbish, even—but now he purposely railroads the black and white keys, all in the name of composition.

His unseeing eyes never leave the ivory keys, and it's like his hands have a contemptible mind of their own.

I'm not a psychologist, but I'd say they connect with the thread of loss and injury, yes, but hope.

He's a battering ram, a nomad, a burdened traveler. The boy's an unidentified and under-appreciated street performer. The keys are his railway. He doesn't wish to stop.

Usually, I'd just join him at the piano, but I don't want to ruin the mood. Plus, I only took like three piano lessons when I was eleven.

When Luther's fingers slow, the sustain pedal connects all the dying notes.

I wheeze. Play it off by stretching my arms high above my head with a yawn. "You know, if I could play like that, I'd open my home and sell tickets for a show."

His hair hangs in his eyes as he rubs his forehead with the back of his thumb. "It wasn't too . . . melancholy?"

"Oh, it may have made me want to ball my eyes out, but in a good way!"

His glassy eyes stare into mine, sucking me into his morbid world. As the grandfather clock ticks in the background, those same eyes search mine as if he's trying to decide if he *should* tell me what's going on.

I want to know—I *thought* I wanted to know—but what if it involves finances and illness and gout? I already have a heap o' trouble of my own.

My legs are kinda draped across the back of the couch, so I pull them down. Lurch to my feet, 'cause the last thing I want to do is pile on the problemos.

Time to check on Rosalyn and Mom.

I dig into my back pocket for my phone.

Ah, but it's dead. Silly me forgot it died on the way over.

Sighing, I'm tempted to spill a few of the deep, dark secrets in my heart, but I settle with something superficial. "While I must admit you are excessively good looking, it really is past time for me to run along."

Luther doesn't look at me as he grazes his fingers over the top of the ivory keys. "Do you believe you are in danger here?"

"The fact that you jumped to that presumption really freaks me out."

While he studies me through his hair, the itty-bitty hairs

on the backs of my arms stand on end. His eyes soften as though he wants to say something sweet, but, all too quickly, his gaze hardens.

I pretend to read a message on my phone. "Well, it's been real! I think . . . anyway, thanks for the hospitality!"

Luther plunks out three low keys on the piano.

The extended string of notes he plays next makes me think of a demonic rainbow. Stepping around the coffee table, I add, "I'll just . . . be going now!"

Luther cowers even more, so I do my best to make myself invisible as I stride toward the halls. "Guh-bye now!"

He plays a few random keys that I have to say don't go all that well together. And his voice rises. "I *thought* you liked my playing."

"I do!"

"I thought you wanted me to explain . . . why aquariums explode and . . . why slugs pour from my eyes."

Now he admits to seeing them?

I scamper—trip—past the kaleidoscope table. Why's he suddenly acting so sinister and evil?

Standing, Luther impassively watches me as I get swallowed up in the halls. I certainly wish there was a straight shot to the front door, but it seems as though the architect was an overachiever.

I meander and zigzag past sconces, beads, and urns; purple petals suddenly flutter from the walls.

When I make it to the dim and dusty foyer, I am so outta breath, my head's altogether hijacked by that helicopter from before.

Need to focus. Breathe, y'all.

I twist the brassy, lion's head doorknob.

Though it keeps spinning.

And spinning.

The metal is cool and slick, and *why* doesn't the mechanism catch like last time and open the door?

Luther's footsteps behind me echo the frantic beat of my heart.

I don't wanna see an angry Luther.

I want to go back to when he was a mystery—clandestine and surreal—but now I'm quite sure he's the psychotic neighbor everyone warns you about.

A sudden breeze snakes around me and pries open the door.

A gust from the *inside* of the home.

And outside? Outside . . . it's raining bullets in a typhoon.

The raindrops crash against my head, and I'm not really sure why we're getting so much rain in Arkansas.

I stagger—stagger!—to the front yard stairs, the stairs that lead to the street that really need a sign that says, "Slippery when wet, fools."

I tuck my hands into the sleeves of my sweater and tell myself I've gotten past the worst of the worst.

Luther's not who I thought he was.

It will be okay.

He's just a moody guy who likes to play the piano.

I'll get home, do my breathing treatments, and clear my head. Make sure Mom and Rosalyn are all right from that guy who broke into our house and stole Dad's hammer.

Wish I didn't have to worry about pneumonia.

Wish I didn't have to worry about infection, but . . . life.

I'm only seven or so steps down when I spy a little white and blue mail truck.

Idling at the curb.

The sun still hasn't come all the way up, making it a misty, murky dawn, and I don't know why the mailman's already out.

Maybe he's getting an early start on his route?

Maybe the Christmas rush got pushed back to before Halloween now?

I wait. Convinced he will soon drive past the house.

But he doesn't.

Doesn't.

What if he's watching me? What if he's got night-vision goggles on?

I *really* hope that's not the case.

I'm tired.

Surely, after a few more seconds, he'll be on his merry way.

Ah, but the rain floods me with shivers.

Tick, tick.

Grandfather clock's plumb gone to my head now.

Tick, tick, tick.

I really shoulda grabbed my broken umbrella from the porch.

Why is the mailman taking *so long*? Something tells me not to approach, something about his time of arrival or aura.

We're at the beginning of a shootout at high noon, but I need to get home and see if the police got the guy who robbed my house.

Meanwhile, the wind makes chicken skin on my arms.

I clutch them in front of me, never more certain that I'm gettin' pneumonia.

Why doesn't the guy lean outta the door, stick a package in the mailbox, and drive on?

He can't honestly be looking at a map of his route.

Maybe . . . he's sorting through packages?

But I thought organization was a precursor for getting that job.

A pair of long, gangly legs are the first of him to emerge from the truck.

Next comes the long torso . . . and a shirt that's so blindingly white, it looks brand new.

White cap, white sneakers . . . he looks to have dressed up as a Lego set's "retro mailman."

Aw, I shouldn't be rude. I wave in the dark . . . feeling like I belong in *Leave it to Beaver*.

The mail guy leers at me from behind a pair of fogged-up glasses. He's also got swimmer shoulders and arms. True, he's very far away, and I'm sure he's not here just for me.

Oh, and his hands are empty.

Could this be Luther's cousin, or perhaps an uncle?

"Nice night." I recite the first line of our Western show.

The mailman's lips twist into a smile that's plumb awful.

The light from the streetlamp glints off his glasses. "Good morning." Wait, was that an accent?

I feel like that would be an important detail.

Maybe . . . and I know this is really far-fetched, but maybe *he's* the burglary guy.

He robbed my house. Tailed my mom when she came over, and now he plans to rob Luther's home!

He mounts the first of the steps, and I'm standing smackdab in the middle. Scrambling, I scoot to the right, and he moves to the *exact same side.*

I scurry like a lobster-hamster to the other side, and the psycho follows.

My breath lodges, not unlike a cough drop in my throat, and this has to be a coincidence.

A misunderstanding!

He wants me to sign for a package.

But he has nothing. Nothing!

Discreetly, and pretending I've come outside to bask in the rain, I lower myself from the step to the grass. . . . *He does the same.*

I stagger back two full steps.

He walks way faster, and I'm tripping over my own feet until my butt splashes in a mud puddle. "Good thing I'm wearing rain boots!" I chortle at my own joke.

Only, he's three . . . two steps away.

He smells like moldy cheese, and his glasses are still fogged. I swear, he's guesstimating just how many steps it would take for him to grab me—and carry me to his mail truck.

Please, sir, comes Granny's voice in my imagination. *Don't worry yourself over these old bones.*

Standing, I take a few hefty steps back.

The mailman catches up.

Surely, this is beyond bizarre. There's a rational explanation for *all* of it.

He thinks I have a package . . . my lungs feel like they're being snipped with scissors that I wish I had to defend myself.

Altogether slipping in the mud, I catch myself, palms striking the edge of a step.

The mailman's hands clamp round my waist as he showers me with his day-old bread breath. "I have been waiting for you to come out all night."

I crab-walk in the muddy grass. His hand grabs my waist, and why's he grabbing me? Why's he grabbing me? Never more terrified, I tear off for Luther's house.

The sky decides to open up.

Shotgun shells rain down, and while I can only see about three inches in front of my face, I imagine this is what it'll be like if I ever decide to go to boot camp. So. Much. Work.

When the mailman wrenches my left arm painfully back, I give him the dog-scratching of his life.

Gotta say, it feels glorious as my nails dig into his face's doughy flesh.

His stubbly beard scrapes across my neck, and I tear off

his glasses and chuck them at a pillar. Once, I took a self-defense class where the teacher said that you can actually claw a person's eye out. Isn't that amazing? All you have to do is form your hand into an ice cream scoop . . .

As it happens, I like digging.

Consider me a geologist.

I'm just raising my clawed hand when something like a lightning rod flips, head over heel, through the air.

Thwaps me across the face.

My knees buckle.

Air gushes past my teeth, and my chin slaps the rock-hard cement.

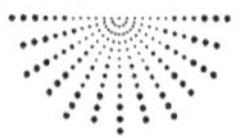

CHAPTER TEN

SOMEHOW, I've gone and conjured up Granny's actual bedroom with my old lady voice.

Frilly bed . . . pink, ruffled pillows.

I'm on a crocheted comforter with aged, dolloped edges. The lacy curtains are drawn, and murky light spills over the whole of the room.

Man, it's already mid-day. I must have been conked out for a while.

That mailman? He was going to *kidnap* me.

Where's my phone?

Oh, yeah. It's gone the way of the dodo bird.

The room's so pink, I can practically smell the Pepto-Bismol, and *I have been waiting for you to come out all night,* the mailman had said.

I don't know, but he has to be the one who burglarized my home. What are the odds of two stalker-y guys coming after my family and me in one night?

How did he even know I was here?

Did he follow Mom over?

Is Rosalyn okay?

I need to call them . . .

Dumb pockets come up empty. I know my phone's dead, but maybe Luther has a charger somewhere? Maybe I left my phone outside . . . in the monsoon . . .

Rolling around on the bed in my filthy, sticky jeans and sweater, I try to get comfortable, but everything feels so sweaty and awful.

Who in tarnation even crocheted this comforter?

Luther must have a grandmother living with him . . . or great-grandmother.

She's the one playing peekaboo in the walls!

Silver lining: my throat's not nearly as scratchy anymore. Something slick and slimy slides along my nose, and what the—?

Hunter green vines snake like centipedes across my cheek. They un-suction-cup from my nose, leaving my face uber cold.

The skin right there feels so empty, so clammy.

The vines slip from the bed and retract into a hole in the wall.

Yeah, that's completely normal . . .

I move to clear my throat, but I don't even have to cough.

Guess I hit my head harder than I originally thought.

Dried periwinkle flowers hang on the walls, necklace-style. I'd be lying if I said those framed doilies don't look an awful lot like human skin.

Tan colored; rice crispy.

Pastel figurines rather ostentatiously line a lowboy dresser, and, I hate to say it, but they all look to have made a recent visit to the amputee doctor.

A missing arm, a missing leg . . .

Granny appears to have a temper.

I still can't believe I conjured up Granny! How does that work?

The walls look like two people couldn't agree on styles of wallpaper. In stripe-y, mismatching vertical patterns, shimmery lilac alternates with a vomit-y pea green color.

And I thought Mom had design issues . . .

Throwing my leg over the side of the bed, I remind myself once again that it is time for me to go.

Hopefully, Luther doesn't catch me.

Hopefully, the mailman is long gone.

"You're awake," a soothing voice floats from the door.

I straightaway go all statue, and I know I shouldn't be so affected by visuals, but Luther's damp hair curls a bit against his forehead, and he's wearing a clean, collared shirt.

His vest is a little crooked, although the scratches on his face have already begun to heal. If he's got the hookup for some super speedy antibiotics, he'd better pass the meds on!

While I'm still not exactly sure what his earlier mood swings were all about, and if he or somebody else threw that pole that nailed me in the face, I choose to give him the benefit of the doubt. "Hello, sweet thing!"

Doesn't take me long to spot the silver metal tray in his hands, and that glass of water has my mouth priming to pump the well.

Tearing from the bed, I snag my foot on the frou-frou bed skirt. I shoot Luther a smile that says, *No worries—I do that all the time*, and haul my butt closer to take up the glass.

I down it like a fat kid on a seesaw.

"Got the Sahara Desert goin' on in here." I tap my throat. "Thanks, hon."

Luther glances over his shoulder to make sure *the moths* aren't watching us before crossing the room and ultimately lingering at the bedside table.

Clutching the tray to his chest, his shoulders relax, but he still glances round the room with no small amount of paranoia. "How are you feeling?"

"That metal pole certainly threw me for a loop, but I expect to be right as rain soon!"

Luther's face washes yellow. Guess he feels guilty about throwing that pole.

At least he scared off the mail guy.

If he *did* throw that pole.

"How long was I out?" I ask him.

Luther's lips draw into a thin line. Gosh, his upper lip's got a fair amount of facial hair, and, despite everything that's happened, I'm tempted to nibble it off.

Oh, Cate. Don't get ahead of yourself.

"I hope you like toast." Luther lowers his tray to the table alongside the vase of crusty, dead flowers and a wide, metal brush.

Truthfully, I hadn't noticed the tray had anything else on it, but, sure enough—there's toast. Next to the toast is a big, fat jar of orange, gummy stuff, the likes of which I've seen before. "Ooh, I love marmalade!"

I survey the green and white fuzzy spots spread over the toast, though, and I'm not real sure Luther's granny's marmalade is all that edible.

Luther's staring at me like he expects me to eat it, though, and it's probably just peach pits, so I pick up the piece of toast and take a hasty bite. "Mmm!"

Luther all but collapses on the edge of the bed—as if I've just eased the weight of the world from off his shoulders. And I'm not really a natural at knowing what to say or do, so I try to think of something poignant to say as I work around the stickiness in my mouth. "Whose room is this, anyhow?"

Casually, Luther rests his hand on the crocheted comforter. In the name of quiet solidarity, I make sure to sit real close.

Surveying my face with uber soft eyes, he says, "You seem hotter than usual."

"So you *do* like the perm!"

"Do you, in any way, feel fevered?"

I lay the back of my hand against my forehead, turning quasi prima donna. "Hard to tell." I lean in close enough to smell the licorice smell. "Could *you* feel it for me?"

Luther raises his arm, and his vested shirt brushes against my sweater, sending me a barrage of heat fumes.

He places his hand on my forehead, and he's altogether gentler than I presupposed.

Though he did act all fishy after playing the piano, so my goal is to *get away* from him, not co-sign on a loan.

"What happened to the mail guy?" Mayhap my voice squeaks a little.

Luther snatches his fingers back like he's just been bitten, and he searches my face, looking super sad. "He won't be bothering you again."

"How long has it been since he left?"

"I didn't mean to hit you." He ignores my question and looks down. "I didn't expect you to jump in front of the pole."

"I was gettin' ready to pull an eye out!"

"Remind me to never get on your bad side . . ." Luther shudders, and, *somewhere* beneath his cultured ways and nonplussed exterior, I know there's gotta be a smile lurkin' deep down in there.

What I would give to see it—just once.

"I called the police." Once again, he rubs the ring on his finger. "I expect they should arrive soon."

I don't know whether to hug him, thank him, or remind him that this day was weird even *before* the mail guy showed up.

Except, now . . . I don't exactly feel like leaving . . . I don't know.

Everything feels so intricate and cozy around Luther.

Is that weird?

Yes, I know. But for the first time in a great, long while, I've actually been rescued by a boy. I mean, ugly mailman tried to abduct me, and *poof!* Luther came to my rescue. Technically, he did knock me out with that pole, but we can consider that rehearsal.

I don't exactly know what's up with those vines, but I can also actually breathe real well.

Maybe someone's pulling the vines with a pulley system inside those walls.

Mom told me to stay and knows where I am, anyhow.

When she's ready, she'll come and get me. After what happened with the US Postal Service, I don't exactly feel like going solo.

Between all this thinking, *somehow* I've managed to put my hand on Luther's leg. Can't tell if the heavy breathing is coming from the walls, him, or me.

"You're not one of those guys who likes to trick girls . . ." I glance at the head of the bed, since this is the second time I've woken up, completely disoriented and . . . more flirtatious than usual.

The cold, hard truth of what I just said blankets between us, and I can see *exactly* when my meaning hits Luther.

He slips from the bed.

Like me, he trips on the ruffled skirt.

Turning beet red, he doesn't have time to articulate his words. "I'll . . . see if I can hurry along the police."

I am the cruelest girl in the world.

But if I believe him—and I do—then there's nothing to be scared of.

Feeling a giant pang in my gut, I jump to the floor, which squeaks not a little. "I am *so*, so sorry for saying that. Sometimes . . . I speak before I've had time to digest my words."

Luther's hands rest, immobile, at his sides. "I understand this house is . . ."

"Shuddersome? Ominous?"

". . . Not exactly forthright."

I don't know whether to laugh or cry or yell.

I mean, I like layers. I *love* layers. Onions and parfaits. But is this the way our conversations are going to go *every single time* I try to get one of us to be honest?

Sensing my unease, Luther mumbles, "I tried getting you to leave . . . "

I laugh—this crazed, lunatic asylum woman's sound. "I know!"

Rubbing the backs of my arms, I find that they're both cold and hot. Everything in Monkshood is mixed up. "I deplore John Keats!" I add, 'cause if we're going to be honest, let's begin with that.

Luther draws so close, he's half an inch away from my face. So much warmth wafts from his chest, I feel like an orphan in January, stuck without a coat.

"I do want to hear *your* poetry," I murmur as my heart goes faster still.

"My poetry?"

"Assuming you've written some."

Luther's eyes stretch all wide. "Why, yes." And it's a little magical when all the lines in his face soften.

"Then read it to me!" I do my best to shake out my crumpled sweater. "Not everyone can be a parfait, Luther."

CHAPTER ELEVEN

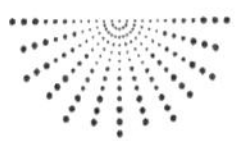

So many blankets surround us, things may not stay PG. Who knows?

'Course, the "us" part is a little forward thinking on my part. Luther's currently stoking the fire, and as the stubborn logs hiss and groan, I'd say he's setting up the backdrop for a romantic movie.

For the first time since getting here, I feel relaxed.

Relaxed enough to pull my knees in all cozy-like and cup my hand along the hollow of my neck. I've never been into poetry—we all know how John Keats was a bust—but maybe Luther will dab on a little Shakespearean violence.

When he finishes with rearranging the logs, he joins me on the couch, all sophisticated and graceful as he moves, and holds his book with such impressive posture that he could be Mr. Darcy in the next *Pride and Prejudice* retelling.

With the bag o' bones twirling above us, Luther takes the time to thoroughly clear his throat. He appears to be waiting for me to give him the green light, so I nod, praying he's somewhat gifted.

Nodding, he opens his perfect lips . . .

"She dulls our life," he reads with his uber smooth voice. "Chokes. Rips. Maims . . ."

Well, three points for a violent beginning!

Gripping his book harder, he adds, "She is the *antithesis* of love. The fair one is patient, yes. But also vindictive, morbidly selfish, and controlling—"

No longer do I have the wherewithal to keep my mouth shut. "Sounds like you gotta mean girl on your hands."

"Her somnolent nature is quite unsettling." He doesn't raise his gaze from the book, so I'm not sure if he's answering me or if he's still reading.

Reaching up, I tap the back of his hardback. "Your poem certainly has a 'high drama' quality."

Luther's eyes crinkle round the edges as I catch his eye above the book, and I'm pretty sure he doesn't understand my meaning.

So, I reach out and pat his hand. "If she's an enemy to you, she's an enemy to me." My heart does this unexpected twist. "Is this why you're so sad all the time?"

Flinching, Luther snaps his book shut. "Poetry helps me express my woes."

"And do you have many woes, Luther?"

His eyes flash.

"Do you wanna talk about it?"

Again, Luther's only like two inches away. His facial hair has even more scruff, and being around Luther is like tiptoeing too close to the fire. I can't move away. It's like accidentally eating a ghost pepper, swallowing it, and chasing it down with Dr Pepper.

Luther Dvorak is elusive and evasive, and . . . he bloody well won't crack a smile 'til he's ninety.

But . . . he's also empathetic.

And gentle.

As long as you don't listen to him play the piano, then immediately try to tuck tail and run.

This foreign emotion splits apart his gaze. His cheeks tighten, his eyes go taut, and, I swear, he's going to tell me something important.

The bag of bones creaks and drops—a full twelve inches.

The scare takes three full years off my life, and I've clutched my chest, laughing now that I realize I've just gasped. "Sorry! Sorry . . . wasn't expecting that. Where are your parents, anyway?"

Luther presses his lips together in a firm line before rubbing the middle of his forehead and standing.

In two stiff strides, he's made it over to the fire.

Bracing his hands against the gray, stone mantle, he leans toward the decorative egg-and-dart wood etchings—a Victorian detail Mom once told me about. "Tell me . . . are you innocent?"

What in the heck does a girl say to that? "Does your entire family like to read poetry?" See how he responds to that.

"Can you be trusted?"

"Can *you* do the whip and nay-nay?"

There's a sudden rush of wind that sends the pages fluttering in the books.

A door closes . . . somewhere . . . and Luther's arms become so stiff, I half-expect him to, I don't know . . . grab the gramophone and chuck it straight into the fireplace. Not because he's been violent (except when he threw that metal pole), but 'cause that's what angry men *do* when they're angry.

The milky mirrors do little to show me the emotions on his face. His shirt collar is up, and I half-wonder if he's always dressed this artistically . . . Rosalyn would have loved to grab her sketchbook and pencil before . . .

"There was a time," Luther says, loosening his grip on the mantle, "when my family liked to read poetry."

"But they don't appreciate it like you do?"

He pushes away from the mantle. Rounding on me, he shows me his impassive face. One of his eyebrows is pointier than the other, and his hair's just as wild as it is cobwebby.

"They do not appreciate *anything*." His boot kicks off from the fireplace.

Pushing back the blankets, I try to decide if I should be empathetic or take charge. We go round and round, trying to ascertain what the other one's hiding, and I'm afraid that if I do lower my guard, we'll both grow bored.

Though . . . we can't live like this forever. Finding my hidden authoritative voice, I say, "Luther, I thought you said you'd spill the beans about why I'm here after you finished playing the piano."

He flinches—as if completely clueless to what I'm saying.

"What in the gosh darn tarnation is going on?!"

Slowly, the boy absorbs what must be an exasperated expression on my face. The fact that I'm still wearing my old clothes and they've gotta be wadded up like a Kleenex doesn't really speak to my reliability as a trustable source, but I *do* have nice skin. And I'm pretty sure I've got on the non-running eyeliner.

"I am in the throes of explaining what is going on. And" —Luther breaks eye contact— "you have an intriguing face."

I don't know whether to shout *hallelujah,* or wring his neck.

Clenching his fists in frustration, Luther takes two heady steps closer. "Do you know why I am absolutely drawn to you, Cate? You have the face of someone who's holding onto secrets even *you* cannot fathom."

"Um, thanks?" Now I can't decide if I should feel deflated or ecstatic.

Leaning down, Luther rests his long-fingered hands on the coffee table two inches from mine.

I absorb his sweet, licorice breath, and . . . does his shampoo have tea tree oil?

The wiser part of me believes he's buttering me up. I don't know why. 'Cause he's about to break up with me?

But we're not even together!

I don't think.

Never thought to ask him if we're exclusive.

When his lips stop a few inches from mine, he lingers there for a few long seconds before moving them to my ear. "You . . . are torturing me . . ."

A cloudy pile of dust suddenly puffs up around us, and I end up coughing so hard, I have a heart attack.

By the time I'm crawling to the finish line, Luther's sorrowful pupils darken. "Tell me once and for all, do you have the asthma?"

Can't stop laugh-coughing . . .

I am "torturing" him and now . . .

"You talk like you're ninety!"

Luther's deep, gray eyes absorb my eyes. Perhaps he's deciding whether or not he *should* talk to me . . . but now the heat's so tangible, I could bathe in ice buckets.

Sweat drips from my neck to my chest.

My forehead's a furnace.

Luther snakes a gentle finger through a tendril of my hair and murmurs, "Ophelia . . ."

Wait. . . .

I flinch as Luther's eyes widen when he realizes his mistake.

Thankfully, I am with it enough to slap his hand away, but I still do not understand how he could call me the wrong name. "Why in the Samhain did you call me that?!"

As I jump to my feet, the rest of the blankets tumble to the floor.

Trembling, Luther holds up his hands. "I . . . am sorry."

What is happening?

"Why did you call me that?" It's the type of name that never should have been dreamt up.

And I don't know . . . I start stacking up books. Part of me feels the need to organize and reverts to school mode. "Is that what you've always called me in your head?"

Has he ever called me "Cate"? Now I have brain fog.

Luther, though, runs a shaky hand through his hair. "Sometimes . . ."

My mind automatically darts back to the moment when Luther and I first met at the library. I was standing in line to check out some books and puzzles. I accidentally dropped my card, and *he* ever so gallantly picked it up. Looking down, he read the Sharpie lettering that spelled both my first and middle name, middle name first . . .

I was thrown and excited 'cause he was fixated on *me*, truth be told.

So, in that moment, I didn't mind it that he called me by my real first name, Ophelia. Of course, I clarified that I go by Cate, but that was a fluke. A fluke!

Maybe . . . he has a fetish for old names.

Deciding that it's high time I leave, I check that I'm still wearing my boots. "My name is Cate."

Luther gulps, giving me this look like he fears that he's just made the gravest mistake of his life.

Maybe I should ask him the names of his past girlfriends —Beatrice, Judith, Nancy!—and, lifting his hand, he actually has the gall to try to stroke my face. "Both Ophelia *and* Cate are lovely names."

I jerk back so fast, I knock all the books off the coffee

table. One of the mugs crashes to the ground, and I cry, "Ophelia's an awful name!"

The walls shudder, almost in answer, and Luther shoots me such a deep frown that he'd be giving me the heebie-jeebies if he weren't so pretty.

I grab the fire poker.

Saunter close enough to poke him in the chest with the cool, metal tip. He looks so apologetic and so dashing that this unexpected impulse to kiss the hollow side of his cheek flares through me, and *oh,* no. He is trouble, so I jab him harder. "I think it's time you told me *exactly* why you wanted me to come here. Don't. Lie."

He opens his mouth to answer, but I'm not finished.

"And I need you to know, that marmalade was disgusting."

Taking a heavy step backward, Luther paces over the rug that *probably* isn't bloodstained. He rakes his hand through his hair and stops in front of the wall of plants near the lead, glass-fronted bookcase. Sticking his hands in his pants pockets, he marks me with his eyes. "Do you want to get to know me?" His rage settles partially. "*Truly* get to know me?"

My breath tightens as the rope from the bag of bones twists and squeaks.

Walls rumble.

I nod.

"Then come with me." He grabs my hand, stalks to the back door.

I follow, 'cause Imma immune from livin' a dull life.

CHAPTER TWELVE

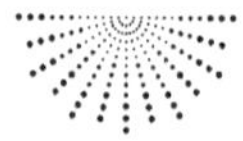

MY FACE IS ATTACKED by skinny, witchy fingers.

The wind!

Just the wind. My sensible side pleads, *Go back go back go back,* but Luthy's going to show me all his deep, dark secrets, and I'm really liking this "Luthy."

In semi-quiet solidarity, we march down the creaky back porch steps to pause before a sad, little outbuilding.

Looks to be strung together with two-by-fours, rebar, and chicken wire.

Dead plants chaotically slip in and around these teeny-tiny oval wires, and I'm not even sure what could be in there.

"Is this where you keep all the dead bodies?" I think I'm pretty clever amidst my laughing.

Luther slips a secondary skeleton key inside the padlock. "I know it doesn't look like much. But I built it during happier times . . ."

Oh, he built it? Leave it to me to be the royal jerk.

Sad to say, half the building looks like a gust of wind will blow it over, and the other half's overtaken by moss. Scrounging for something positive to say, I add, *"Love* the perpendicular corners." I give a firm knock on the wobbly two-by-fours.

Luther mutely pulls the padlock off.

"Worried all the plants will make a jailbreak?" I ask.

Luther wordlessly holds the door open.

Well, okay, then. "Why, thank you, kind sir."

Really, truly, it *is* an honor that he's showing me another part of his life, so I swagger on in.

Catching sight of the dew-covered, bluish-purplish flowers, I beam. "They're so pretty!"

Between their upside down, long lobes and stacked grouping, I have no idea what kind of flowers they are, but it is pretty darn remarkable that they're still alive, being that we're at the end of October.

Once inside, Luther examines a thin crack in the copper drip line before pulling a cream-colored roll of tape from his pants.

Tearing off a piece, he carefully wraps the old, metal pipe like it's a long lost friend.

"By the way . . ." I graze the edge of my fingers along the pretty, silky flowers. "Have you seen my phone?"

With his back to me, Luther slips the tape back into his pocket. "When you were running away . . . it broke. I was going to fix it, but . . ." He casts a sidelong glance at the metal gutter system that climbs a lot like a daddy long-legs along the back wall of the house.

Hmm. Wonder how far he got in fixing it. "No worries!"

Without actually touching the flowers, Luther examines a trellis that drapes across a splotchy, windowed wall. "Whatever you do, *don't* touch anything."

Oops. Guess I wasn't supposed to touch those silky petals earlier. "Is this a secret society for plants?"

Luther frowns at me, so I halfheartedly salute him. "Aye aye, Sensei."

Dried petals melt into the ground, reminding me of the petals that suddenly appeared in the labyrinth halls.

Some of the petals nearly brush my face, and Luther tugs me away so fast, I 'bout lose my lunch.

Staring down at me, he looks at me like I'm the only girl he's ever seen in the world. Is all this part of some weird charade?

Water bubbles in the drip-line as it comes on, and Luther releases my waist.

Gotta say, that whole area spasms and tremors from his touch—like thunder, actually.

While my heart goes catawampus, Luther pulls on a pair of very sturdy-looking gloves, and I try to wrack my brain for any sense of small talk.

Not coming up with anything . . .

Luther grabs a trowel from the wooden shelving and digs around in the ground. Exposing a gray-white root, his silent yet deadly eyes rest upon me, as if invoking me to respond.

"Lemme guess." I scrounge around for answers. "It's the same thing that's hanging in your kitchen. Ginger root, right?" Haha, I know it's not *ginger* root—he looks far too terrified for it to be that—but Imma tryin' to see what kinda reaction I can get out of him.

Ultimately, Luther glowers, but he doesn't say a word.

"Hey," I cry, "it's not the most colorful of specimens."

Pulling the root from the soil, Luther delicately holds it out on his palm. "What if I told you that it can *kill* you, Cate?"

What if I'm happy that he got my name right? "So why do you hang it in your kitchen for unsuspecting visitors to accidentally slip into their mugs?"

"Most of us do not mess with unidentified substances . . ." Lowering the root in his hand, Luther adds, "It can cure many heart anomalies."

He still hasn't told me the plant's name, though, so I hold my breath.

"I fed you some earlier," he says, and back up—undo—*rewind*!

He's openly admitting he poisoned me?

"Why would you do that?!" True, I play Russian Roulette with my health all the time, but other people have to tell me what they're doing *before* they secretly whip out the poison.

"I thought it would help with your disease . . ."

He knows about my condition?

Rosalyn swore she would never tell him. Mom! . . .

Not wanting to talk to Luther about the overproduction of my thicker mucus—or the fact that I sometimes use an oval-shaped thing called an acapella at my visits with the school nurse—I nod at the dead-looking plants in cylindrical cages at the back.

Tall, scraggly leaves hang similarly to the way I'm sure my hair looks, and a crusty, old chart's nailed to the wall, covered with extensive, loopy writing.

"Look who's a master gardener now!" I cry, not even having to feign the enthusiasm.

Crow's feet stab Luther's eyes, and looks like I've hit another glum topic. "Unfortunately, I do not give them the time they deserve . . ."

"Hey, I got a black thumb." Speaking of which . . . "Doesn't anybody else do chores around here?"

Luther ducks away from answering by lowering his chin to his chest.

I've obviously hit a sore spot, so I pat him on the elbow. "Your tomato plants look grand."

Luther's eyes actually soften at that, and I'm getting somewhere. "You could make salsa. Ooh, and spaghetti!"

The boy's suddenly gazing at me with so much kindness.

Looks like I've stumbled onto one of his key interests. Hey, better than video games or fake wrestling.

Spotting an overturned bucket, I formulate a very risky plan.

"I don't know about you" —I sashay over to the bucket— "but I have been *dyin'* for some fresh tomato paste."

Luther's eyes shine brightly as I lean over to turn over the bucket. Climbing atop it, I hold up a finger to address my audience. "We shall allow *all* men to grow whatsoever plant they like! In any season or location. Let them be prosperous and bear *many* tomato babies!"

Luther gazes at me for so long, he's probably thinking I'm delusional, but I've definitely been called worse.

I give a stiff little bow.

Climbing back down, I make a big show of brushing off my hands on my pants. "Got a B-minus in speech, don't mean to brag."

Face slack, Luther tries to fill his pockets with his gloved hands. When they don't go in fluidly, he suddenly pulls them out. Taking several random steps, he makes this quasi-abnormal noise in his throat, hunches his shoulders, and rips off his gloves. Tossing them to the nearby wooden shelf, he seizes a pair of pruning shears and shoves them into my hands.

Leaning in oh, so close, he murmurs, "You need to get out of here, Cate. *Now.*"

The hair on the back of my neck stands on end, though I don't rightly know how to take that. "There you go, trying to chase me away again . . ."

He snags my arm in his grip. "You need to *leave* before he wakes!"

"I thought you said it was a 'she.'"

Something sharp scrapes along the door, and ooh, mercy, that sounds very much like claws.

Thwap.

Thwap.

What's makin' that noise?

My mind automatically flops to the wild boars while Luther full-on blanches.

BOOM!

The door rattles and shakes.

It bounces a total of fourteen times before a caramel-colored paw suddenly breaks through the glass.

A feral growl comes from Luther's once-loveable dog, and I don't have a clue what's makin' him so mad.

Glass crackles beneath Bastian's paws.

Saliva drips in heavy ropes from the dog's mouth, and I wanna be approachable. I wanna say, *Hey, doggie, doggie.* But his thick, black lips are already peeling back . . .

Hurdling through the air, Luther throws himself between me and Bastian. "Cate, RUN!"

CHAPTER THIRTEEN

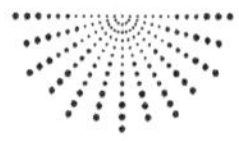

I STUMBLE, half run past the purplish flowers.

Must not let the deadly plants touch me.

Why is that?

Ducking around a bunch that seem to have grown taller, I wind round a shoot that's somehow sprouting up near the trellis.

Bastian proves he's way too street-smart by tracking my every step.

He's practically a killer horse.

In a blur of layered jacket, ripped pants, and vest, Luther leaps to grab Bastian's collar.

Bastian snaps at his owner, and, *I swear,* all the plants are swaying and applauding at what's going on.

Thankfully, Luther's able to lure Bastian a few paces from the door. I make it to the doorframe, pruning shears in hand, glass crunching beneath my boots as I run.

In a warm, puffy cloud, Bastian's moist breath creeps over the little hairs on the back of my neck.

Remember that other phobia I mentioned before?

It may or may not have to do with hot breath.

Any breath, really.

I'm not picky about it.

Wrenching open the door, I lob the shears in the dog's general direction—only for them to slink to the grass.

I slip outside real fast.

Trouble is, Bastian tears off a mouth-sized piece of my shirt.

Doesn't matter.

Doesn't matter.

Didn't spend *all* my time sewing it.

Mud slings every which way from my boots; hair flies in my face as I run like an Olympian. Actually, I never rightly thought of myself as a sprinter, but a career could be had.

As I leave Luther and Bastian in the dust, I trip through the fog.

It's dusty. But wet. How is that?

I nearly run smack-dab into a muddy, tin wall, and ooh, another outbuilding.

I need to get to the property's edge.

If I can find a gate, I'll be able to get out.

A rustling in the grass makes me turn, and as I do, thick, sharp claws suddenly hook into my back.

I'm being crocheted; someone's gone and grabbed me with the hook of a tow truck, and I know it's Bastian—it has to be Bastian—but it helps to pretend I'm not at the end of a fishing hook.

The taste of slippery metal slips over my tongue. I elbow him in the head, and he throws his body against me.

I fall.

Bastian's really part jaguar.

Growls curl from his teeth, and it's just a matter of time before I cash in my chips.

Maybe, with a bit of imagination, I'll be able to pretend his cool, wet saliva is really Tabasco sauce . . .

I have become a dog's toy.

I squeak, and I didn't think this is how I'd go out, but, because of what I did to my sister, I always knew karma would pop up.

By the time Bastian's done tossing me, my ears ring a heck of a lot.

Rain drizzles across my face, and my cheek rests on a pretty, flat rock. When something *thwaps* Bastian between the shoulder blades, he falls on my left leg.

Pain shoots from bone to skin, and Bastian does this horrible, undomesticated growl as Luther grabs my hand and pulls me close. "WHY AREN'T YOU RUNNING OR FIGHTING HIM OFF?"

Exhausted, I push off from the rocky ground. These ol' bones are just about spent. And, to be clear, I have learned to pick my battles.

I always knew I deserved to end up dead.

Luther jabs Bastian twice with a garden spade when the dog suddenly lunges at my feet, and, somehow, the stars align when I actually succeed in kicking him right on the neck.

I didn't want things to go like this.

I didn't want to hurt the dog!

"GO!" Luther screams.

In one swift bite, Bastian rips a hole in the leg of Luther's pants, and I suppose now's as good a time as any to listen. I may have been exhausted, but I'm feelin' a second wind. And I need to fight for Rosalyn. And Mom! When push comes to shove, Mom would actually care if I lived or died. Yes?

As I tear off for the back part of the yard, though, I realize there's no way in Hades I'm leaving my favorite boy behind.

I'm not that cold.

So, I turn as Bastian growls.

He and Luther tussle as Bastian nips Luther's sleeve, and Luther smacks a hefty rock against Bastian's striking face.

I *hate* that he's having to hurt his animal, and I'm just stupidly standing here like a quasi-cool lava lamp.

So, I crouch behind the rotting wood and tin outbuilding, assessing the situation. I *need* to rescue Luther.

I should be some bait and run?

My foot prematurely snaps a twig.

Bastian rears around to face me, and I search the fog for a way to run. But I have *no* idea how far back the yard goes, and Bastian's a freaking cheetah.

Forget my running glory days.

I need to get to Luther. Maybe he's base—like in baseball—or he knows where that is.

Though I can't see him anymore through the fog, and I need to see how badly he's bleeding.

All I can see on the ground is wild patches of grass. I've already abandoned one person in my life. I'm not abandoning another.

While I approach what I think is the back porch steps, I do not find a body. Nope. Zilch. Nada.

I do not find Luther standing *or* lying down. He's completely erased, melted into the fog.

He's not by the greenhouse door . . . I don't think. Maybe he ran back inside?

As I stagger back, my leg's hit by Bastian's warm, moist snout, and I sprint for the house. Scampering up the steps, I am sure sure sure my life depends on escaping him now.

Half ripping the door from its hinges, I scramble inside.

Luther has to be in the house!

Snout clogs the door, so I kick Bastian, guilt clawing at me all the while.

With shaking hands, I grab the chain on the wall, slip the round thingee in the track, and zip it tight.

Bastian throws himself against the door.

Luther screams from outside.

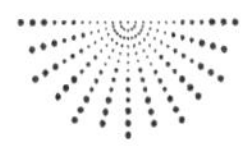

CHAPTER FOURTEEN

"LUTHER!" I scream, hand frozen on the chain.

I have to go back.

Have to go back.

Bastian claws and throws himself against the door.

I need to find my phone.

Call the police. Didn't Luther tell me he called the police? What happened with that? We need to *tell* them to come before the only occupation I can dream of having is the world's flirtiest chew toy.

Luther said my phone was somewhere . . . and smashed, but I can fix it. I can fix it! Even with my back screaming for Neosporin and Band-Aids.

Squinting through a window clogged with more dead plants, I try to find the boy, but all I can see is a black haze.

Trees and mud.

A smudged, army puzzle.

BANG!

Bastian jumps into the window, his ears and nose pressed into the glass. My heart nearly jumps outta my chest, but the glass doesn't break.

I need to get past the dog.

Hide in another place.

But Luther . . .

Something willowy groans from upstairs, and I do not like the idea of being stuck in this house without Luther.

Something *else* shudders overhead.

BANG! Clank, clank . . .

The bag hanging from the rafters reminds me of a more macabre version of a piñata we once got for Rosalyn—a unicorn for her fourth birthday.

Why would Luther invite me over to begin with if he had a bloodthirsty dog?

Can dogs conspire to be a human's friend while plotting their death the entire time? I knew they were smart, but this is just nuts.

Again, through the plant-covered window, I search for Luther. But the greenhouse door swings and swings, all alone, in the wind.

Maybe . . . Luther went to the other outbuilding?

The one with the tin and board siding.

The grandfather clock *chime-chime-chimes*, and something upstairs just dropped something real fragile.

The sound of a scuttling lobster scampers above the second-story floorboards, and I *really* hope that isn't Luther's secret, hidden girlfriend.

She has a pegged leg.

Or . . . his grandmother does?

Time to find my phone.

Where might Luther try to repair a cell phone bedazzled with Rosalyn's glitter?

Hmm . . . the dining table!

Oh, but the Dvoraks don't seem to have a dining room.

The couch?

The couch!

Spinning round, I comb each and every square inch of the couch's musty, old cushions.

Lungs burn like a cast iron boiler, but I'll be right as rain once I'm able to get out of here.

Breezy plumes of dust curl toward me as I search the couch, and I can't believe there isn't even a Cheerio.

Cough.

Wheeze.

Cough.

Maybe . . . Luther deposited my phone on the kitchen counter?

There could be worse ideas.

I tear off for the witchy-woo, root-dangling kitchen.

My left side clips the side of the counter, but don't cry for me, Argentina—Luther could be bleeding out.

Phone's not behind the silver tea kettle.

Not behind the cocoa packets canister, either.

There's not *anything* near, above, or around the square sink with the nozzle and high knobs.

Should I be brave and look upstairs?

Luther's   peg-legged   granny-girlfriend   could   be reasonable . . .

And I suppose—I guess—I might have left my phone in Granny's room.

But I didn't see it when I looked around when I was in there.

Maybe . . . it's in Luther's room—laid out and all organized on an antique worktable.

I tear off for the stairs. Can't help holding onto the willow-wisp of hope.

On the way, I haul my butt over to the fireplace and grab the gnarly fire poker. I could run back outside, grab Luther, and fend off Bastian, but if Bastian gets me before I can get him, there will be *no one* to call the police to help us out.

Must check upstairs.

Must check upstairs.

Biting my lower lip, I glance out the window a final time, but the army puzzle of trees and mud swish in a blur.

Greenhouse door whips madly in the wind, and no Luther . . .

Shoes trailing fresh dirt, I scamper up the stairs. Mom would have my head if she knew I was doing that to the carpet draped down the center of the wood, but I don't have time to grab a vacuum and be all redeemable.

At the top of the stairs, I'm greeted by photograph after old photograph.

Dead people are looking at me—no one cracks a smile—and I don't have time to stop or think about it. Nice to know I'm not the only unphotogenic one, though.

Pea green walls flank me on the left and right, and I stalk past Grandma's room with my eye on the prize—Luther's.

Every single footfall results in a squeak that does nothing to calm my nerves. It also smells musty. His room's gotta be up here.

Reaching a door that's held open by a wooden pickleball paddle, I pause to pick it up. I could use that along with the fire poker to fend off Bastian. But that'd be like fencing with the Count of Monte Cristo.

I do a few jabs with the paddle before dropping it to the floor.

Inside the room lies a partially-made bed and . . . a pretty extensive collection of maps pinned to the walls. They're ripped in so many places, but taped back together, again reminding me of Rosalyn's unicorn papier-maché piñata.

Why would Luther have such an extensive collection of maps hanging in his room?

Random pins mark several countries, tacking up sticky notes.

An old globe rests on a chest of drawers, and it looks like Africa's been torn away.

The peeling plaster near the ceiling definitely has black mold. On Luther's desk, though, lies the lonely, old bones of my phone.

Just like I had foreseen.

It all feels so surreal.

Sad to say, the device is in so many pieces, there's no way I'll be calling the police or Mom. Luther said the police was headed over, but . . . what if they're not?

What if he was only telling me what I wanted to hear?

My breath hitches. Gah, my throat always houses a baby rattle.

I struggle to breathe, but all that comes out is *hack! hack!*

There is no time to panic.

Things are supposed to be looking up.

In a few minutes, I'll be calling home. Going out bowling and treating Mom and Rosalyn to frozen yogurt.

But our place was robbed. So we wouldn't be doing that.

Feeling extra woozy, I take an additional step. The hardwood floor creaks lobster-style in a trio of low clicks and groans, and I grab one of the four posts of the bed, determined to settle my nerves.

Chest's feeling mighty heavy. I could hook up to my ventilator and medicate for hours and hours.

Breathe, just breathe, Cate.

Don't think about CF . . .

I need air.

I need—

I turn for the window, but it's been boarded up.

Dainty, glowy things dance on the low, slanted ceiling, and I'm definitely seeing spots. Imma goin' to pass out.

Why wasn't Mom more concerned about me chumming it up around so much black mold?

Soon I'll be in the hospital.

We all know there will be complications.

I'll end up staying for weeks.

If I ever get out.

Lungs feel like they're a forest fire . . .

Cough.

Hack.

Cough.

Throat tastes like cauliflower.

Hey, is that a bathroom? With an extra murky sink and mirror . . .

Steam, I love steam! Woo, baby, you know that could fix me up.

CHAPTER FIFTEEN

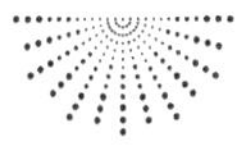

Every single person with cystic fibrosis loves showers.

'Tis good for our lungs.

It's *great* for people who love to be exhibitionists, all alone, for themselves . . .

Of course, the steam is amazing. It's akin to flooding Vicks Vapor rub through my chest, and the hot water caresses, prods, and massages my back.

I could go nighty-night right here, right now—if it meant Mom and Rosalyn were taken care of, and I could go by way of steam that feels like liquid crack.

Oy, I can't believe I left Luther outside.

Oh, you're bleeding? Excuse me while I put on my birthday suit and shampoo my hair!

This is why I'm zero for four in relationships.

Yowza, the water's getting *really* hot.

I reach up to turn the old, metallic knob when the water temperature suddenly drops.

Piercing needles of cold suddenly stab into my arms and back, and goosebumps erupt from my skin in half a flash.

I *try* to turn the knob, but the metal is blazing hot. Hot handle, cold water? What the—?

I'm living in a crescendo. The water temperature slowly rises again, and tubas and bassoons are drilling music into my shoulders and shins.

Fiery liquid slides its fingers into the wounds in my back, and I didn't know I could withstand hot water scalding me like that.

The knob is stuck.

Both the water *and* the metal handle are so hot, they shock, and the knob is shrieking like a dolphin as my hands twist and twist—it won't gain any traction.

I thought there weren't supposed to be showers in old, Victorian-era homes—only claw-footed tubs.

Something must be wrong with my eyes, 'cause now the water's turning black.

It's getting heavy.

Thick.

Feels . . . but doesn't smell like molasses.

It smells like mothballs, more like. And heavy. So heavy, weighing me down.

My skin's blistering, well past red, and with a shaking hand, I reach out to push the shower curtain back, but the tar's too heavy and thick.

I can't see.

I can't see my arms, my legs . . .

The water suddenly shuts off.

For all I know, Luther's goin' to be out there on the other side of the shower curtain, pipe wrench in hand. He's going to ask me why I happened to use his shower without permission, and I'm not going to explain the real reason to him.

With shaking, tar-covered hands, I grab the thin, gauzy curtain and pull it back, but there's no Luther.

I don't think.

Only that lone pedestal sink on a fancy Ionic column.

Thank the Maker.

I've still gotta wipe away the tar.

Still gotta wipe away the tar!

It burns. So much.

Grappling along the wall for a towel, I seize the thin, scratchy fabric from a wall hook and pull the towel to my face.

I look down.

Tar's gone.

CHAPTER SIXTEEN

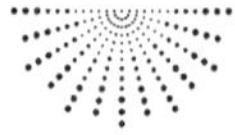

Molasses?

Surely, I was seeing things.

Just like the slugs dripping from Luther's eyes.

Luther, himself, told me this place makes you see things that aren't really there. So . . . what does that mean? The house is haunted? If I'm lucky . . . or unlucky . . . all of this isn't just my CF.

The Monkshood plant messes with the minds of dogs who like to be scratched behind the ears and nuzzle your hand.

Oh.

Guess I fell asleep while wrapped in this towel, 'cause I'm lying on Luther's bed.

Totally forgot I climbed on here after that shower escapade.

I do not recommend Luther's shower.

I am terrified to leave this room.

Weird noises have been going on for hours and hours. It could be the hot water heater—old pipes—but I can't get the foolish image of a girl with one eye and a pegged leg outta my head.

Oh my gosh, it's *so* relieving to be able to breathe again.

Something thin and slender slithers along the base of my nose and—I reach up to grab the strand of whatever it is, but it's just skin.

Just skin.

No vines.

Hmm. Whatever that was, it was fast.

Looking to the walls with the torn-up maps, I halfway put together that a string of hazy notes are being played by someone somewhere in the house.

Luther's got another melancholy, stringed instrument?

He's okay! He's all right!

But what instrument is that?

A ukulele . . . a banjo . . .

Shoot, here I am, lyin' on a cute boy's bed in nothing but a towel, and I said my vixen days were over.

Ahead of me stands a fancy chest of drawers. Dollops on the sides, chaffed edges—the whole shebang would be making Mom giddy, all right.

That light, honey-colored wood is what they call "birds-eye" maple. It's super expensive and rare. And with the beading on the trim and unscratched surface, Mom would be scouring the Internet for comps, ASAP.

Luther has got to have some clean clothes in there.

Skipping the top drawer—don't need to tempt myself with no underwear drawers—I go straight for the second.

Sort through piles and piles of vests and scarves.

Landing on a pretty, soft red fabric, I totes find a flannel shirt.

From the third drawer, I snag a pair of slightly too-big pants, and by the time I reach the top of the stairs, I'm a bona fide lumberjack cover model.

Downstairs, twin trumpets croon from the gramophone, playing twenties music.

This shrieking sound of whinnying ropes cuts across the stairway, and from the plant side of the room, a fair-haired guy in a jet-black robe literally comes sailin' from the rope-hanging corner.

For real, he's an acrobat on a trapeze.

A flesh and blood magician who's just missed his show.

Hovering about three feet above the coffee table, the guy kicks out his black shoes to land on the furniture as I inadvertently wander around the piano.

Who the gas is he?

He's got immaculate, pale skin and a dimpled chin and toothy smile. Something about the combination doesn't strike my fancy at all.

Whoever he is . . . he isn't Luther.

The guy releases the ropes, and when they whinny again, they retract and disappear into the far corner where they hung all mysterious-like before.

Dramatically clapping his hands, the guy struts toward me, theater performer-style. "She's awake!" His authoritative presence strikes me as how Henry VIII would be if he were here.

Wait . . . he knew I was upstairs?

Hopefully, that towel was doin' its job.

Taking in the guy's powerful frame and purple lining in the hood of his robe, I stagger a step back as he gives me a long, exaggerated bow.

"I am hurt that you failed to notice my stage before!" He winks at me, and I gotta say, I'm not really in a laughing mood. Sauntering way too close, he adds, "And yet, she still looks tired."

I stare into his flat, gray eyes. Why does he behave like we're already friends? Maybe he doesn't get out much. Still,

I'm way past the point of joking around, so I try to be as direct as possible. "'She' only slept for a few hours." I would suppose. Feels like it, anyhow.

The dude's blond hair is combed back and a little to the right, and hey, his hair's the same color as that honey-colored dresser upstairs.

As the guy smiles, the gramophone serenades on and on, and, for no apparent reason, goosebumps flare and pucker on my arms.

Pulling out a blue and black deck of cards, the dude leans toward me, reeking of . . . a yeast-y smell.

"Pick one," he says with an awful sparkle in his eyes. "Don't be rude."

What he doesn't know is, I'm a sucker for pretty much any card game in general. Dad used to play with me when I was little, Rosalyn has me play Old Maid when she can't sleep, and Mom's always had a soft spot for Hearts.

In a bit of a flurry, and feeling unnecessarily obedient, I take one of the boy's war-torn cards.

I don't know who he is—what exactly he knows about Luther—but I hold onto the third degree like an arsenal on the tip of my tongue.

Showing me a shiny queen of spades in his hand, Magic Guy doesn't bother to take the time to look at it himself.

"Remember this card," he says in an overly ominous tone.

And . . . he shuffles.

He shuffles so fast and forcefully, I can practically feel it in my pulse.

The grandfather clock chimes two times, and, yeah . . . card tricks at 2:00 AM is perfectly normal.

Looking past the bushy plants crowding the Eastern—Western?—window, all I can see is the outline of trees amidst the moon and fog.

Where is Luther?

Magic Guy drawls, "Now, put it back, please."

I slip the queen of spades back into his hand while he whistles this playful, jaunty tune—completely at odds with the gramophone.

This sick feeling in my stomach has me battling how I should be feeling. Should I be trying to have fun and living in the moment like this guy is, or drilling him about Luther?

When the dude splits the deck in half, he doesn't so much as look at the queen of spades as he shows it to me once more.

"You're going to see it *three* more times." He playacts an emcee on a radio.

Flipping it over so only I see the card, he warns, "Once."

Flip.

"Twice." His eyes are trained on mine, and he lifts the deck to show me the queen of spades on the bottom a third and final time. Making a pretty fan of cards, he smoothly places my card at the edge of the deck. "Push it in now."

When I do, Magic Guy closes the fan, collecting all the cards in one hand, and when I look up, my queen of spades is suddenly hanging from his mouth.

"Hey!" I truly am shocked. "How'd it get there?"

Pleasure shines in Magic Guy's eyes as he retrieves the card. "Shhh!" He holds a slender finger with a longish fingernail to his mouth. Eyeing the ceiling, he looks at me meaningfully, like I should know who is up there.

But the only other flesh and blood person I've ever seen around is Luther—apart from my imaginary, peg-legged, granny who may or may not like pickleball.

As the music trails off, I up and decide to take the friendly approach.

"So, are you Luther's brother? Or no?"

Maybe Luther didn't tell me about his brother, 'cause the dude looks like the Grim Reaper in his robe.

Magic Guy shushes me. Again.

He does this fancy Vegas dealer thing where, with one hand, he shuffles all his cards. "Now . . . pick a card."

What, is he on a loop?

Glancing down at my ankle booties—bare feet, whoops! —I turn Miss Sassafras and cross my arms. "Well, thanks for the card tricks, but my laundry won't starch itself!"

Magic Guy rolls his eyes, making him just about the least likeable person in the world. "Have care, Cate. You do not want to be a spoilsport."

He knows my name?

I . . . try not to stiffen, but I can't help it. He *has* to be Luther's brother. Same pointy cheeks, same old, tattered clothes. "I would like to point out that I have been talking to you for a full five minutes, and you haven't even offered to help me find Luther."

"You have to admit," Magic Guy drawls, "that you like me better than my sententious brother."

Say-ten-cha-wha?

"*Everyone* knows how he's too self-punishing for his own good."

I open my mouth to tell him I'll do a few things for *his* own good before clamping it closed. I don't need another argument. I simply need to point out that I won't be his gal pal when it comes to naysaying Luther. "Now that wasn't a kind thing to say at all."

Turning, Magic Guy suddenly slaps a fistful of piano keys. "Don't *tell me* you're defending him."

Like Luther's guilty; like he's done something wrong . . .

"Where is he?" A scaredy-cat takes over my tone.

Magic Guy leans in so close, I can smell the noxious pomade in his hair. "How was your shower?" Closing the lid to the piano keys with lightning speed, he seizes my wrist and grips it real hard with clammy fingers. "Did you view the portraits, hmm?"

Automatically, I am shaking my head, 'cause, *really*, I didn't study them at all. But then I nod, because, if I admit to not seeing them, then he'll insist on giving me a show.

Magic Guy's lips twist into a ghoulish smile. Forcing my hand into a fist, he clutches it close to his heart. "I *like* girls who know how to be creative with the truth."

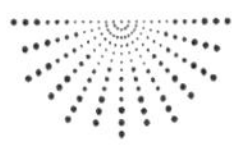

CHAPTER SEVENTEEN

LUTHER'S BROTHER strolls up the stairs like he's God's gift to the Bellagio.

If *I* were into magic, I'd invest in one of those cute spandex outfits with sequins, but whatever!

Lucky for me, the dude carries Luther's candelabra, which highlights every few stairs. The power company still hasn't turned the lights on, but Mom always says utility company employees are always underpaid and overworked.

Prolly 'cause Mom works there.

"You must excuse the condition of our home," Luther's brother says as the steps groan under our footfalls. "My mother would be beside herself if she were with us now."

"Looks nice enough to me." I can't help feeling like he's intending this as a jab at Luther.

But I don't think this dude's even listening. His eyes are settling on the first portrait on the wall, where the *faintest* outline of an old lady stares at no one in particular.

She's kinda smudged, kaleidoscope-style, and mostly, all I can see is her eyes and like fourteen different chins. Not because she's on the larger size, but because the film's been overexposed.

"Who is she?" I keep a sizable distance from both the portrait and the brother of Luther.

"Eighteen hundred and ninety-nine," Magic Guy says. We'll pretend that's what I wanted to know. Puffing out his chest, he tucks both his hands into his armpits and gazes at the picture. Can't say what he's thinking. Hard to know.

When the dude slinks to the next portrait, he carefully blows off the dust that's settled on the frame's corners.

Cough.

Hack.

So much coughing ensues.

As dust and dirt clog my nose, my skull's metaphorically split apart by a migraine-y syringe, and Magic Guy flinches back.

"Er . . . Bastian?" Have no clue why I just called him Bastian. "I'm ready to go home now . . ."

He laughs so hard, an unsettling vein throbs in his temple. "So, you admit it!"

I'll admit whatever he wants as long as I can be back in my aromatherapy and bubble bath by noon.

Leaning in real close, Magic Guy takes my cheeks in his hands. "She's not only a rule breaker, but also discerning . . ."

I don't like his octopus hands, so I jerk away from him.

Also, I'm *really* disliking the way he's now running a long fingernail down the length of the portrait's glass.

Pretty sure I need to get my ears . . . no, my eyes checked, 'cause his fingernails are growin' *long*.

Real long.

They can't be.

Can't be.

I swear, they've grown half an inch now.

They're brown and pointy. Gross.

Unwilling to blatantly accept whatever voodoo is in front of my eyes, I quickly blurt, "What happened to Luther?"

Magic Guy's upper lip curls, and this menacing, animalistic growl curls from his throat.

Clutching the backs of my arms, I hold them real close and close my eyes for a sec, 'cause *none* of this can be real.

But I'm not really in my room *or* asleep in Luther's bed.

Magic Guy's normally white teeth elongate and darken. A startling amount of facial hair suddenly sprouts from his neck, and *none* of this can be real!

He smiles at me like he'd love nothing more than to have me for lunch.

I scream—half a scream—when he presses a furry finger to my lips. "Shhh!"

Raising his semi-translucent eyes to the popcorn ceiling, he adds, "*She'll* hear you . . ."

Who in the gosh darn heck is he talking about?!

As his teeth further sharpen, I'll admit it right here: he would *sell out* in a Vegas magic show.

"You . . . are quite the illusionist!" My voice quivers as I throw out the compliment.

Teetering at the top of the steps, I tense to turn around when red and purple flowers snake and slither from the sleeves covering his arms.

"You have no idea." His eyes turn raw hamburger red.

Please, let me stop seeing things.

I'll stop seeing things!

And he leaps, eyes torched, as I plunge backwards to my rainbow bridge of death.

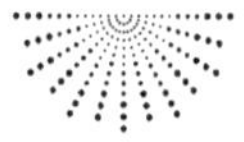

CHAPTER EIGHTEEN

IT'S JUST him and me.

Me and him.

About to join the rainbow bridge's prematurely killed baby raccoons and wolf-nibbled bunnies.

Bastian's eyes glow candy apple red, and his hood rises all tentacle-esque from his back.

I'll break my neck.

Break my neck.

I wonder if Autumn will greet me when I get to the other side. Will she blame me for not administering her medication more regularly for her heart defect?

Neck wrenches painfully as my head smashes into the cool, wrought-iron railing midway down the stairs.

Feels like I've just been hit with a sledgehammer, but I'll live.

White and black splotches dance in my vision.

I'm seeing the Big Dipper, Ursa Minor.

When Magic Guy lands on the stairs, he perches a mere step up.

Extending a matted, furry hand, he casually plays with

the front of my hair. "I suppose, *now*, you're ready to pay attention?"

He smells like wet fur—half-transformed dog, half-man. Black and blond hair still prickles over his body, and a little bit of drool trickles from the corner of his mouth. He reminds me of a werewolf, but he's not.

He *is* the Doberman, holy, holy crap. How is it that such a sweet dog could turn so vicious and now human?

This guy . . . *this* Bastian . . . is far too calculating and enjoying every moment. He seems to be relishing every minute of my terror, and, between his glowy eyes and his hair-covered human form, I'm pretty sure he's the creepiest thing I've seen my entire life.

Regardless, I smile my biggest, brightest smile that in no way says that I would love nothing more than to introduce his face to the garbage disposal.

Guh-bye orange peels and black lips!

Peeling myself from the stairs, I grab the rail, hunching my shoulders as I ascend the steps.

If I playact being all moldable, I'll get him when he least expects it.

Wrenching my arm, Bastian pulls me forward so that I'm forced to straighten my stance. "Come along," he growls, hair disappearing from his hands and arms.

I don't rightly know what he is, I don't know how to react, but I do allow him to lead me back upstairs to the heavy, stagnant darkness that envelopes us at the second portrait.

The hollowed-out cheeks and clay-colored eyes prove this portrait is of Bastian.

But it looks like it was taken in the 1800s. Can it really be him?

"It's just as well you didn't know me back then." With his long fingernails, Bastian tap-taps the glass.

The real and photographed versions look exactly the same, with identical, slicked-back hair and a large, dimpled chin. "I was a sickly little thing." Bastian glances at the walls with exaggerated reverence. "You could say that this house has shaped who I am."

What, an antagonistic douchebag with a car salesman haircut? Instead, I nod like I agree. "Oh, yes."

Taking a predatorial step toward me, Bastian asks, "Did my brother tell you how this place became 'Monkshood'?"

"Gang of monks heard you were havin' a fashion party?" I nod at the purple lining of his hood.

A feral twinkle shines in his eye as he raises his fist to strike me, but, alas, he lowers it.

"A long, *long* time ago," he says, "society ostracized my kin. Long story short, the Dvoraks were unable to bear children."

"Oh, you mean you can't reproduce? Dang!"

Bastian's robe flaps wildly as he lunges forward. Stopping about two millimeters from my face, his eyes flash vermilion. "*Naturally*, my family did not know what would cause them to fail to produce offspring." He backs off. "So, a few of them began to experiment—with herbs and the like." Pulling out a deck of cards from his robe, he begins shuffling, as if in a trance. "One of those herbs was a purple-petalled flower called aconitum."

"Riveting!" I comment just to piss him off.

Bastian snarls with his uber-sharp canines. "Otherwise known as Devil's Helmet, or . . . *Monkshood*."

"Well, call me a naked mole rat." I joke like I don't have a care in the world. "It's been right in front of me the entire time!" But that doesn't explain how Bastian's able to grow unnaturally long fangs and nails . . .

"So, you decided to take the name literally." I dig for more background. "Got yourself an outfit that makes you look like a monk with a hood and everything."

Bastian's upper lip curls, and his teeth look moldier than a pair of grandpa buns. Not really wanting him to rip out my throat, I clasp my hands together in civility. "I am *so* sorry to hear of your ancestors' baneful tragedy."

"It is not just—" The dude's robe swoops as he spins. Gesturing to a string of empty portraits I hadn't taken the time to notice earlier, he drawls, "*These* were supposed to be for our children—the ones who would carry on the Dvorak line."

Wha—?

As in, hypothetically between him and . . . ?

"For generations" —Bastian's strut resembles a jaguar's as he swaggers up and down the hallway— "newly married Dvoraks were plagued with the fear that they would not be able to bear children. As it turns out, frequently only one sibling could."

Seizing my elbow, Bastian drags me the five or so paces to his mother's kaleidoscope-prismed portrait. "That was *her* fear."

I can't move away fast enough. His breath *reeks*. Salmon breath.

"She became consumed with the terror that she would never again see another Dvorak child."

"So she wanted grandchildren . . ." I bite the inside of my cheek. *Please* tell me that I don't know where this is going.

Bastian just stands there, apparently waiting for me to say something else. But I've never been real good with verbal affirmation, so I let out a long and chipper exhale. "Well, *I'm* bored. I know, let's go brush our teeth!"

Bastian wrenches my arm toward him so fast, pain radiates from my shoulder.

I think he's about to let it go when he twists it further.

"What do you want?" I try not to gasp.

"To explain why you're *ours*."

Ours? I guffaw, only to end up coughing up a marmot.

I don't know how, but a spray of blood covers my fist.

Oh, laddie.

Seeing the blood, Bastian's callous eyes widen. And taking in a shuddery breath, he steps back.

Glancing at the walls, fear and vulnerability splits open his eyes.

It's clear that my ability to shoot blood from my mouth is a game changer for him. "*What* is wrong with you, child?"

I never got to pay him back for chasing me around outside. Or nearly breaking my neck. So I cough right onto his lying, self-absorbed mouth.

Blood splatters kinda like the salsa on the carpet.

Dog Boy's face fills with so much rage, I *almost* feel a twinge, a spark of guilt . . .

Nope. Not happenin'.

I don't know what he is, but this dude deserves whatever he gets. He gives me the heebie-jeebies, and he gets a rise outta freaking me out.

Smiling my close-lipped smile, I reveal the peaceful warrior that I am: all the nights I've spent in ICU, all the times I've never had anyone to tuck me in or say that it would be all right.

Sure, Rosie would show up a day or two later, but I'd already gotten through the long night by myself.

Bastian wants to know what is wrong with me?

He likes girls who are creative with the truth?

"Tuberculosis," I lie through my teeth, lifting my chin. The fear in Bastian's eyes tells me that he'd like nothing more than to make me permanently vanish.

So, I make a mighty show of wiping the blood from my lips *all* the way across the back of my hand.

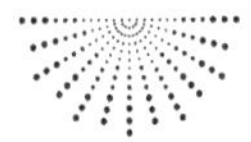

CHAPTER NINETEEN

Bastian reaches out and slams my head against the nearest portrait.

Crack!

Temple throbs not a little.

"DO NOT LIE TO ME!" Bastian spits. He's gone completely back to his human form, with his pale hair and face. His head shape is longer, more oval than Luther's, and his countenance screams "murdery bastard."

"I understand you're upset," I say with a huff, trying to get my bearings. "But you don't need to make me your visual aid just to point that out."

Pain shoots through my skull in rockets, and that fear in his gray eyes? Makes *every single bit* of the throbbing worth it.

"Had the disease for a while." I make a messy show of coughing at least thirteen more times.

Too bad the blood stopped coming up.

Bastian's ugly teeth elongate further as he grabs the hair lying against the back of my neck. "Tell. Me. You're lying. Or . . . I'll grab that baby sister of yours and deflower her instead."

Whaa?

My heart pauses. Shrivels up.

What'd he say?

But Rosalyn's barely even ten.

What is wrong with this guy?

How could he *ever* threaten that?

Adrenaline shoots like a geyser in my head, and I've got a fever; a heat wave's burnin' me up. As I take in his nasty, pallid face and the complete lack of light in his eyes—I know this is much more than a threat.

He means what he says.

Liquid venom rushes through my veins. I spit—right on his dimpled chin.

Bastian recoils, but I have surely made my mark. Gritting his teeth, he pulls out a linen-colored handkerchief and wipes away my spit. "You are *lying*." Fear still rings his eyes, though, and the walls? They hum as if in agreement. Muscle pulsing along his jaw, he adds, "Though *she* does not wish for you to leave."

I am ready to pull my hair out. "Who the gas is *she*?!"

Amusement simmers in Bastian's eyes, and I know he's not going to tell me. He straightens the sleeves of his robe, lips curling in an evil smile all the while.

"Imaginary girlfriends aren't real, you know." I lean away from him, pretending I'm not terrified one bit.

Bastian peels back his robe's sleeves, one after the other, revealing vicious burn marks—scars—that run up and down his forearms. Running one hand over said burns, he snarls, "*I* possess a love you will never experience. A love that I would throw myself in a burning building to keep intact."

The floor below us rumbles, and what's he saying? That he willfully became a human torch for "his love?"

I can't imagine being with him. He's like a self-absorbed,

entitled lord who prematurely spent his inheritance and still suffers from the delusion that he's actually a catch.

So . . . what will it be?

Should I stay, or should I go?

Ditch the weirdo, or . . . be his poppet?

In a fit of impatience, Bastian tugs his sleeves back down. "Tell me you're not so self-absorbed as to be *really* willing to risk me taking your little sister."

"Of *course* not," I snap, but I am not having this discussion with this guy. He threatens Rosalyn? There's a specific ring of hell for souls like his.

Though I can't show him how much he's getting under my skin. "I'll stay with you," I whisper, wishing more than ever that I could run his face through with scissors. "I *can't wait* to make babies with you, Bastian."

The sheer revulsion that twists apart his face hurts my pride only a little bit. What, he doesn't think I'm cute?

"Hey, I'm not that bad! I thought you said you like girls who know how to be creative with the truth. Luther would believe me." I shrug, playing up my indifference.

"*Luther* wouldn't know a good thing if it smacked him upside the head."

"So, Luther *is* still alive!"

Bastian's eyes flash, like he didn't mean to let that one slip. "The only thing that matters is, he'll always do what is required in the end."

"The only thing that matters," a tenor voice shouts from the base of the steps, "is that *you* are mistreating our guest!"

Cue the symphony.

Luther?!

I knew he would be okay, and he would forgive me for running away . . . and for accidentally falling asleep.

When I look down the staircase at him, though, I find Luther's jacket is hanging on by a thread. And beyond the mud, I can barely make out the whites of his eyes or his exotic features. A few more gashes have torn open his cheek, and oh my, Dalai Lama, his hair is a *train wreck*.

Leaping over me, Bastian becomes a supervillain dog-man. His ears rise higher on his head as he sprouts his obsidian fur, and he really is Houdini, just about to reach his brother.

All at once, Luther turns and knees Bastian straight in the neck.

Dog squeals. Bastian's nearly in full dog-mode now, and boy howdy, that was a good move, Luther!

Buckling, Bastian goes down far enough for Luther to raise his foot and pin the dog's head against the floor.

"Hurry!" Luther shouts up at me, warmth shining in his eyes.

He doesn't have to tell me twice; Imma already trippin' down.

Squeak, squeak go the stairs that have somehow been infested with ants.

I gotta run faster.

Once I hit the bottom of the stairs, I graze Luther's ripped sleeve with my fingers in a thank you as I scramble past. "You going to be okay?"

"You need to go now!"

Well. I guess I'll take that as a yes.

The mailman has to be gone, dog's in here, so I sprint for the halls.

I'm in the zone—hit about three scarves, two urns, and several potted plants. All of these spin and clatter, and one makes a masterful *crack*.

The noise is an angelic symphony. So grand.

By the time I'm able to reach the front door, I'm clean outta breath. The cool, brass lion handle turns and turns, and it's not catching.

Why's it not catching now?

"LUTHER?!"

Something *BANGS* from the other side of the door. Tall. A dark shadow hovers on the other side of the stained glass window in the door.

Shrieking, I jump back. Who is it? Mailman or Mom?

As witchy fingers scratch the broken glass, I see that it's just the newly broken branches of a tree.

Just a broken tree branch.

Reaching out, I try the handle again.

Spin, spin, spin goes the stripped mechanism.

More brawling comes from the other end of the halls while more glass shrieks and breaks.

I throw my weight against the door—gotta get out, but my shoulder screams with pain.

The claw wounds on my back certainly don't like my strategy, and stupid friggin' door!

I'm stuck in freaking *Groundhog Day* meets *The Blair Witch Project*.

I hate this helpless feeling.

Everything shakes—from my hands to my arms to my legs. I've got low blood sugar. Should really eat something. People burn more calories when they have CF.

I have to go. I have to go *now*.

I don't even realize I'm headed for the back door until the screaming statue nearly rips my nose off.

Sidestepping the statue, I kick a few pottery urns outta the way, which smash like crash symbols.

Silks and scarves flutter in ghostly whispers as I tear past them, and it's like Bastian's secret girlfriend's attached to the house. She can *hear* me, but that's nuts.

By the time I make it back to the boys, they're actually halfway up the stairs. Luther's got a half-transformed Bastian in a headlock.

Not wanting to get sidetracked, I tear past the piano.

Clipping the edge of the kitchen island, I swear the dead plants look greener than they formerly did. Healthy. Something tells me this is bad.

When I make it to the back door, with shaking fingers, I slip the cool, metal lock from the track.

Pulling it from the latch, I try not to freak out that my fingers are spasming so hard, I can barely control my movements.

Uhh, how did Luther get inside just now? Did he slip through another door?

Don't have the time to answer that, and I rip the door wide, wide open.

The yard's still awash in fog and mud, and as the cool, wooden porch greets my feet, I remember all over again that I'm still barefoot.

Don't have time to find my shoes. Must clamber down the steps, and I'm eighty-nine percent successful at avoiding slivers of any type.

More threats and shouts blast from the boys, so I run faster.

Must get away from them.

The fence on the property still has these pointy arrow tips, and I'd have to be a ninja to climb to the other side. But Luther urged me to get out, so there must be another way, right?

I tear past the greenhouse.

Leaves bite into my toes and *slish-slush*.

I zoom past the other outbuilding and round a pair of statues with missing hands and heads. The hair rising on the back of my neck tells me there truly are eyes on me through the fog.

But how can that be?

I sprint past a postcard's collection of toadstools and

seventy acorns only to snag my foot on a raised root.

I fall flat on my face.

My chin and nose are implanted in a pink plastic backpack.

Dazed and confused, I stare at it for a great long while.

Ordinarily, I wouldn't give it a second thought, but it's on the *boys'* property, and the name *Ophelia* is embroidered on the top.

I take a few extra deep, measured breaths.

Must calm my breathing. Egad!

Why couldn't Mom have named me after my other grandma, Delilah?

Forcing myself to investigate this clue, I lean down and pick up the backpack. Silk embroidery meets my fingers.

When I reach for the zipper, I find that I am unwilling to waste any more precious time, so I must hurry this little investigation along.

A piece of strawberry blonde hair's stuck in the zipper.

Strawberry . . .

Rosalyn's hair color.

The zipper purrs as I pull it along, and my heart suspends midair as I peer into the dark abyss of the backpack.

A small, doll-sized head covered with hair, resides inside. Yup, it's the *exact* same shade as Rosalyn's. The pink and white polka-dot shirt tells me things are worse than I thought.

Pulling out the plastic—or porcelain—doll by the arm, I find a miniature replica of my baby sister—right down to the soft features and splattering of freckles on her cheeks and nose.

Her eyes are scratched out.

From a razor or a knife.

I drop the doll and scream, 'cause somebody knows what I did.

CHAPTER TWENTY

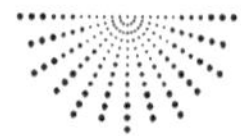

A MILLION DOLLARS.

A million dollars would've been grand.

Then I could buy Rosalyn enough jellybeans to fill a swimming pool. We could afford that eye procedure the doctors keep asking us to get, but we know we can't afford.

The fence—the stupid, freaky fence—is only a million meters high, and I don't see a gate anywhere. Doesn't help that the whole yard's cast in shadow. At least the moon's big enough to help me see through the scratchy needles of the pines.

For all I know, that mailman's still hanging around, patrolling the perimeter like a freaking stormtrooper.

Would it be completely lame of me to admit I want my mommy? Not that I believe she would want to be here for me, but she could be in the other room. See me when she unloads the dishwasher and such.

Don't call me crazy, but the back of that Rosalyn doll stares back up at me like she's got eyes on the back of her head.

I feel bad that I left her face-down.

Reaching down, I pick her up and hold her arms so that we're facing one another.

"What'll we do, Rosie?" Gosh, I haven't called her that since I was five or six. Looking at my baby sister's small, thin chin, I settle my gaze on her thin nose that she likes to wriggle when she's imitating a rabbit.

Never give up, I swear, my little sister says. I do everything I can to avoid her white, scratched-out eyes.

I know the real Rosalyn's not here, but part of me has to believe she is in a way. If she knew I was trapped in here, she'd do everything she could to give me the pep talk I need and help me out.

Fun fact: despite going blind, Rosalyn's the *only* person I know who cheerfully gets up in the morning. She springs outta bed like she's part lemming.

She's memorized every single car in the neighborhood—knows them by speed and sound. Oh, and she taught herself to read braille when Mom and I thought she was listening to *Aladdin.*

Question is . . . can I *really* trust Luther when he says there's a way to get out?

He never exactly said how to leave. For all I know, there could be a big highway of underground tunnels, but I can't very well use them if I don't know the entry point.

The doll's smooth, plastic hair is so much like Rosalyn's. She even smells like my sister, with her freshly laundered clothes and young, smooth skin.

My sister's young enough that she can jump on the trampoline for hours.

Eat way too much candy, and nobody gets mad.

Rosalyn's favorite band is Fitz and the Tantrums, and, every once in a while, she still pulls out her blue, satiny blankey.

I cannot *believe* Bastian threatened that he would . . . I can't even.

I need to find Rosalyn. Get Mom. Together, we can leave town. We'll stay with Grams in North Dakota until we know everything is safe. Yeah.

Slowly, feeling like I have a little bit of direction, I slip the doll back into the backpack.

Can't let it distract me from moving on and finding a way to escape.

Slinging the strap over my shoulder, I tell myself there *must* be a gate.

Sticks and acorns dig into my feet, and my bare toes are starting to sting from the cold. How does the Bastian in that old 1800s photograph and *this* Bastian look exactly the same?

And Luther . . . can he also shift into a Doberman?

The pine needles and fog are so thick, I'm in a snow globe —dizzy and mixed up. I do have to admit that the boys aren't the only ones who are cursed.

'Cause I've been "off" since I was about five years old.

Never been able to make the right choices in life . . .

I cut my baby sister's hair without permission.

Refused to set the table when it's lunchtime.

Actually, the universe won't let me go until I pay my price. The universe, and apparently someone here, knows what I did. I can't go to sleep at night without thinking about it . . .

Somehow, I've arrived at a thick wad of trees. Stalking around the tall, prickly branches, I find the pine aroma almost soothing.

From the home's old, sandstone walls, I don't hear any more fighting or yelling. Guess the boys stopped brawling. That's good.

Is it good?

I hope it's good.

Wonder how long their brawl lasted.

Hopefully, Luther was the grand champion.

You know, if Uncle Jimmy's death taught me anything, it's that *every single* structure or abode has an exit, even if I'm not ninja enough to climb the property wall.

There *must* be a way to leave, to escape.

Taking a resolute step forward, I feel like I'm pretty much on the right track when my breath rushes up my throat, and I fall through the air, dropping five or so feet straight down.

CHAPTER TWENTY-ONE

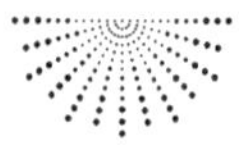

WHILE FALLING, five feet feels like a grave.

I wonder . . . when Uncle Jimmy jumped, did he regret his choice?

Did he worry he'd never again eat lime Jell-O salad or go fly fishing? Did he wish he hadn't left his wife and babies?

My leg hits first. I'm plumb lucky, 'cause it folds and collapses just right. My tush hits, too, and, *yeah*, I wanted to get out, but who would have thought I'd be so talented at falling?

Looking around at the dirt and damp, I find a smallish, rectangular room.

Pretty sure I've fallen into the root cellar, of all things.

Here's a pickle.

Just as long as I don't *get* pickled.

Hehe.

Fun, little mush-filled jars line wooden shelving, and, in the corner, lies a heap of yellowish, undergrown potatoes that smell a whole lot like the dust and dank of the house.

"You really shouldn't have tried to run!" Bastian yells down, flexing his tall, hulking frame. He reminds me of an anti-tobacco ad people post to get you to quit smoking. His complexion's so pallid, so wrong.

What happened to the cute, snuggly creature who crawled on my lap and wanted to be scratched behind the ears all night?

"I liked you a lot better when you were a dog," I mutter, kicking the ground.

Bastian's slicked-back hair flaps in the wind, and I *really* hope this doesn't mean Luther lost their fight.

Holding up the pink backpack, I give Bastian as much sass as I can. "Hey, your mom called! Said you forgot your tea set and Barbies."

Bastian glares so hard, a vein throbs in his forehead. "LUTHER!" he roars.

And he goes trompin' across the grass like a mobster in the twenties.

For Rosalyn, though, I should watch my mouth. Keep things more civil. I don't want Bastian saying that my smarting off made him go find her.

Somewhere above the cellar, leaves and twigs snap à la Rice Krispies when a dark-haired figure with torn clothing comes barreling down the hatch.

Ah. Luther.

I attempt to catch him, only to succeed in clipping my arm with his.

Landing in a fatty cloud of dust, the boy's got a gnarly-looking scratch beneath his eye and another one down his jaw.

How very Cap'n Jack Sparrow.

With bound hands and a few more rips in his vintage vest, the boy looks up at me, and I'm always gonna be a sucker for that dark, wavy hair that hangs in his eyes.

When his eyes settle on the pink backpack, though, his

shoulders draw up tight. I'd pay *all* those swimming pool jellybeans just to know what he's thinking.

Suddenly feeling wary, I sink to the ground and hug my knees. I could ask Luther if he happened to bring any s'mores or beef jerky, but snacks look to be the last thing on his mind.

"I worried things would turn out like this," Luther says mournfully.

There's not a whole lot a girl can say to that, so I cross my legs. "What's up with your bro, anyway?"

The boy fumbles with—ah. His hands are tied . . .

As he twists and tries to loosen them, taking forever, I lean over to finish the job. "Here." With a swift tug, I pull apart the knot, which is awfully coarse and frayed.

With a nod of gratitude, Luther rubs his swollen wrists. "You must really . . ."

"Wish your brother was more civil?"

He sighs. "Yes, that."

I raise my hands. "How are you . . . *you* . . . and he's about as lovable as a poltergeist?"

"We were raised differently."

The wind howls above us, apparently interrupting his train of thought, 'cause he doesn't add anything else.

I pluck up a jar of pink and white ingredients, pretending I'm merely inspecting the canned goods at the local Safeway. "He's older than you?"

"By a few years, yes." I think Luther will give me more, but he scratches the side of his head, obviously lost in thought. I could wait and wait for him to talk to me, or I could get myself something to eat.

Using elbow grease I didn't know I had, I unscrew the lid.

Feeling brave, I take a mighty whiff of what's inside.

Whew! Burns like crazy.

I wave my hand in front of my face, coughing. "I wanna

be an embalmer or a mortician, but not sure I can handle all the fragrances." *Cough, cough.* "Know what I mean?"

Luther gazes at me with the softest of expressions, and *this* is why I am obsessed with the boy. Mom lost all sympathy for me and my CF ever since Rosalyn went blind. While it certainly blows that Luther and I are trapped, at least we're together. Big, bad Bastian wouldn't let his own brother die . . . right?

Stomach rumbles.

Man, I'm so starved, I'd be willing to eat *anyone's* mystery meat.

Well . . .

Outta options, I dig into the jar with nothin' but my bare fingers and secure a slimy potato and onion dipped in vinegar.

Slipping it into my mouth, I pretend that it doesn't burn like hydrofluoric acid.

"Mmm!" I can't help but cough as I pound my chest. Part of the gooey yumminess sticks somewhere between my throat and chest cavity. "Yum."

Luther just continues to sit, staring at me, probably realizing that I *do* look like a model for all lumberjacks. It's a gift, see.

Setting the jar back on the shelf with an extra loud *clink*, I figure it's time to drill him some more about Bastian . . . and the house, and pretty much everything else that's going on.

"I am sorry . . ." Luther says, suddenly standing and turning his back to me.

I'm not entirely sure what to say to that, so I offer something rather complimentary. "Hey, it's not your fault you're on par with Zac Efron."

Luther turns, history professor hair coming out to *here.* And between the dark circles under his eyes and fifty shades of guilt in his gaze, I have to say that I will never, ever grow tired of looking at the boy.

He surveys the other mason jars I have failed to eat yet.

"I am sorry for inviting you *here* . . ."

So, he does feel bad! I lick my lips, which have grown crazy salty. "In all fairness, I've been diggin' for an invitation ever since we met."

Not really sure how, but we've ended up standing super close. The sides of his shoes brush against my feet, and *maybe* he's finally going to explain what's goin' on—or, at the very least, why he extended that original invite.

With a heavy breath, he sinks again to the ground, taking with him all my hopes and dreams. Leaning back on his hands, he glances up at me, looking about as innocent and adorable as a boy could be.

"So . . . " I make a show of not wanting to sit *too* near the dark corners before joining him on the ground. "You lured me into your house to . . . ?"

Luther stares at the pink backpack rather forlornly. "You wouldn't believe me if I explained."

"I will believe anything you say. Except how to organize hallways, 'cause y'all need to invest in some Tupperware and cubicles."

Drawing in the dirt with his pointer finger, Luther makes two giant, concentric circles before scratching them out. "I shouldn't have promised to explain what's happening. I'm sorry. I can't."

Reaching over, Luther tentatively strokes my fingers, effectually making me forget every single bit of what I was thinking.

Holy guacamole, is he ever usin' his masculine wiles on me.

I should know better. *Do* better. But I do not seem able to gather the willpower to pull away.

He threads his fingers through mine, and when he smiles —*almost* smiles—it's the most tender expression I've ever seen.

Little lines gather round his intoxicating eyes, and his lips twitch up, ever so slightly. Firmly, yet gently, the handsome boy reaches over and lifts my chin.

"What are you doing?" I am near outta breath.

"It has been a *really* miserable last few days." Luther's breath hitches. "And it helps to gaze at you for a while."

My chest floods with super sharp sunshine. He likes gazing at me? "You go ahead and gaze as much as you like."

Eventually, the boy does release my chin, and when he pulls away, his voice comes out hoarse. "Do not think, even for a second, that you haven't successfully wooed me, Cate Ophelia."

My heart does a double backflip.

He just switched my first and middle names.

I kinda like it.

He murmurs even softer, "We should be safe for a bit."

CHAPTER TWENTY-TWO

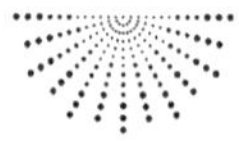

I . . . must have been knocked out.

A golf ball-sized bump throbs on my head, and I wake—hunched over a desk . . .

Shimmery lilac alternates between pea-green wallpaper, and . . . I'm in Granny's room. Again.

A tea-stained tulle and lace dress hangs over my curves in thick cobwebs, and this can't be right, 'cause Luther and I were just having a moment.

True, he did switch my first and middle names, but the way he said it—so gooey and warm—I'd say he's my yellow canary. My one bright spot in all of this.

But I'm not in the cellar. I'm in a dress.

Headless figurines and framed doilies mock me from Granny's lowboy dresser and the bedside table. Bastian must have hit me from behind, but wouldn't I have seen him get the drop on me?

Actually, I do remember a robed figure barreling down that hole, come to think of it.

A male voice laughs. It's awful. Spidery. I try to turn in

my chair, but my arms have been shackled by long, semi-pliable vines.

Craning my neck, I try to see who's laughing.

Deathly pale skin shells the darker soul of Bastian. When he smiles, black gums line his teeth. His slicked-back hair doesn't wriggle even a little as he hums the jaunty tune the gramophone played earlier.

Oh, and my feet have been partially cleaned.

More firelight flickers from the bedside table almost in time with Bastian's humming.

Wisps of smoke tease the dust-laden air, and what if I could burn the entire house down? Mom would have a panic attack from wiping all that history.

"We do not want to have what happened *last* time . . ." Bastian clamps his sweaty hand on my shoulder.

Last time?

He sets the blind Rosalyn doll on my lap so that it seems like she's staring directly at me. I try to avoid the scratch-marks on her eyes, but it's kinda hard to do, seeing as it's evidence of the singular worst act of my life.

"I can put my hair in pigtails," I offer, "if younger girls are more your thang."

Bastian snatches the back of my hair so hard my neck twists painfully. I try not to think real long and hard about the fact that he and Luther must have been watching Rosalyn and me for a long while to be able to dress the doll in an *exact* replica of one of Rosalyn's shirts.

When Bastian's empty, soulless eyes reach into mine, a dark shudder slithers down my spine. What kind of evil is he? And how in the golliwog can he and Luther be related?

Feigning boredom, I tap my index finger against the chair's side. "Yo, what's a girl gotta do to get a little popcorn around here?"

"Caaate." A brittle wind bristles and floats through the broken window glass.

Uh . . . that wasn't Bastian, and it sounded decidedly female.

My heart steamboats and ricochets across the Mississippi. It's the elusive "she," and I don't see her one bit.

"Ophelia Cate . . . you believe you are ready to take my place?"

The curtains dance with her every breath, and I must still be dreaming, 'cause everyone knows curtains don't speak.

Bastian shoots me a tight smile while the vines constrict round my wrists. And all of this—*all of this*—would just be so much better if I had a sip of Mountain Dew paired with salt-water taffy.

The elusive "she" makes all these weird breathing noises. Maybe she's hiding in the walls because she really does have a peg leg.

Hold on . . . she asked me if I'm ready to take her place? Like, in the walls?

I'm not exactly an overachiever, but I *was* thinking I'd at least graduate.

"I'm good," I answer way too late.

The curtain swooshes and swirls as spiderweb roots emerge from the floorboards, scuttling toward the baseboards akin to some terrible disease.

Three of the roots' fingers peel back two sections of the wallpaper—one lilac, the other pea green—and, while I do not know what exactly all of this means, I *do* know, for once, that heavy breathing isn't coming from me.

"You know what to do." Curtain Lady flaps her argyle fabric like she's got crows in the panels.

If she's Bastian's long-lost mom—or grandma—I should be offering to throw a big ol' Dvorak family party.

Raising his crazy-long, serrated knife, Bastian points it in my direction.

There's no way I'm subjecting my immune system to that. So, I spit.

I try to, anyway.

My throat is drier than the Gobi Desert. Actually, I'm not able to do any real spitting at all while Bastian wrenches my hair from my scalp.

"*Immortality,*" Curtain Lady breathes, her eyes and mouth becoming slight indents in the fabric. "*Are you ready for it?*"

Oh. Whoa, whoa, whoa. I'm not sure if this whole extemporaneous pow wow is worth entertaining. There's a reason why the Holy Grail's a thing. Everybody wants to live forever.

Bastian wraps his clammy hand round my shoulder for a second time, though now he jabs my throat with his fatty blade.

"*Another place!*" Curtain Lady shrieks, and at least we can agree with that. Bastian glances back to where her feminine features stare back from the argyle fabric, and, oh, mercy me. I can't believe this is my life.

Lowering his blade, Bastian presses the tip to my left shoulder, but I don't want him cutting me.

"You'll get blood on the fabric . . ." I stoop to whining.

Bastian yanks down the neck of my dress, exposing my left shoulder, and, yeah, I shouldn't have whined about that.

"*Yesss,*" Curtain Lady says. She flaps faster, wilder, and where has Luther gone?

Pain blazes in my shoulder as Bastian twists the tip of the blade into my flesh, and he bequeaths me with a smile he must have stolen from Ted Bundy.

When he smiles wider, the dude's gums appear to have maggots lodged inside.

Maggots. Inside.

Consider this to be your friendly reminder to floss, girls and boys.

"You really don't have to do this," I plead. I'll go ahead and assume that I don't want Bastian and Curtain Lady's idea of immortality.

"*Only enough to fill a cup.*" Curtain Lady's cloth nose twitches as she ignores my plea.

Seems as though Bastian's already got an eighth of a cup, and my shoulder's hurting like a banshee.

The floorboards rattle in a frenzy, and I'm really beginning to think I need to hit the escape hatch. From my back, all my wounds scream, and they're connected—interconnected—to my shoulder, where Bastian digs deeper, like I'm a sandbox.

I don't really wanna die.

Sure, the idea of death can be intriguing at times, but now I just wanna go home. French braid Rosalyn's hair. Put away groceries.

Besides, what did I ever do to Dog Boy?

It's been hours since the mailman attacked, so I'm beginning to think the possibility of the police showing up is not really a possibility.

"*Keep her alive!*" Curtain Lady hisses as my head bobs. I'm losing so much blood I might lose consciousness.

More blood dribbles into the cup, and I'm way past feeling.

Surveying the stripe-y wallpaper, I wonder how the vines creep out. Curtain Lady must control them, I guess.

Powerful Curtain Lady.

Four more vines worm and coil their way round the chair's wooden legs.

They prick my heels, too.

Wonder what Rosalyn would say if I died.

Wonder if Mom would have an open casket.

When Bastian releases my neck, I barely have the where-withal to press my palm over the wound. But . . . oh yeah.

Arms are tied.

Maybe it would be better not to think about what's happening.

Instead, think about the good times.

Easter dinner! Pulled pork. Green beans. Or the time Rosalyn stole my favorite earrings and came bounding outta my room with the most joyful look on her face.

I'll think about that.

A blurry, disoriented form near the door leaps toward me.

The messy hair and torn, creative layers tell me it's *Luther*, and he looks about like he's ready to kick Bastian's trash— hallelujah, yes-sirree, Bob!

CHAPTER TWENTY-THREE

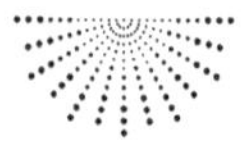

WATER FREELY DRIPS from Luther's body as he lumbers across the room. Bastian lifts the cup to our curtain gal pal's freaky lips, and I don't know why it takes me seeing that for me to *finally* register what's happening.

I know what to do.

I know what to do!

Straining against the cords binding my arms and legs, I yell to Luther, "Cut me free, you beautiful boy!"

Luther glances back at me, hair in his face, as Curtain Lady gulps my AB-negative.

Grabbing the knife Bastian left on the bed, he sets to work on severing the vines that shackle my wrists.

Pop!

Hiss.

The vines are so greedy they think I'm a bloody trellis.

I do everything in my power to lift my hands to help Luther. Doesn't matter that, by doing so, the blade slices into my wrists.

Burns a little, but, finally, the vines snap and break.

I jump from the chair, diving for the thin cup in Bastian's

hands.

Problem is, two vines are currently tying my legs to the chair, so I rather poetically crash to the floor.

Bastian makes sure to give me a thorough kicking, and he's so generous, his blows don't stop. Feels like I'm in a back-alley mugging, and as skin and ribs ring with pain, I can't help thinking about what he said about hurting Rosalyn.

How can he be that ugly?

Stretching my arm as far as it will go, I extend my fingers to reach for the teacup in his hands. Must get it if that's how they mean to grant my "immortality," shady as that sounds.

But it's just too doggone far away.

Bastian leans in close enough to kiss, and I kung fu punch him in the gut.

Cup lowers just enough, and I grab it just in time and down the contents.

It tastes like tomato juice—mixed with a healthy amount of battery acid.

When a heavy hand strikes my face, I fly back like a paper doll into the bed-frame.

Guess Luther cut the vines holding my legs.

Blood from the cup sprays all over the curtain, and Curtain Lady puckers her lips, trying to find as much liquid as she can.

But she's just too darn slow, and the sound of her shrieking is glorious.

Her anger rattles the floorboards. Dust floats throughout the room, and some of the skin doilies slip from their hooks on the walls.

Luther smashes a candelabra over Bastian's head, and the entire house shakes like it's in a toddler's fist.

While I wipe the blood that's dribbled from my mouth, the ground rumbles and rattles some more. I attempt to get up when two floorboards open up, and I end up falling toward the likes of Jabba the Hut's pit.

Ooof!

Luckily, I am saved by my bubble butt.

Lodged halfway through the floor, feet dangling, I am ever so grateful for this one significant and magical curve in my body.

As I stretch toward Grandma's rug to grab onto something and pull myself out, a small collection of femurs and skulls roll toward me from under the bed in a percussion concert.

It's a good thing nobody's downstairs, 'cause I just remembered I'm in a dress.

A girlish voice giggles from one of the skulls, B-movie style.

"Feeling . . . guilty?"

Little patches of hair stick to the side of the head, and there's no way I'd touch that.

"What do you want?" I lean as far away from the skull lady as possible. Kicking, I try to clamber outta the hole. Problem is, the floorboards are jabbing into my thighs and aren't letting me budge.

Above me, the two boys full-on brawl. More porcelain figurines break while ol' Patchy rolls closer to me. *"What* do you *want, Ophelia Cate?"*

I elbow her on the side of the head, sending her a good six feet away. "I wanna get out!"

She releases a slew of airy giggles. *"That, sadly, I cannot grant."*

The orifice of her mouth doesn't move, and between the mothballs and old scents, she even smells like Granny.

Planting my hands on the floor, I do my best to shimmy out. "Come here, sweetie pie." I mimic her era and voice.

Skull Girl giggles when, to my horror, little gray and

white eyeballs suddenly fill the hole around me.

I wouldn't be all that worried . . . 'cept for the fact that they keep coming.

Gumdrop-sized.

The irises are blue, and all of them are laced with ugly, red veins.

I know what she's doing . . .

Amidst her crocheted bedspread and skin doilies, this new BFF of mine is trying to make me remember that day . . . but I absolutely refuse to think about it.

The eyeballs—just like the vines—hiss and pop, and to calm my nerves, I temporarily close my eyes against the growing pile.

They slip over one another, becoming roly-polies. They ram against my arms, feeling like partially cooked eggs. One tries knocking into my lips to slip inside my mouth.

From my own illness, there's so much water pooling in my lungs I may physically drown in the middle of Bingo night. Not the way I wanted to go, so I plant my elbows on the ground on either side of me.

I wheeze . . . don't know how I do it, but, lungs burning, I do manage to crawl out.

By the time I've officially escaped, I look around for the boy.

Luther gives me an almost, *almost* grin, and, from that one look, I know he wasn't in cahoots with Bastian and Curtain Lady.

A set of sturdy hands grapple for my hair and wrench it back.

That would be Bastian's signature move.

He's got me. He's really going to offer me in a blood sacrifice. But I do remember another tidbit my favorite self-defense teacher taught me. Not pretty, but it'll do a semi-respectable job.

Spinning, I grab hold of Bastian's meaty fist and take a giant, greedy bite—straight outta his thumb.

It works! Just like my self-defense teacher said it would.

Thumb snaps off like a carrot.

Bastian howls, bloody well confirming I'm a genius. But, hey, we need to give my teacher credit.

Clutching his hand to his chest, my newfound foe kneels, screaming sonnets.

With no time to lose, Luther seizes my arms. "Cate, we need to go. Now."

Truth is, I wanna trust Luther. More than anything, I wanna trust him a whole, whole lot. But what if his plan truly is to eventually offer me in that blood sacrifice?

"You knocked me out!"

"That wasn't me!"

"Then why in the heck don't I remember getting hit on the head?"

Luther's eyes stretch wide. The hole's overflowing with more eyeballs than the coins in Scrooge McDuck's money pit.

Yanking on my arm, Luther still looks pretty when he yells, "Come on!"

Eyeballs spill every which way. We tear outta the room like Bonnie n' Clyde, and the hall rumbles as we dart for the stairs.

Woo-wee, it reeks out here quite a lot.

Placing his arm over his mouth and nose, Luther says, "Breathe as little as you can." That pretty much sums up my life. "We need to get outside!"

Feeling agreeable, I throw my arm over my mouth. But one solitary question needs to be asked. "How do I know you're not going to chop me in pieces and stick me under the bed?"

Luther grunts with disbelief before tugging my arm with

his free hand. We scramble down steps covered by old branches and ants, and by the time we make it to the bottom of the stairs, I know it's time for me to make a final decision.

To trust him, or not . . .

Should I be at this boy's mercy? Or pretend it's opposite day and not listen one stitch?

I've spent my entire life flirting with the reality of dying. Once, I had a scare at thirteen, when my pneumonia got real bad. I could see it in Mom's eyes that she believed I really wouldn't make it.

I'm tired of waffling, but I just don't have enough information yet. First thing I gotta do is get outta this house, and, for the time being, Luther's all I got.

Bending down before the halls, the boy pulls a three-foot-wide screen from the black mold-covered wall. "Climb in!" he whisper-shouts.

Yeesh, Curtain Lady's making the house rumble quite a lot. I'd say it's a six or seven on ye olde Richter scale. But he wants me to climb *into* the wall?

"Seriously?!" I remember not to pull my arm away from my mouth. "How do I know you're not tricking me into climbing into a trash compactor?"

He throws out his arms. "I would never do that!"

As we gaze at one another, Luther's blazing eyes sparking into mine, the air becomes so powdery yellow, he drops the screen—and dives right in.

I do believe he says, "Shortcut," but I don't have time to psychoanalyze everything going on.

Crossing myself with three Hail Marys, I choose to abandon ship.

The duct's coppery, and everything clangs as we crawl like crazy. When we do eventually climb through, he and I pop out right next to the foyer, where the front door stands wide open . . . like it's been that way the entire time.

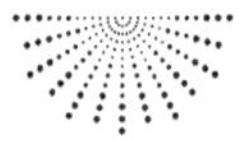

CHAPTER TWENTY-FOUR

Luther and I catch our breaths while sitting at the top of the front steps.

Apparently, inside's biological chemical warfare level of toxic.

I need Luther to talk to me. What I don't get is why we don't just run off. Mailman's not anywhere in sight; far as I can tell, it's an empty street with enough clouds to make us think we're in Washington or something.

Luther suddenly turns toward me, hair so wild he could keep a beehive in it. "I think it is time we are honest with one another."

"Bring on the truth bombs and lie detectors!"

"I lured you here . . ." He glances away, shoulders slumping. "So that you might take Ophelia's place."

Wha-huh?

And . . . *Ophelia* is Curtain Lady's name?

"There is much to say." Luther's cool ring grazes my knuckles as he covers my fingers with his hand. How can I pass up the chance to hear what's really going on?

But he just openly admitted that he "lured" me here.

Can I trust him?! I know I can't trust him!

I'll "listen" whilst creeping down the steps . . .

Pulling my hand from his, I tense to stand by pushing off the step.

Mid-stand, though, he gently clutches my arm. "I wouldn't do that."

"Why?" Fighting him off is hard 'cause his touch is trés cozy.

"You were going to leave . . ." He reads my mind. "I would not blame you. But if you try to do that right now, Ophelia *will* have Bastian retrieve Rosalyn."

In one fell swoop, I sway a little as I stand. "What are you saying?" My gauzy, bloodstained dress flaps like demented birds in the wind. Luther's not supposed to threaten such things. He's supposed to be gentlemanly and chivalrous.

Pulling off his jacket, he stands and somberly places it around my shoulders. A little bit of glass is embedded in the collar from the bursting aquariums—or mirrors, I guess—and I begin to shrug it off. But, you know, I'm bloody well cold, and I can't believe I still don't know what's been going on.

Leaning over, Luther fastens the top two buttons of his jacket and lingers for several long seconds. "We can beat her," he eventually says. "But we have to think cleverly. Whatever we do, we mustn't do anything to make her upset. Ophelia is a force to be reckoned with when she is angry."

I still feel like I'm in a vacuum. "I can't believe you didn't tell me that's her name."

Not able to wear his jacket anymore, I shrug it off, and a button pops off and rolls down the steps.

"It is why she targeted you." Luther stares down at the discarded button. "She believes in the power of symmetry."

"I'll show her symmetry," I grumble, wishing it was her when I kick his jacket. "How do I know you're not just making up what you know I fear most to keep me around? You know Rosalyn means everything to me."

Luther closes his eyes, guilt corroding his chiseled features. "Because . . . she . . . made me make the doll."

How in the heck does he think admitting *that* will get me to trust anything he says?

He's been lurking outside our windows, watching Rosalyn and me?

Lurky Luthy!

How else would he know my sister's blind, and that she wears polka dots?

"You told me that you can't leave." I grit my teeth in frustration. "How do I know I can believe you? I mean, we met at the library!"

"Day pass," he mumbles, as if to himself. "That, and because . . . I am sorry. I cannot say . . ."

I throw my hands in the air. "You told me you would explain everything!"

He glances left, then right. "I want to. I . . . can tell you the history." He raises his eyebrows meaningfully.

I cross my arms over my chest, 'cause I've about heard enough history for one day. And, *still* not knowing where our relationship stands, I pace down one more step.

Will they really try to get Rosalyn if I try to leave?

"Okay, spill." I pause, feeling like I'm standing on the edge of a cliff.

But if Bastian will truly get Rosalyn, I *have* to stay. There's no ifs, ands, or buts about it.

"Once upon a time," Luther says while I wander to the next step, "my brother fell in love. The object of his affection was a beautiful girl with long, dark hair, and it is said that she did not love him back."

"Ophelia." I tap-tap my foot.

"Yes." Luther slumps. "You must understand that my

brother was very different back then. Entitled but deferential. Submissive. Our mother was woefully controlling. When either one of us disobeyed, she grew very, *very* upset."

Images of old school switches and paddle-boards swirl in a funnel through my head. "What's your mother's name?"

Luther's eyes twinge, fearful.

"It'll be a lot easier if I can assign a name to each figure you're telling me about!"

He looks both ways—to the clouds and mist—before whispering, "Henrietta Pearl."

"Pretty. Though, she did look a lot like Attila the Hun in that portrait."

Luther nods. "Yes. One of the things our mother liked to do was focus on *possible* negative outcomes." His voice rises a few notches. "'What if my boys never marry?' 'What if they never have children?' 'What if I never become a grandmother and use the charming nursery we have planned?'" He scrubs his face with his hand.

"She had my brother and me . . . when she was well past her prime. By the time we became of age, she had matured— much more than she liked."

"So, you're telling me she went crazy pants."

Frown lines linger between Luther's brows, though he doesn't debate it. "Our mother became obsessed. She believed that she *needed* her children to marry. She became preoccupied with obtaining toys for the future nursery." Twisting the big, black ring on his finger, he adds, "Just like all our ancestors, she was terrified the Dvorak line would end."

Dvorak. . . . I pause on the fourth step. "But she's a girl."

Luther stares at me, eyes open and honest.

"*Dvorak* should go from father to son."

Dropping his gaze, he murmurs, "She and my father were distant relatives."

Add that to page ten of the "what-not-to-do-at-family-reunions" rulebook. But the joke's on Luther . . . he's their kid. I don't need to be a jerk by making him feel even worse, so I nod like that makes perfect sense.

"You were teens at the time?" I fold my hands like I'm part of the historical narrative. "How come you and Bastian haven't aged, hmm?"

A fatty tickle rises in my throat, and I have to lower my head to cough in the crook of my arm.

"Bastian told me," Luther answers, marking me with his gaze. "About the tuberculosis."

"Oh!" I let out a rip-roar of a laugh only to hack up a bucketful of mucus.

I'm half-tempted to admit the truth about what I really have, but there could be a chance that the boy's still lying, so I refold my hands and wordlessly survey the next step.

"When Bastian proposed to the young woman," Luther continues, "needless to say, she refused him."

"Ooh." I can't help smiling. "Wasn't fond of the mood swings and neck hair?"

"She had her eye on someone else." Luther's cheeks flare as he looks down. "Mother grew very upset. After she pronounced Ophelia dead—"

"Whoa, whoa, whoa!" I hold up my hand. "I think you skipped a few steps."

"Little did we know that we'd unleashed a shifter's power."

Okayyy, looks like we're not going back to the moment leading up to Ophelia's death. But he did just say "shifter," so I put on my Nancy Drew ears and listen to that.

Luther falls silent, staring at the crimson, rustling weeds like he's stuck in an old photograph. If he's a contemporary of Bastian and their mom, I guess there's a reason why Luther struggles to say what's what.

Obviously, the girl—Ophelia—is still haunting—er, becoming—the house, appearing in the curtains and whatnot.

But how does one gain the power to create plants and control vines?

She can shatter aquariums, make whatever she wants break in a snap.

"What does she want from me?" Knowing that I don't want to hear the answer, I stop on the second to last last.

Luther glances east, then west, as if surveying the property. "Why, to become the house."

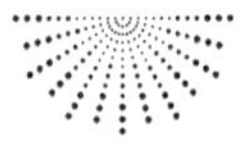

CHAPTER TWENTY-FIVE

"Become . . ." I sputter at the wacksadaisical nonsense. "That's crazy." And yet . . . I've known for a great long while that "Hellström" is a Scandinavian name. My grams used to ramble on and on about our ancestors being berserkers who shifted into wild animals and stuff . . .

She wasn't off her rocker?

To think I was just coming over for a hot date. This is *way* more than I bargained for or expected.

People can't really become an entire *house,* right? We can't walk around inside other people. That's nuts.

"How does she propose I do that?" For demonstration purposes, I up and pretend I'm on the same page.

"For one, you thwarted her when you drank your own blood."

The boy didn't answer my question, but, by the way he said it, I'm a flippin' vampire, and I didn't even know it.

Still, it's come to the point where I must choose: either turn around and sprint the seven or so blocks home, or . . . stay. Because Rosalyn may or may not get kidnapped.

I could just protect Rosalyn when she shows up at the

house. Or run away with her, but, with my health, I'm not sure I'll be fast enough.

Can I truly, truly trust the boy? Objectively—*extremely* rationally speaking, probably not. But I want to. My gut tells me I can when all is said and done, but what if my gut is wrong?

"Cate . . ." Luther locks eyes with me before he pauses. "I know I have given you no reason to trust me, but I really do esteem and adore you. Please know that."

Why does everything he says have to sound so cryptic?

I'm the biggest hypocrite ever. I *invented* the word "cryptic." Which means, really, we're the best match. I can't even imagine a boy who gets me better than him, and I haven't even shown the full me yet.

Watching his wind-swept hair and Johnny Depp clothes, I have to say what's in my heart. "Okay."

His eyes flash with surprise. "Yes?"

"I mean, in the very least, I should hear your plan. Show me how we beat her?"

Cautiously, I lift my foot to the second to last step.

The boy stands, seeming to sense how monumental the moment is. "It's around back."

Gosh, every word he speaks creates so much heat and chemistry between us. *It's around back* isn't supposed to come out so sultry and hot. What if I'm willing to believe him only because I'm attracted to him?

"Or we could just make out." I shrug.

Laugh lines frame his eyes, but I still haven't earned a full smile. Not yet.

"I am trusting you," I warn him.

"And I am trusting *you*," he whispers back.

Feeling dutiful, I stomp across the yard and head toward the west.

East?

West.

Luther follows, content to let me take charge.

This boy's a keeper.

"So." I all but clap. "How do I become the house?"

"Ophelia is a shifter," he says as we turn to tromp around the nearest corner.

Wait . . . is that a *gravestone* in the grass a few paces from us?

Scampering over, I kneel in the weeds and make out the faint, blocky etching of letters. But the weathering and mildew make it so hard to read. The stone's pretty little and rectangular. If everyone around here was all born in the 1800s, I guess that makes perfect sense.

"This is where you buried her?" My throat is scratchy. I look around to the flowerless rose bushes, some witch hazel, and a red-trunked, paperbark maple. "Where are your mother and father's graves?"

A bit of color floods Luther's cheeks as he ducks his head.

Huffing, I stand real close to him. "If you want me to trust you, Luther, you have to talk."

His eyes mark mine. "I am explaining everything I can." Taking my hand, he squeezes it once, and ooh, baby, his smooth, calloused palms shouldn't feel so good.

His gaze reaches into mine, and I think—I don't know . . . maybe he's going to kiss me—but instead, his gaze raises to the kitchen window.

Nothing seems to be lurking there, so I get us outta this awkwardness. "Let's keep walking."

I certainly don't know everything about the boy's past, so I must find ways to urge him to talk.

We wander past the rubble of a few broken statues— rock-made hands and faces sink against Mexican feather grass—and when we've rounded a giant mulberry tree, Luther whispers, "She simply wants you to swap places."

Simply.

"Wait . . . are we secretly ant people, living inside a crazy bird box?" That would make slightly more sense.

Luther quirks a sexy eyebrow.

"Hey, that would explain all the illusions. Smaller things are easier to manipulate, you know."

"And do you think I am manipulating you?" He's standing so close I can't help smelling the sweet sweat on his neck.

"Nooo." Even to me, it sounds like the biggest lie in town.

Luther inches forward another step. "The truth is, it takes a great amount of ambition and energy to shift into an entire house."

My breath hovers, trapped in my chest. "That's why her powers seem to come and go?"

He tucks a piece of my hair behind my ear. "That is why her powers seem to come and go."

"Okay . . . so why does she care that my name is *Ophelia*?" I pick my way around the brittle branches of a thicket of cedars.

"Because there is power in a name." He glances back uneasily at the kitchen window. "Some say the name means 'help.' Others say it means 'spirit demon.'"

Mom named me something that basically says I'm evil?!

Did she know that?

She always said she had me before she was ready, but did she really believe I was her demon child?

'Course, Luther doesn't have to tell me that *Ophelia's* not exactly a name that comes around all that often. I imagine it was all the rage back in the 1600s.

A pinecone digs into my foot like a set of knives—still barefoot, ugh—but after I hobble round the murdery thing, we eventually make it to the last stretch of the side of the house.

Veering around another mulberry, I find another question popping outta my mouth.

"So . . . what's the deal with all the vines and tiger moths?"

Luther gently releases my hand. "The vines are her—Ophelia's—way of retaining control. The tiger moths . . . come because they're attracted to the plants."

"There's nothing magical about them?"

"No, not by themselves."

Yeesh. He's basically saying that anything can become magical once Ophelia puts her grubby hands on it. Kinda sorta freaks me out.

The mulberry tree scratches another stained glass window near the corner of the house, and everything's so wonky, it makes me wonder if the windows are her eyes or nose.

Luther leads me round the final corner of the back of the house.

"My ancestors' choice to take Monkshood in an ill-advised attempt to have children followed them to our current time. The thing about Ophelia is, she likes to flaunt her power. She enjoys finding all the ways she can behave as the plant—choke, rip, maim . . ."

"Ah, your poem!"

The corners of Luther's lips *nearly* tilt up in a sheepish smile. "Yes."

As we veer around the second mulberry and a clothesline, which, due to the mud, doesn't look to be used much at all, part of me wants to say, *Look, I'm sorry about all the family drama, but it's all a bit much . . .* but what kinda person would that make me?

I reek drama. I *exude* drama. I'd be a drama major if I ever thought I'd make it through college.

As the prickly needles of a nearby pine tree tickle my

neck, I can't help thinking that we've reached a crucible in Luther's and my relationship.

Maybe now's the time to spill about my CF.

All that comes out, though, is the most watery of coughs.

"I do not fear the disease." Somberly, Luther takes my hand. My insides turn into a great, big pile of murlush.

He thinks I'm contagious, and he's willing to risk being infected.

Oy, I have to stay logical. Logical! He's just a cute boy I've decided to trust. "If Ophelia's the house, then what was your family living in before she shifted?"

Luther nods toward the other outbuilding past the greenhouse—the tin and wood one, with the missing shingles and three of the four walls caved in. "She can't control the entire house at the same time. It's too exhausting. That's why some of Monkshood Manor is more dilapidated at times. Though *our* home existed before her shift."

"That was your house?"

"It used to be nicer." He does this adorable, full-body shrug.

But that doesn't explain all the vases, sconces, and statues in the main house.

"My family" —Luther calmly approaches the greenhouse — "picked up a few possessions in our day. Especially my father, before he misspent my family's fortune. But most of the Estate is her. She can become and grow anything she likes."

Chicken wire rattles in Luther's hand as he grasps the metal handle and opens the greenhouse door for me for the second time.

I don't know if I wanna go in there. I should have taken buckets of enzymes and be donning a hazmat suit, 'cause he said those flowers are poisonous.

Sensing my unease, Luther reaches toward me and runs

his thumb along my jaw, sending little shimmers of heat through my skin.

"I will protect you." His voice comes out hoarse enough to make me think he truly means it.

"But what if she comes out and gets me? I still don't even know the plan . . ."

Luther casts a heavy, sidelong look at the house. "I will not let that happen. We still have a little time."

CHAPTER TWENTY-SIX

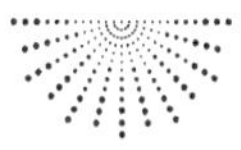

"Each of us has a job," Luther explains as we trek past the mountains of flowers inside the greenhouse. "Mine" —he extends a hand to the wine-colored petals that have grown along the walls overnight— "is to tend the plants."

"You're a master gardener." I examine a trellis with its swatch of freshly bloomed buds.

The top petal of each flower really *is* like a hood, flamboyantly hooking over the top.

I wonder if Ophelia has Bastian wear that robe, or if the 1800s made him as cray cray as Ophelia.

Feeling the lure, I extend my hand to pet the pretty, purple flower.

Luther catches my fingers. "Don't."

There's a softness in his eyes that couldn't be counterfeit.

Needing to understand more about the role of the greenhouse, I nod toward the plants. "Why does Ophelia need you to tend these if she can grow them herself?"

His gaze sweeps over the unruly garden. "Because maintaining a house requires a great amount of effort. She . . . tends to sleep a great deal."

Running his finger along the top of my arm, he then slips on a pair of gloves and tucks an errant stem behind the trellis.

Gaze skittering to the door, it's like, even now, Luther's afraid we'll be caught, or he'll say too much. But I'm not about to let him wuss out on me when he has a solid idea of how to protect Rosalyn.

Also, maybe, possibly I *don't* wanna die. That little thing called self-preservation . . . well, it's strong. Maybe I'll find a renewed dedication to life after stopping Crazy Lady and Bastian.

"So, what's the plan?" I square my shoulders. "Burn the bloody place down?"

Luther's untamed hair flutters as he shakes his head. "Already tried that. What we need to do is make her go to sleep . . . for good."

My breath hovers in my chest. "How do we do that?"

Pulling off his gloves, Luther watches me, his eyes becoming icy stars as he tucks another piece of my hair behind my ear. "You . . . are a hallucination."

I can barely hear the words in his breath, and we'll go ahead right here and make that my epitaph.

In a messy blur of petals and fog, the boy leans down and kisses me, his lips softer than velvet.

Trickling his finger down my throat, he kisses me surer, stronger.

Words melt like sleet, and his lips are a gentle massage.

Something inside me tells me that he's trying *really* hard to ascertain how I'm feeling—how I'm probably not too thrilled about being trapped at Monkshood Manor.

But another part—a hidden part—almost, kinda, sorta feels that I never wanna leave.

There, I said it.

I know it's idiotic and moronic. *I* don't believe I would ever admit it aloud.

I'm a masochist.

As the pretty, honeysuckle-ish flowers spin and whir around our heads, I lean into the flames that flicker beneath his lips.

I might be filthy in this strange, tea-stained dress, but part of me thinks, I dunno . . . I might actually look good in it.

Luther breaks away, and all of that happened *way* too fast.

His eyes are telling me there's something else he wants to say, and I not-so-gently rub the back of his neck.

Maybe it's the driplines leaking ye olde love aroma, but his lips reconnect with mine, and I go and rove mine over his.

He's both tangible, yet not.

Actually, if I'm being honest, a large piece of me believes that Ophelia's going to reach up and tear him away from me any second.

Everything feels so temporary, too fleeting with Luther.

When he pulls away, we both have to pant. His hand rests on the small of my back, and it pretty much feels like my skin's glowing from the inside.

With the first real, genuine smile he's given me since the moment I arrived, Luther gazes at me with way too much softness. "Let us get to work, my love."

Lucifer! Judas! I . . . don't know how to react.

Are talks of love premature? Don't you know it.

Does it bother me?

I gotta say . . . nope.

Zilch.

Nada.

Actually, if I'm being a hundred and ninety-nine percent

truthful, I always thought "main squeeze" would be my first title in a relationship.

He just called me "his love" . . .

"So." I have to force my lips and cheeks to stop their perma-grin. "What's the plan?"

Shoulders relaxed, Luther pulls back on his gloves and, bending down, he actually rips up one, then two Monkshood plants.

Uhhh . . . is that allowed? Sure, whatever! I don't care if it's allowed. Still. "Won't she just grow more?"

He uproots another with an itty-bitty smile I could just nibble off. "Not if she can't . . ."

I have no idea what *that's* supposed to mean, but hells bells, yeah. I'm game. Spike, homeroom, touchdown!

Opening his arms, Luther confidently says, "Our captor maintains a great amount of pride in these plants. She has me tend them, because *maintaining them uses strength she doesn't have*. Shifters are not supposed to be so large. It is why she rips apart and eats more than either one of us would care to admit."

"Rips apart . . . and eats?"

He raises his eyebrows with meaning, and he doesn't have to say more. I already knew about that bag o' bones in the living room and secretly hypothesized that it wasn't merely for décor purposes.

Though something else doesn't quite add up. "Why is Bastian able to become a dog?"

Luther glowers. "Because" —he uproots another six-foot-tall plant— "my brother is connected to Ophelia."

"So . . . that's why we were able to escape after I bit off Bastian's thumb?"

Bowing his head, Luther laughs—truly laughs! "When one is wounded, they both feel it."

"Well, call me the Thumb-Chomper. Dude, let's bite off the other one!"

Laughter shines in Luther's dark eyes, and, ooh, I'm in trouble.

Trrrouble.

Feels good.

This I can take. This I can handle, booyah. I thought I would only like Luther when he was all layered and complicated, but I gotta say, I like him even *more* now that he's being all open and honest.

I can almost imagine hitting a few softballs with him.

Playing a round of mini-golf.

Pigging out on popcorn and, er, *not* making out.

Pausing before pulling up yet another plant, Luther warns, "My brother will not be foolish enough as to allow an incident like that to happen again."

Grumpily, I kick one of the stalks of an uprooted plant. "Well, of course not."

Setting down another handful of Monkshood flowers on the ground, Luther slides off his gloves. He's going to grab the rake or pruning shears, yeah . . . but instead, he reaches over and plucks up another thin strand of my hair. Rubbing it between his fingers, he says, "You are the first ever to weaken them." His shining eyes offer me congratulations.

Cheeks blazing, I giggle, nervous. "Oh, gosh. It was an accident."

"You accidentally bite off thumbs?"

I laugh again and slug him on the arm. "Whatever you do, *don't* make me mad."

CHAPTER TWENTY-SEVEN

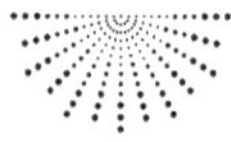

I NEVER THOUGHT PULLING out flowers could be so fun.

And I know it's still *way* too early, but I really feel like Luther and I could have something solid. Obviously, there's that initial attraction—and one good make-out session—but, I don't know . . . I've gotta say, I'm smelling Christmas and birthday presents.

The boy actually builds me up.

Called me "a hallucination."

Okay, he may not be the most natural when it comes to contemporary flirting and stuff, but that's what makes his kind words even more grand.

Yep, there's an earnest sobriety about Luther.

An unmatched sobriety I cannot get outta my head.

I don't want to, honestly.

Is he involved in the drama in the house? Well, he lives here, so, yes.

But he's not the one pulling the strings!

Dude's getting by, best he can.

Plus, he even said he tried burning the place down. That

takes out like three months of trying to unravel this rather complicated relationship.

He doesn't like evil, haunted buildings? Check.

Doesn't mind cooking? Double-check.

An excellent kisser? Check, check, check.

I pray he's not duping me . . .

I mean, he *can't* be. He's so gentle and earnest.

Doing my best to pull up a Monkshood plant by its roots, I grab hold of the meaty base and *yank* for all I've got.

It lifts pretty easily from the ground, and I'm right grateful for the gloves Luther found for me beneath a potted plant.

"Take that!" I go ahead and kick it in the goods.

Leveling out the dirt with a trowel (Luther thinks it "unwise" for me to slide the dirt around barefoot), I'm actually quite careful to do a grade-A job.

Luther smooths out his pile of dirt with a round-mouthed shovel like an expert, and yeah, I'd say we have a good rhythm going.

Glancing round at the tall, pulled up plants that look a lot like abandoned, uprooted cornstalks, I have to ask, "This'll get rid of her? Or hurt her, at least, to start off?"

Discretely, Luther takes my hand. Right when I think that's all he's gonna do, the boy plumb tugs me closer and grabs my waist.

Chills run down my spine.

Boy's got better moves than Enrique Iglesias and smells better than a candy shop.

We sway back and forth—back and forth—and we can forget about my dreams of playin' softball and whatever other activities I've spouted off before. 'Cause Luther and I? We're more uncategorized than that.

We're gonna dance.

On my hip, he gently secures his hand, and I don't think I've ever felt this desired or loved.

His warm fingertips graze the skin above the waist of my jeans, causing a blowtorch to flare up my shirt.

"If you could go *anywhere* in the world," he asks, "where would you go?"

In a fluid motion, he lifts his arms and sends me in a spin, à la "Dancing with the Stars."

Hmm. He's asking me about the world? That might be 'cause the boy loves maps.

"Bot-sa-wana," I say. It's the first thing that pops outta my mouth.

But, seeing as he's got a giant papier-mache map taped on his wall, I decide to be real frank. "I've always wanted to go on a cross-country train ride with Rosalyn. I know she can't see, and . . . I have my issues and stuff, but it's something I think she would like to do. You know, feel the ice at Glacier National Park. Go up the Space Needle. Maybe even hear all the hubbub at Times Square . . ."

Really, I know the idea's far-fetched, and I cough, 'cause the timing feels just right. "It's not like my condition is kosher for travel."

Luther nods with understanding, and my giant web of lies isn't making me feel real comfortable.

Time to turn ye olde proverbial table. "How about you?"

Silently, Luther gazes at his lonely tomato plants.

I glance behind me, feeling only slightly jealous. "Do I need to learn how to photosynthesize?"

He spins me, quickly veiling his look of hopelessness. "Please don't."

His tongue's still not wagging, so I give him a little nudge. "Why do you care about them so much?"

Lifting our arms, Luther spins me in yet another circle. His eyes lock on mine, and I could die a happy lass.

"You ask a lot of questions," he observes, taking my waist.

I nuzzle up real close, basking in his manly smell. "And you don't ask enough."

He spins me faster and faster, slowing down at the perfect moment.

"Some answers cannot be supplied," he says.

I give him a look that says he *better* start talking, so he pulls me in real close and whispers, "Some things are not what you'd expect."

His breath is like a hot fudge sundae. I want to argue—*oh,* I want to argue—but the only words I can seem to find are, "You are an incredibly secretive boy."

"My father was a peddler."

Not real sure what his father has to do with anything, but I pretend we're in tandem as we sway.

Lowering his hands, Luther stoically shows me the black ring on his right ring finger. "He couldn't afford diamonds, so, when my father proposed to my mother, he gave her a ring of ancient obsidian."

"Isn't obsidian made of lava?"

"Volcanic glass, yes . . ."

"Hey, at least your mother got to keep her jewelry! My dad up and sold my mama's ring for drugs."

"Oh. I . . . am sorry."

Leaning down, Luther quietly rests his soft, lightly bearded cheek on my head, and heck if I've ever felt more adored than this.

Not that I'm good with the whole "possibly becoming a house" scenario, but . . .

"So, you wanna see the world," I murmur. "Find volcanic glass." *Cough.* "Like your daddy did."

Luther squeezes my hand, sending little shockwaves up my wrist. I can tell that there's much more to the story, but, as usual, he doesn't open up about it.

Holding me closer, he says, "I am sorry you have the tuberculosis."

He had to go and bring up the fact I'm not exactly being truthful.

Since I've never been real good at managing guilt, I blurt, "Luther, I don't actually—"

An unseen force suddenly rips him from my hands. Amidst blowing leaves and stems, he's thrown a good twenty feet—smashing through the greenhouse window's glass.

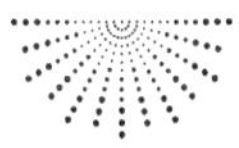

CHAPTER TWENTY-EIGHT

THERE'S THIS SHARP, sickening, sucking sound.

"LUTHER!"

Another powerful gale rushes through my hair and ravages my limbs. It stirs the purple petals in the air like the kettle in a witch's brew.

Pausing only half a second, it—Ophelia?—rips up each and every one of Luther's tomato plants.

Wilted leaves flit to the ground, and they look so crestfallen, so wimpy. Below them, *below them* is . . . a man's charred, shriveled remains.

Jet-black hair sparsely interweaves with a half-smashed head.

Fraying fragments of an off-white shirt lay across the limp remains—along with a pair of dark slacks that have most certainly seen better days.

I'm *way* past the point of thinking I'm seeing things.

The man's skin looks like stretched saltwater taffy, and in his palm lies a handful of black obsidian rocks.

Exactly like Luther's ring.

Is this Luther's dad?

"Noooo!" From outside, Luther screams. He pounds on the window—the other window that didn't break—and his eyes are stretched so wide with fear that I'm backing up.

How is it that his dad's suddenly lying on the ground, no longer concealed by those tomato plants?

Was he actually alive? Is *that* why Luther cared about the plants so much?

In another rush of wind, Ophelia wrenches Luther back so far I can't see him through the fog and mist.

All right . . . time to show this heifer who's boss.

Grabbing the shovel, I stab the closest mangy stem while Ophelia shrieks and flips on the lights.

Momentarily, I go blinder than three blind mice.

While lifting my hand to block out all the rays of light, I'm hit with a gnarled, twisty vine that snakes up my hand. It pries my fingers from the shovel's handle—one at a time.

Snatching the shovel from my fist, Ophelia purrs, *"Do not look away."* The lights burn hotter, brighter. *"Your sister certainly didn't."*

I can practically feel Ophelia's cruel words being written inside my veins. Her anger boils lava hot, menacing, and hungry.

Fighting back the tears that are starting to burn in my eyes, I try to squeeze my eyes shut. But she must have me in some sort of trance.

Can't. Look. Away.

I already knew it, but she really knows what I did to my sister.

She knows that because of me, Rosalyn looked into the lights.

One of Ophelia's sneaky tendrils creeps and crawls across my face. I think she's going to attach a breathing tube to my nose, but, gradually, she slides her stem all the way across my cheek.

Dips into my ear, tickling my cochlea and eardrum.

Sifting and wriggling inside, she eventually finds what she's looking for—a memory. A memory I have been avoiding for a very long time . . .

Mom, all decked out in her stretchy pants.

Hair's slipped into a ponytail.

She pauses at my bedroom door, gym bag in hand.

"Honey, do you know where the suntan lotion is?"

I'm too busy to look up from my computer. "In the bathroom, I guess."

Fists pound and rattle the door—not my bedroom door, but outside the greenhouse.

CRACK! The wood around us visibly splits, and Luther must be trying to get back in.

Ripping out the tendril Ophelia attached to my ear, I spin to go to Luther, but Ophelia flings the door wide open, hitting him so hard, he flies ten feet backward.

I'll grab a lighter. Burn *every single* one of her plants.

Except, Luther said he tried using fire. Why in the heck didn't it work again?

Even through the adrenaline and the questions, I have to force myself to keep a clear head. "What did they do to you to make you like this?" I ask Ophelia. "Did they kill you? Is that it?"

"'Kill' is such an unfitting word." She rattles the lights as she talks, but nowhere does her face imprint. Maybe she talks through the flowers themselves. I guess that makes sense, her faux-sweet voice coming from all directions at once.

Looping her tendrils around one of the lights from above, Ophelia ensures that it flashes directly into my eyes. *"'Murder,' too, is an awfully short word for what they did."*

I gulp. Not exactly cheery dinnertime fodder. "Bastian wanted to marry you, but you didn't want to marry him back."

A messy bouquet of flowers slithers like snakes across the ground. With an enormous whoosh of air, that *same* bouquet gives me a mighty shove.

I land right on my bubble butt.

"Okay, okay!" I *oof* from the ground. "I'm sorry they killed you . . ."

"*I'm not.*" The subtlety of Ophelia's power hums from the walls and driplines. The lights crackle and buzz, and Imma pretty sure Ophelia's decided to breathe on the back of my neck.

'Cause I'm feelin' wind. It's so unfair that she knows it's a real phobia of mine.

Kneeling, I ready myself to stand, though everything's way more awkward in this dress. If I can grab the garden spade by the shelf, I can start knocking out lights. Then, at least, I won't be seeing spots.

"*I am actually quite happy about my death,*" Ophelia adds. I'm half-tempted to tell her that no one cares about her sicko reaction. "*Otherwise, I couldn't do this.*" Gathering all the purple flowers, she loops and curls them into a macabre, choreographed dance. Skulls imprint in wilted hoods. Thorns protrude from regularly smooth vines. When a fresh wave of thorny fingers snatches at my skirt, though, I smack them off.

Yep. I'm ready to use that spade now.

A puff of pollen flits over my nose, and I cough through her latest gust. The smell of B.O. is worse than death.

Ophelia growls so loud, and dark veins suddenly snake from the underside of Luther's dad's skin. Glass shards whip through the air, and something tells me, the time for battle is over. I need to run.

Which direction?

To the back of the yard . . .

But there wasn't a gate. Just that pink backpack that led

to some pretty freaky sorcery in Grandma's room. The front door is wide open, but it's so far away . . . and Luther said, if I ran, Bastian would take Rosalyn.

I'm out of the greenhouse and halfway to the other outbuilding—Luther's family's original house—the world feels topsy-turvy as I stagger toward it.

It's a structure that existed *before* Ophelia and the Dvoraks met . . .

It can't be under her power.

Can't be under her power!

It's gotta be "home base" in our tricksy game of cat and mouse.

CHAPTER TWENTY-NINE

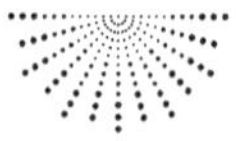

I SHOULDN'T RUN into a condemned house.

I shouldn't run into a condemned house!

But there isn't anywhere else to go, and I kinda like the look of moss and randomly strewn floorboards.

Ooh, is that a spinning wheel?

I give it a little nudge, and the wooden wheel spins with a creak, echoing the frantic rhythm of my heartbeats.

Luther lurks a few paces away, looking as disoriented as a drunk driver at a three-car pileup. Digging his hands into his hair, he doesn't say a word, his complexion pale and wildly sick.

"She just killed him," he mutters in a trance, looking in the direction of his dad. "Just killed him . . ."

He covers his face with his palms. Fresh dirt coats his nails, and another set of scratches shine through the sleeves of his shirt.

"You shouldn't be in here," he mumbles.

Back to his mantra . . .

I glance at the warped two-by-fours holding up half the ceiling and the moss that's nearly taken over the building.

Maybe he's right.

I don't care. I rush over and give him a big, fat hug—the kind that says I'm not only his kissing friend, but his *friend*, and I do care about what happens to him.

His body's so stiff that I know this has hit him hard. He doesn't move his shoulders or his elbows. He doesn't so much as pat me back, and this is how I know it's hit him in the gut.

I embrace him even harder.

"I am so sorry." I try to wrap my mind around his grief, which must be razor-sharp. His father from the 1800s was buried beneath a big pile of tomato plants. How is that even our reality?

Relaxing a little in my arms, Luther does allow me to hug him for another thirty seconds.

Ultimately, when we're ready to let go, I end up wandering over to a chaise lounge. Stuffing's popping outta the sides, and Mom would definitely be inspecting the cherry wood frame, inch by inch.

"I truly believed pulling out all the Monkshood flowers would stop her . . . I never dreamt she would dig him up. I always believed—hoped—he was alive. Or, at least, a part of him." Luther stares without seeing, still in a trance. Clearly unaware of what he's doing, he begins clearing off the debris from the chaise lounge—a broken snow globe, three volumes of pocket-sized textbooks, pouches . . . and, very fondly, he removes a locket from the back cushion with a pretty intricate maze etched in it.

"These were your dad's belongings?" I nod to everything he deposits on a nearby mahogany table with scrollwork and legs etched with vines.

Still in a daze, Luther doesn't hear me or see any of this.

Everywhere he looks, I'm sure he's seeing his dad.

How long was his dad trapped and shielded like that?

And *was* his dad actually still alive before Ophelia pulled him out of the ground?

A melancholy wind whistles over the room, and I wish I could tell the boy that everything's going to be hunky-dory, but the truth is, *I* haven't lost my parents to death. So I don't have a clue as to what to do or say.

Somewhere to the left—right!—loose sheets of aluminum rattle in the wind. Or Ophelia, more like. Chances are, Luther and I don't get to stay tucked away in here, canoodling as long as we like.

"We *have* to make a plan." I do my best to focus on our priorities. For all I know, it won't be long until this building isn't even standing.

I pace.

Past an old, half-smashed lamp.

"I'm *really* sorry you lost your dad. I can't imagine what you must be feeling . . . but, just so we're on the same page, *she* can't get to us when we're in here, right?"

Luther surreptitiously wipes at his wet eyes. "She couldn't before . . ."

The walls prickle and rattle—we're inside a fatty tambourine in a monster's hands.

None of this does *anything* to instill confidence.

Spidery whimpers groan from the boards, and all of this feels an awful lot like . . . actually, I have no idea. I've never been stuck in a random structure with a super-hot boy and a vengeful ghost-slash-shapeshifter wanting me to take her place.

If I were to liken it to something I *have* experienced, I'd say it's like I'm the runner in one of those Alien movies. Eep! Why'd I have to go and think about that?

A pounding—thumping—bangs from directly over my head.

Someone's on the roof.

On the roof.

They're dancing Michael Jackson's "Thriller" . . . or "Beat It," and the hyper, scamper-y paws tell me it's Bastian.

Luther's ashen face washes so white *he's* the one who looks like he has the chronic illness.

A very loud *boom* rattles the entire structure.

Dirt and dust rain down like confetti.

The shrieking aluminum on the walls tells me it's only a matter of time before the entire structure collapses, and boards and aluminum shingles *would* crush us to death.

I never got ahold of my family.

Never talked to Mom or Rosalyn.

Egad, what if this is it? What if Ophelia's about to give up on her original plan and just kill me now?

Nervous, I scamper over and take Luther's strong hand. While I know, I don't exactly deserve to be safe, deserving something and *wanting* something are very different.

"I don't suppose you can shift?" I ask him, scrambling for another strategy.

More dust rains down while Luther shakes his gaunt face. "Long ago, she suspended that ability in me."

A three-foot clay lump tumbles through the air. Lands on my boot, thick as cement.

"Why does Bastian get the special treatment?!" I shriek, my big toe throbbing like it's just been hit by a hammer by Tom or Jerry.

Dust, timber, and clay drop like hailstones every which way, and there's so much noise, it's the freaking Fourth of July.

Moldy wood groans.

There's a loud *pop!*—the ominous sound of bones cracking.

A feral growl curls toward me from two inches away, and

the black-furred, tall-eared Bastian crouches as we stare, eye to eye.

He snaps his bright white teeth.

Grazes the edge of my throat, giving me razor cuts.

Luther tugs my hand to prevent me from being the dog's munchies, but Bastian pounces on me so hard, I smack my head on the table.

Oof—it's an anvil to the brain, and my eyes flutter shut.

CHAPTER THIRTY

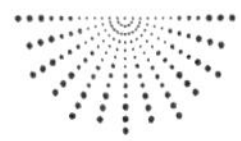

Dumb ways to die! So many dumb ways to die . . .

In a never-ending loop, that song's been stuck in my head. How many times do I need to be knocked out? How many *other* corpses are going to show up? Pretty sure I've been here a few days . . .

A pink, croqueted comforter lies beneath me. Tan, skin doilies . . .

Ugh, I've been dumped in Granny's room *again?* Stupid, freaking Twilight-zoned house.

Hey, I thought the whole house was in toxic mode.

Either I'm gonna die, or that was a passing phase . . .

Fact is, I've long come to terms with the fact that I'm going to cark it.

For years, I've made random visits to the hospital. Stripped down to a hospital gown and got hooked up to enough machines to power a small planet. I've actually grown quite fond of hospital food. Never understood why it got such a bad rap.

Usually, Mom and Rosalyn come around. They bring flowers, and I fill out Madlibs and such.

Gah, I miss my baby sister's laugh.

I miss how she makes those crazy facial expressions when I turn up the music for her to pretend she's singing along.

Okay, yes, we've already established that I caused my sister to be blind. The thing is, she's still my greatest sunshine. She's the biggest clown I know, always insisting that I paint her toenails teal while she cracks jokes about Teletubbies.

I roll over on Granny's bed. Ophelia's? Whoever's.

Seriously, how many times am I gonna pass out?

More green vines snake over my face—one un-suction cups from my nose—and I grow uber still, 'cause what kinda sick power does Ophelia have over me?

Tiny, green tentacles retract from my face. They slither over the bed, and Ophelia may want me healthy to be a house for a very long time.

She can supply me with whatever medicine I need. Apparently.

Good thing I'm not a crack addict. We'd be a dangerous combination.

Girlish giggles emanate from the walls and bounce off the broken mirror's glass. As the final vine retracts, it slinks over the bed, nudging my arm, as if in friendship.

Friendship. Yeah, huh. I think all the creepy vine stuff is over when this dark shadow flits through the window. Like, across the windowpane itself.

It's a somber presence.

A ghost of an old woman suddenly zooms over the room, dark gray hair tied in a high bun, and ohmygosh, this can't be Ophelia. Who is this?

The old woman snatches at my feet before disappearing just as fast as she came, and a creak at the door tells me I gotta pretend I saw nada; it's time to put my big girl face on.

Bastian's human, muscular form lurks in the doorway,

and at least he looks more sickly. His hollowed-out face reminds me of one of those skeleton masks in New Orleans, and a deep gash runs along the front of one leg.

I'm tempted to ask him about the ghost I just saw, but seeing as he just tried to rip out my throat, I keep my new round of Twenty Questions to myself.

Lumbering toward me, Bastian tightens his fist around the silver tray he's holding. A big, black welt covers one side of his face, and it seems as though I may have had more ninja skills than I thought.

The nub on his hand where his thumb used to be, though, gives me the giddiest feeling of all. "Cat got your thumb?" I cackle at my own joke, still nervous about the new ghost lady I just saw.

A ribbon of muscles feather along Bastian's jaw. Hey, he could be cute if we changed his hair, personality, interests, *and* outfit.

Nope . . . not even then. Sorry!

"If *I* were you" —I make sure Bastian sees me nodding at his missing thumb— "I would be *so* embarrassed. Hey, since you're tied to Ophelia and all, why don't you just grow it back?"

Bastian sets down the tray so hard the tea does an avalanche. Hmm. Guess that's a sore topic.

Some of the tea hits his fancy robe, and I can't help it. I'm laughing. Hard. Even though Ophelia just temporarily healed me with her vines, and, apparently, I have another supernatural foe to deal with.

Using whatever resources I have, I keep up my ruse of "the tuberculosis" by coughing up about fifteen ccs of mucus.

Bastian grinds his teeth together so hard he's gonna knock a tooth out—which might actually solve his failure to floss quandary.

Narrowing his eyes at me, he grouses, "You are revolting."

"Hey." I gesture at his One True Love that once appeared in the curtain. "Not everyone can afford chiffon."

"You *do* realize that you do not have long to live . . ."

"Longer than you." Playfully, I jut out my chin. Wonder if he knows Ophelia's been helping me with her vines. Wonder how she's "doctorly" enough to know what medicine to give me to clear my air passages.

Bastian's greedy paw suddenly snatches up my wrist and stuffs the teacup in my hand. "Bottoms up."

I don't wanna drink it, so I try pushing it back. But his fingers are as unmovable as iron. "Pretty sure I'd rather not."

"This has *nothing* to do with what you want!" Bastian snarls, clamping my fingers round the handle, which cracks, but doesn't break, thank goodness.

Guiding my hand, Bastian overpowers me to the point that my teeth are knocking into the porcelain. He forces my shaking hand to lift the bottom of the cup, tipping whatever nasty liquid's inside.

"I thought the tea was bad," I protest.

Clamping his hand over my mouth, Bastian plugs my nose to make me swallow.

And I do—I have to.

As the room-temperature tea slides down my throat, he lets go of my face.

"Now that's a gum-tickler." There's nothing to do but smack my lips. Really, it tastes like gasoline straight outta the mower jug.

Satisfied, Bastian turns away from me. Running his hand over his already perfected hair, he clenches and unclenches his other fist. "You should learn to be grateful for *any* power that falls into your hands."

I shoot him a look that says I'd rather stub my toe. Repeatedly. But that's not even true. Despite the tea, those vines made my throat smoother than a baby's butt.

Toying with the brittle edge of the teacup, I muse, "Why do you want me to take Ophelia's place?"

Bastian spins around, fireballs for eyes, saying nothing at all.

I thought he was supposed to be the fun and "magical" one. "Is it so you can have your 'happily ever after' with her?"

Still, he doesn't talk.

"You *know* . . . I'm not real sure she's still into you," I add. "You might consider Match-dot-com. And Christian Mingle's a *riot*, last I heard."

Exhaling, Bastian taps an agitated finger against his leg. "And why would you say that?"

"Maybe because you *killed* your would-be fiancé for refusing to marry your sorry butt."

Bastian's eyes grow so thunderous, I can't help adding a little more salty-salt to the wound. "No worries. I'm sure it's only a matter of time before she reveals how much she hates your guts."

Bastian twists his lips into the sort of smile that might keep me up in future nights. "You know, I have had many a friend die from the tuberculosis."

I bust up laughing so hard I end up spraying his cheek with blood. Guess Ophelia's treatments aren't as sure-fire as I thought . . .

Meh. I'm sure I'm fine. "Looking forward to it!"

CHAPTER THIRTY-ONE

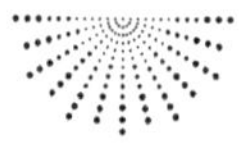

Passing fancy over. Trusting Ophelia to be my doc would make me terminally stupid.

I liked the medicinal properties of the vines and such, but what's to stop her from overdosing me? Or refusing me altogether? This needs to stop . . .

Never more brokenhearted, I stare at the teacup, already jonesin' for another hit.

Maybe I could ask her to hook me up just one more time?

I need to find a sponsor, support group, stat.

Actually, I'm tired. *Real* tired. How many times have I been knocked out in the last four or five days since I came? Imma tired of being the victim in Ophelia's twisted drama.

Sure, I've had a few bright, shiny moments, like when I bit off Bastian's thumb, or when I kissed the boy, but couldn't I have at least kicked the trash out of the mailman when he attacked me? I should've done that stomp-down on his ankle and kneecap thing I learned in my self-defense class.

Rosalyn always liked that move. She's the reason why I took the class . . .

The plain, rotten truth is, Bastian and Ophelia have the upper hand. They know I can't—won't—escape if it means jeopardizing Rosalyn's life. And as helpful as Luther is, he's never really been party to their entire plan.

Maybe they mean to do some other blood ritual sacrifice thing during the next full moon or some such. That's the sort of thing magical people do, right?

Though Luther said Ophelia was tired from being the house.

Not tired enough to stop feeding me the mystical medicines from paradise . . .

For all I know, Luther must be stuck in timeout somewhere on the grounds. What does she do to him when he's away from me? Looks like the brunt of our quandary falls directly on me.

I've gotta sort this out.

When I stand, the ground's a little ripply, and I'm walkin' on waves. Must be the medicine and my biology evening out.

The bedposts offer what little support they can, and if Bastian weren't so lurky, I might even entertain the idea of doing a little victory dance.

There's one thing, though, that's been wriggling around in this wee little mind o' mine. *Could* Bastian have been the mailman? He can shift into dogs . . . so, why not become the creepiest guy who made me stay to protect Rosalyn?

His scare tactics certainly have been enough to keep me here . . . and trust Luther.

I wonder how many Ophelias there are in the world.

Is this one also *Ophelia Cate*?

Ophelia Catarina Hellstrom?

Gah, I sincerely hope not . . .

Staggering toward the gaping hole I fell through earlier, I wonder for the fourteenth time how Ophelia had Luther make that Rosalyn doll. Did she just conjure up random odds and ends from around the house? Or did she make him special order it?

From the corner of the room, the doll does its super creepy staring thing, and I would do *anything* to see the real Rosalyn again.

But I should keep her as far away as Africa.

Though, if my little sister were here, she'd make this into a sort of game. She'd insist we stay away from the "hot lava" on the floor. Claim there's a dark monster inside it.

Staring down at the deep, dark hole that shouldn't be all that deep *or* dark, I gotta say, Rosalyn wouldn't be far off on that hot lava analogy.

Wonder what part of Ophelia it is, that gooey orange membrane that's grown in the hole overnight.

With the cutesy-wootsy, framed doilies hanging over the dresser, I also have to wonder how many people Ophelia's skinned to decorate her room, thinking they're so gorgeous and pretty.

Hey, flowers are pretty . . .

While Luther thought uprooting the flowers in the green-house would make Ophelia permanently go to sleep . . . what if they're not the heart of the problem at all?

What if they're just a limb or something?

Maybe Ophelia *does* have a heart, but . . . it's all covered up in a place where she has the most power. She and Bastian *did* insist on doing a blood ritual in *here*, ladies and gents.

The dame was strong enough to drink my blood.

Tenderly, I examine the fabric of the argyle curtain. It still boasts the splotchy stains from my blood. While I don't see any indication that this is the source of her power, I've got a sneaking suspicion that the source is in here. It's gotta be. I know it.

I'm not going back in that hole. And I'm *not* going under the bed. Besides, I didn't see the heart in those spots earlier.

Really, that just leaves the walls. The oldie-moldy spots behind the desk and tall dresser.

Ooh, the dresser!

The source where *all* the spiderweb roots seem to be leading.

I shove the figurines off the dresser so fast, Imma Muskogee percussionist.

Luckily, Bastian doesn't seem to hear it, 'cause dude doesn't come in.

Behind the dresser, though, lies the thickest, healthiest-looking swatch of wallpaper I've ever seen. True, it's covered in thick, black mold, but the pea-green paper *itself* proves thicker.

Like someone's taken great care to cover up whatever's behind it.

Not really in the mood to grab the Purell, I wipe off all the gunk and cobwebs with my arm.

Comes off like dust.

Behind the second layer of mold, though, the pea green paper appears to be almost strong. Healthy. Reaching down, I search the cool, dank wall for a seam, and a little higher than the dresser, I find the thin, raised line. Carefully, *very* carefully, I pick at the stubborn paper.

It's thicker than I expected. Doesn't wanna come off. But it gives, eventually . . .

A faint whimper tremors from the walls. Ooh, Ophelia's sleeping.

"Shhh, shhh," I hush her like I'm singing a lullaby.

Now . . . what exactly had Luther said?

Ophelia gets real tired . . . so *maybe* there's something to that. If I don't hurry, any second now, she could wake up.

Climbing a little further over the mahogany dresser, I give the paper a swift tug. My fingertips connect with sharp electricity—not from a power line—but my teeth flare ice cold, and I fly back into the frame of the bed.

I'm halfway to the window, and part of me believes, Curtain Lady will materialize to lecture me any moment.

She . . . doesn't.

She's licking her wounds. Or still very much tuckered out.

Rubbing the side of my arm where I hit the bed frame, I jeer at the newly peeled wallpaper. "Didn't like that?"

Scrambling across the floor, I rush over to the dresser and crawl atop it, ignoring the pointy lip digging into my stomach.

I peel.

Imma monkey peeling the best banana this side of Arkansas.

Dried, Play-Doh-like blood lays right beneath the surface, and all this paper ripping makes me feel as rejuvenated as if I'm on a spa day.

Digging my thumb into the surface, I pause when it comes away wet.

I set to more ripping.

Pull . . . snag.

Pull, snag, snag!

After about two full minutes of ripping back paper—hope to crap that it's Ophelia's face—I'm breathing hard, so I stop and survey the damage.

Three feet down, three-and-a-half feet across . . .

Herein lies a vista of dark red hues, thinly veiling a bronze, turnip-shaped heart.

CHAPTER THIRTY-TWO

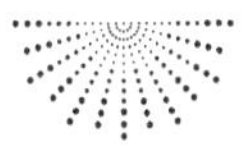

PROBLEM IS, the root-slash-heart is behind the bulk of the dresser.

I need to move it.

Those spiderwebby roots look like veins and arteries. What would happen if I gave them a little snippy-snip?

Grabbing the lip of the dresser, I heave and ho to move it a little to the right.

Thing's heavier than ten wet cadavers.

I rip open the top drawer—only to find an array of hoochie-badoochie grandmother panties. Folded, all satiny with these clippy, hangy-down things.

On to the next drawer.

There, various loopy petticoats lie in wait, so when I yank open the *third* drawer, I accidentally pop it off its tracks.

Oops-a-daisy!

Brunt of the drawer falls on my big toe. H E double-hockey-sticks.

Groan.

When I reach for the next drawer, I slow my hustle. Don't want any more accidents. Carefully pulling out the drawer, I deposit it, along with every other drawer, on the hardwood flooring.

The one with the granny panties actually teeters to the edge of the black hole, so, with a little nudge, I "accidentally" make that one fall through.

Grabbing the lip of the dresser, I, indeed, find that it's now much easier to move.

Screeech!

Fourteen inches later, I do believe I am ready to start my own moving company. By the time I finish peeling off another hefty two feet of paper, I have to wonder . . . how do I stop that sneaky, bronzed heart?

Strangulation?

Stabbing?

It sure is pumping a lot. But it's in sleep mode.

I reach for one of the broken figurines on the floor—an angel, holding her hands in prayer—when heavy footsteps stomp from the doorway.

Bastian's pale, washed-out face emerges from the shadows, and his nostrils flare while fine muscles flicker along his jawline. "I *thought* we agreed you should be in bed."

I look around like I've plumb forgotten the gist of our talk. "I can help if you're having trouble with your eHarmony password . . ."

Snarling, Bastian reaches for my head, so I jab him in the robed stomach with my elbow.

His ribs compress my funny bone, and he howls like I've just bitten off an arm—now *there's* an idea. Think Luther would be mad if I started whackin' off body parts? Though I'm one full sword or knife short. What's he going to do? Do his signature move and grab me by the hair?

All at once, Bastian's whole body drops to the ground, convulsing.

Fur sprouts from his face and arms sorta like a chia pet.

I think he's fighting becoming the Doberman. Maybe it's not his idea? 'Cause saliva's bubbling like sea-foam in his mouth, and his arms sure are thrashing a lot.

Ophelia must be punishing him for leaving me alone. She's not happy I found her heart.

Guess I've never seen him fully shift before, even though he did plenty on the stairs. That . . . seemed like his idea. This, with his gritted teeth and arms flailing everywhere, most certainly doesn't.

Pebble-sized knots bubble up from the sweaty skin on his brow. His eyes wash white, and, hey, he and Ophelia must be having a couples' row.

Leaping over Bastian's sprawled body, I spring for the wall while Bastian's thick, dense nails claw right through the thin fabric of my dress into the small of my back.

He contorts, screams—*I* scream—while he thrashes in a fit, but he and Ophelia can have a spat anytime they doggone like.

When Bastian snatches for my arms, I grab the drawer from the top of the pile and smash it straight into his nasty face.

He howls—half man, half dog—and it's downright bone-chilling.

Twisting to reach Ophelia's heart, I am almost there when, mid-transformation, Bastian shoves me toward the door.

Head slams into the doorframe, and I fall to the floor.

Man, seems like doorframes are a lot harder from the 1800s.

Pain flares through my skull—I'm seeing stars—as foot-falls pound up the hallway.

"Cate!" Luther's wide eyes prove he's ready to hobnob with me. I shouldn't be relieved—Bastian's paws are finding those wounds in my back, and he's pressing me harder into the floor. Burns worse than bacon grease, and, as I lay amidst the dust and broken pieces from the hole, saliva drips freely into my eyes. Bleh.

Luther throws himself against his brother. They tackle-roll past me, to the dusty hall.

"You promised you wouldn't hurt her!" Luther shouts. How much does the boy know, anyhow?

Bastian's voice is riddled with a snarl when he replies, "I said whatever you wanted to hear." Bones pop. Hair covers his nose and neck, but he's still mostly human, fighting the transformation. Or maybe he wants it to go more quickly?

Bastian's paw reaches through the doorway, and he pins my head against one of the door hinges with its cool, cool metal.

Luther pulls something from his pocket. It's gonna be more plant tape like he used in the greenhouse, I know it, but a sleek, black barrel stops me cold.

Pop! Pop. Pop.

Luther's got a gun?

Bastian drops to the floor as my jaw becomes the draw-bridge for this unexpected layer of Luther Maximilien Robespierre Henry VIII.

CHAPTER THIRTY-THREE

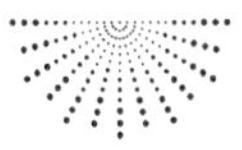

"Dude, you shot him!" I'm ready to bring out the virgin margaritas and whiskey with olives. Does whiskey have olives? "You shot him! You actually shot him!"

"Sleeping dart," Luther apologizes whilst lowering his gun.

Well, we can strip his title.

Not wanting to feel defeated, I try to make sense of the Doberman now sprawled on the floor. Even now, muscles bulge from his torso as he lies half-smashed against the dresser. Everything happened so fast . . .

"Why not shoot him for real?!" I bite back the pain radiating from my injured back and arm.

Luther holsters his "gun" in the waistband of his pants. "I could never do that."

"Are you freaking kidding me?"

His eyes crinkle in the corners as he assesses a deep cut on my scalp. "I am sorry, Cate . . . but he is my brother." His fingers graze the back of my hand.

I snatch my hand away. *Sorry* won't fix what Bastian's threatened and all that's happened.

Bastian needs to be stopped—for good. I clutch my sore arm, fighting the urge to give Luther a hefty whack. "Your bro-dog has no soul."

Luther avoids my eyes. "He's the only family I have left."

Now he's going to make me sympathize with his dead dad?

Surveying the charcoal root still pulsing in the bloody plaster of the wall, I say, "This ends now."

There's a slight noise from Bastian's throat as his animalistic eyes roll beneath his eyelids.

Wha—sleeping dart's starting to wear off.

Unable to believe that this is already happening, I glance around for a machete or a howitzer. A porcelain figurine will have to do. Plucking one up, I prepare to plunge it straight through Ophelia's heart when something furry—and muscular—knocks into my arm.

Bastian's paw.

He readies to swipe at me again, so I lift the figurine to stab Ophelia's heart when Bastian's serrated teeth clamp round my ankle.

He drags me toward the hole in the floor.

I'll burn alive, or dissolve into Ophelia's fungus-y brain matter.

Actually, I'm gonna be granted immortality, so I guess that means I'll be swimming a level *above* the brimstone lakes.

Splinters dig and needle into my waist, and I grab at anything and everything to stop our progress.

The bed leg works, true—it works, woot, woot!—until it plumb snaps in half.

Debris and dust puff up and float pretty much everywhere, and it's like Ophelia *knows* what's happening.

She embraces the dust like a halo, and as the floor rumbles, I just know she's waking up.

Luther unloads so many sleeping darts into his brother that the gun pops at least thirteen times, and Bastian drops like a sack of potatoes.

Feeling giddy, I drawl, "Let's do it, Lewis!"

Luther takes my hand and tugs me away from the hole. I freaking wanna get things over with and stab Ophelia's heart, but Bastian *will* wake any second.

Gahhh!

Against my better instincts, I let Luther drag me out.

"We should be stabbing the crap outta her heart!" I shout.

"You can't!" Luther pulls me faster, but what is he talking about?

A hefty vine slams onto the floor, comin' outta nowhere, and I guess we really aren't going back to Granny's room. We were *this* close to things being over.

While we run down each creaky stair, I bat away the thought that Luther's been working with Ophelia and Bastian the entire time. He's one of the good guys.

Has to be.

I know it.

At the bottom of the stairway, Luther whisper-shouts, "In here!" He darts in the direction of the halls, and something tells me he's headed to the room with all the aquariums.

Nuh-uh, no way am I goin' in there again.

I'm already feelin' real vulnerable, and last thing I need is all those bright lights messing with my semi-stable head.

Focusing, I tear off for the front door.

If Bastian really was the mailman, then I've got nothing to worry about. He may have threatened to get Rosalyn, but he can't do that if I reach her first.

Luther must see my intention, 'cause he's cryin', "Cate, that won't work!"

I'm already swatting away beads and prickly leaves in the halls.

I'd take his shortcut, but I accidentally ran past it.

My breathing's so hollow. So short and ragged.

Seems as though Ophelia's making these beads and scarves antsy; they're moving like Medusa's hair.

Reaching the very cusp of the foyer, I let out a giant sigh of relief and several short, shallow pants. We made it—practically. We made it. And we're not even recording this moment.

I'm just about to smile real wide and shout something smart when a giant, black dog comes barreling down the ceiling hole from above.

Lips peel back, ears point forward, and Bastian looks to be in full-on killer mode.

CHAPTER THIRTY-FOUR

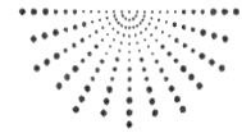

OBNOXIOUS LAUGHTER CLUBS MY EARS, and the half-transformed Bastian's a two-hundred-pound anvil, pinning me to the hardwood floor.

I already got a creak in my back.

Through Ophelia's magic, Bastian's hairy brow and snout slowly give way to baby cheeks and a self-satisfied smirk above a chin with a dimple.

Now Bastian's human face is even more pallid, his eyes an even more cataract-covered gray. If I were to guess, I'd say all this shifting's wearing on both him and Ophelia.

At least Ophelia's supplied him with clothes. His robe transforms from fur to satin, and, I never noticed before, but his hood's lined in the exact same shade of the Monkshood flowers.

With his hands and knees pinning me horizontal, there's nothing I can do but cough.

Cough, cough.

I'm Mad as a Hatter.

Bastian rolls off me so fast, he obviously still thinks I'm contagious.

Pulling out a handkerchief with the initials *BD* on it, he painstakingly wipes off the saliva I sprayed on his nose. Think he's a germaphobe? "Keep your nasty germs to yourself."

Yup, I'd say so.

All I can do is snort-laugh. "No one's ever accused me of being too generous before!"

Reaching down, he wraps his clammy fingers round my throat. His skinny fingers constrict my esophagus, and he sneers, obviously enjoying the pain he's inflicting. Not really seeing anything else to do, I make an ice cream scoop outta my hand and follow through on my aforementioned plan.

Digging through skin and tiny red muscles, I dig out Bastian's eye like it's made of cookie dough.

Actually, a better analogy would be a hardboiled egg, 'cause this sucker feels like it's made of rubber.

While he screams and carries on, I let go of his eyeball and watch it fall, all victorious, to the ground.

As Luther comes tearing into the room—not sure where he went—not only does he have his stun gun, but he also grips the fire poker.

"We've *really* moved past the stun phase," I fill him in as Bastian continues his blubbering and holds his hand over one side of his face.

"What happened to you?" Luther's frantic steps slow.

Bastian drops his hand, about spitting fireworks, revealing a giant, red hole in his face. Now that's a right remarkable crater.

"Another 'accident.'" I shrug, too proud to calm my britches. "You *know* how I can't be trusted to be left alone."

Luther's face goes so pale at my handiwork I swat aside the urge to give a little bow.

Actually, I do one better and lean down and scoop up the eye I mistakenly let go of.

No way'm I goin' to let Bastian get it back now. I squeeze it in my fist, milky membrane firmer than I'd hoped.

Hmm, it won't pop or deflate, and Bastian's scramblin' closer. I don't want him gettin' it back, so I do what any sensible girl would do—I squish it with my bare foot, giving myself a new kinda toe jam.

Finishing with the job, I cough about thirteen times as Bastian screams about me being an infidel.

The wooden panels of the coffered ceiling jiggle, sway, and splinter.

Actually, so does the plaster on the surrounding walls.

Snarling, Bastian holds his face whilst glaring up at the ceiling. "She's awake."

"Gosh, sorry." I laugh, not sure if I should be bored or scared. "Keep forgetting not to wake the baby!"

Something in the other room strikes the keys of the piano, and they're so quick and fast, it's barely even music.

What's going on?

Hey, where's Luther?

Wait . . . looking at the chair with its missing bottom and the "salsa" splashed on the entry wall, I can't help feeling a lump form in my throat.

A brutal, unnatural force picks me up and throws me to the ground.

Knocks the wind outta me.

Ophelia does it again.

Yup, that would be the brittle sound of my ribs cracking. But I just pulled an eye out. Aren't she and Bastian supposed to be weak now?

When my head snaps back, all too soon, it flies forward again *way* too fast, and my chin bonks the floor. Nearly knocks my teeth out.

Little, scampery feet poke my face with their miniature claws, and a pair of incisors clamp my ear.

I try to fling off the rat, but it clings on, dangling like an ornament in my hair. I swat and swat before I finally connect with the hairy side of its body and smack it off.

It scurries its fat rump to the wall's hole, and now where did Bastian go?

He and Luther must have gone outside. But I would have noticed if they opened the front door. Maybe they jumped up real fast to block the halls? But Luther's on my side. Maybe he's trying to stop Bastian from getting the upper hand.

The billowy wind whispers through the stained glass window. Vines emerge outta nowhere, barring the door.

"*Ca-a-t-e!*" Ophelia's dainty voice teases from the splitting ceiling near the hole. "*You don't really want to leave . . .*"

"Uhh, except for the harm that might come to my baby sister, I kinda do."

"*You get to be quite powerful. Do . . . unbelievable things.*"

"Funny." I kick another rat that scurries toward my foot. "Seems to me, all you do is nap. Besides, I just took Bastian's eye out. Aren't you supposed to be all tuckered out?"

Vicious groans shake the floor; rattles my teeth, it does. Something clatters in the distance, and Ophelia purrs, "*We found a new power supply. Besides, you could stay with your pretty beau. Grow plants and play your charming games of Scrabble.*"

What in the heck does she mean by *new power supply,* hmm?

That makes me not marginally nervous.

Backing up a few steps, I accidentally collide with the wooden chair, and *scrrrape!* Chair takes off a healthy piece of wallpaper while Ophelia whimpers. Say, what a good idea!

I reach out and scratch the heck outta Ophelia's newly exposed flesh.

As my nails fill with that weird substance that looks like

red dirt, it doesn't take long for Ophelia's walls to quiver with anger. *"You wanna fight dirty? I can fight dirty."*

A familiar, masculine voice wails from the other side of the halls.

A voice that sounds an awful lot like Luther's.

What is Bastian doing to him?

I dodge the dangling stuff in the halls, mind going as blank as my sports record.

I must reach him.

Must reach him.

Pollen coats the air when I round the final corner, and Luther's long, attractive body's stretched across the top of the piano, legs dangling over the side.

Ophelia's invisible fingers thread a pair of piano strings through his torso, and he doesn't seem to move or breathe, and his eyes are closed.

I can't even tell if he's still alive.

Bastian, new satiny eye patch in place, grandly perches atop the bench at the piano.

Extending his arms, he playacts like this right here is the moment we've all been waiting for.

CHAPTER THIRTY-FIVE

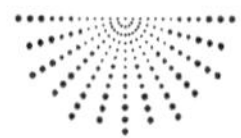

I HAVE A MEMORY . . . of when Daddy took me to see a magic show. It was at some free event in Oklahoma City. I don't remember exactly what happened, but I *do* remember Daddy taking off for a real long time. He left me with a lady with long, gray hair, and she was so nice, chatting me up while we ate peanuts and funnel cakes. That's the first time I learned that I wasn't worth worrying a whole lot about. Daddy didn't know her well, and he didn't come back for hours.

And now? I've currently been left with another stranger. A stranger Mom didn't seem too worried about. Seems like, one way or another, something like this was always bound to happen to me.

Feigning boredom, Bastian plucks a few errant keys on the piano, and the strings tug on Luther's chest in an unhealthy way.

Maybe I can convince Bastian to do a trade—Luther for me.

Then I wouldn't have to suffer through another one of Bastian's magic shows.

Then I could consider myself redeemable. Somewhat. Partially.

Plucking another set of random keys, Bastian slurs, "My brother harbors a great amount of guilt for luring so many candidates to our estate."

Wha—? I'm sure Luther didn't lure *that* many people . . .

I need something to defend myself with. There's the poker, but Luther grabbed it earlier. Now where is it? I don't have a clue.

Jumping up from the bench, Bastian looks like a demented vulture in his robe, air billowing through the silk lining. "He *showed* you the greenhouse!" Bastian slaps another bass key. "Pulled all the flowers!" Another. "Before you even came" —he rolls up his sleeves, exposing the burn marks on his arms— "he tried burning down the house! But I saved her. I saved my love. And you cannot *honestly* believe I can forgive him—after you both hurt my fiancé!"

"Uhh. Hate to be the Debbie Downer here, but *you're* kinda the reason why Ophelia died . . ."

Bastian pounds *so many* keys, Luther shudders and twinges like he's been strapped to an electric chair.

How'm I supposed to defeat a sociopathic, shapeshifting Dog Boy, an entire house, *and* save the boy? Plus, I thought the living room was *supposed* to be the safest place for us.

Holding up my hands, I try to think how I can prevent Luther from going through any more pain. Choosing my words *muy, muy* carefully, I say, "You and Ophelia must've mended fences if you were able to work together to do that blood ritual on me."

Bastian retracts his fingers before playing another key. "She and I shall enjoy a *great* many years together. Unless" — he stretches out his hand again as if he means to play another arrangement of keys— "you're unwilling to lessen my brother's anguish."

I swallow the fatty lump that's lodged in my throat. No way I want Luther getting hurt even more. "What do you need?"

"You *know* what we want." Bastian flings a hand of cards from his pocket to the wall. They stick with a sparkle before becoming absorbed by the wallpaper's gold foiling. "My darling yearns to be a family."

Ophelia doesn't exactly seem to be the "yearning" type, but I nod real quick. "Oh, sure. Definitely. I can see that."

"She wants children who take music lessons, a governess who tends them so we can take a holiday!"

Not gonna lie, that seems to be more of *Bastian*'s kinda life . . .

"She wants a bloody day where she's not forced to be this stupid house and eat another jar of rotten food the rest of our lives!"

If I were closer to him, I'd be tempted to pat his shoulder. "Wanna talk about it? I'm definitely getting the 'repression' vibe."

Throwing another smattering of cards, Bastian stares up, up, up to where they stick to the coffered ceiling. Guess I never noticed how high the ceiling goes before. Something wet splatters my cheek as Bastian says, "I suppose you need me to point it out."

But he doesn't need to point out anything, 'cause I can see what he's talking about.

People. He's talking about half a dozen or so elderly people—hanging like objects from vines.

The mantle squeaks as Bastian leans against it, folding his wiry arms. "To think you still haven't noticed your sister."

What?

Rosalyn isn't here . . .

Amidst all the old people, I-Spy nooses grasping the necks of people in their fifties and sixties, strung up like macabre Christmas tree ornaments. Some of them are even wearing splashes of red and green.

What did Ophelia say? *We have a new power supply . . .*

I bite my tongue so hard it rings with pain. Where's Rosie?

"You're making this up!" I force myself to blink, just in case all of this is a hallucination. A few hours ago, Bastian did force me to drink that tea . . .

"Or . . ." Bastian's bored voice perks up, "maybe they've been here for *hours*, and it's taken you this long to see . . ."

I can't *unhear* the truth of his words—what he's saying. His big, foul mouth confirms that I've been so caught up with my own drama with Luther and getting out of the house that I failed to see how anyone else could be inside the manor.

An older man with a bald head and slit throat twists lifelessly from a vine.

His fingers . . . twitch—are twitching!

With what looks to be a great amount of effort, he reaches up for the stem wrapped around his throat to loosen the vine. It's making it impossible for him to breathe.

As Bastian fiddles with one of the long piano strings in Luther's chest cavity, Luther makes this choking, gurgling sound that I guess is good to hear, 'cause it means he's still alive. But it's awful. So awful. I'm going to hear it in my head for the rest of my life.

I move to cover my ears, but I don't cover them. Not completely. "Stop. Stop!"

"Be the house." Bastian opens his arms like he wishes there could be another way. "Be the sweet, humble abode we've always dreamed of, Ophelia and me."

Why the gas do they need *me*? Why don't they get their own normal house? But I bite back any snarls or retorts, just in case he's feeling murder-y. "Then you'll free Luther and never come after Rosie?"

Sneering with *way* too much satisfaction, Bastian raises his gaze—to the kitchen part of the ceiling.

Far, far in the corner, his gaze locks on a little girl in a polka-dot shirt with bright blonde hair hanging in her unconscious face.

"Rosalyn?" My feet are working, but my mind is not. Her jeans are ripped, and for the first time in forever, she's not holding her white cane.

Rosalyn doesn't move. She doesn't respond, and all I know is my limbs are going numb as my throat is shrinking in on itself.

I stumble past the kitchen island, knocking into the counters with the askew sheets. Luckily, a vine's wrapped around my baby sister's chest, high as it can go, so her arms, at least, are preventing the rope from strangling her.

Bastian tosses another deck of cards, the queen of spades coasting so close to Rosalyn it slices into her vine.

It doesn't sever the rope completely, but Rosalyn does drop a full two feet.

"STOP!" I scream, 'cause pointed directly under Rosalyn is a newly appeared block of inverted knives. Who would threaten a young girl? *What* is *wrong* with this guy?

Dodging a cutting board Bastian or Ophelia throws my way, I scramble to reach Rosalyn. I lift my leg to crawl atop the counter, but the sheet's slippery. Trying to straighten it, I find wormy intestines squirming on the counter like some intestinal disease.

Above me, Rosalyn's rope causes her to twist round and round, and this is all a bad dream.

All I can think of is how scared my baby sister must have been when Bastian probably jumped her and brought her here, kicking and screaming.

Did he put her in the trunk of a car?

Or scare her when she stepped outside our house?

The gramophone clicks on, and this obnoxious, brassy tune steals across the gallery.

"She's a trusting little thing," Bastian says while flinging yet another deck of cards, narrowly missing my face. "When I was in my other form, she scratched behind my ears for a full minute straight." He clucks his tongue. "She didn't even ask for her mommy."

Rosalyn's young neck's so bruised and swollen I find myself clambering over the counter, squishing the pink and cream creepy-crawly worms beneath my shins and knees. When I stand, I jump to graze her shoes—Converses I bought her on a Saturday—but I only succeed in knocking the heels of her shoes, and she twists faster and faster.

It's only a matter of seconds before she falls to the inverted knives.

I reach down to pull them out, but Ophelia's invisible fist suddenly flings them up, each blade flying millimeters from my sister's face.

From the gramophone, jazzy trombones play amidst a clash of cymbals, and, no matter what, it's time to listen to Bastian and Ophelia.

No time for fights, lies, or games.

So I shoot Bastian the most loathing look I've ever made my entire life. "I'll be the freaking Taj Mahal. Now *let* my sister go."

CHAPTER THIRTY-SIX

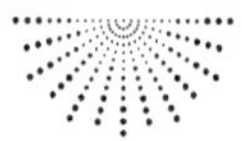

AN ODD SUCKING sound fills the living room as Luther strains to sit up.

Please, let him be okay!

Ophelia weaves a new string round his neck and slams him back so hard the piano frame splits.

I wish I knew what to do—how to make her stop. And Rosalyn? Baby girl, wait a little longer before you wake up.

Heavy, creaky groans ricochet off the walls. They bounce off the filmy mirror that's broken into so many pieces it could be a jigsaw puzzle.

I know what I have to do.

I have to be Bastian and Ophelia's poppet. It may be against my nature, I may end up having to be a toilet, but, really, at this point, we all know I'm willing to cross the River Jordan to save Rosalyn and Luther.

Before I can do or say anything, though, the music grows quiet.

Too quiet.

One of the bodies in the living room releases from a vine.

Thump!

Blood pools on the floor behind the old man's head, sizzling like acid.

Ophelia just went and doggone murdered the old guy. Murdered him when I was already a willing slave.

"Is that really necessary?" I cry.

Vines creep and curl from the walls. The one that was holding the man dips low and *rrrips* him apart like he's made of bread dough.

Wrapping him up in a neat, little cocoon, Ophelia uses her vines like arms to gather the guy in a symmetrical pile of body parts, collared shirt, and khaki pants.

Not much more than thirteen seconds later, sixty-year-old skin drapes from the bag in a newly shed snake coil.

The old guy's glassy eyes stare out, and, through the vines, Bastian pats the old man's cheek before strutting off. "You better act fast, doll, if you want your sister to be released by us."

"WHAT DO YOU WANT ME TO DO?" I run to the bag o' bones, absorbing the mess of appendages and clothing, then scamper back to Luther, who's still wrapped up in those piano strings. Realizing I'm outta my mind for forgetting Rosalyn, I run back to *her*, tripping over the squeaky floor, then stop—'cause, at any second, Ophelia could be dropping more bodies.

What if I become the house just long enough to free everybody?

Then . . . maybe I could bounce back into my original body?

I have no idea how it works. Don't know if I'd be a Queen Anne Victorian or more of a pillared Antebellum. I do know that if I don't act fast, my sister, these people, *and* Luther will join the Dearly Departed.

This! This is how I make amends for not doing the things I was supposed to that day . . . and now.

Oh, and when Bastian and Ophelia made that blood sacrifice, they needed my blood, so . . . I'm sure they still need it now.

Doing my duty, I spin around.

Must run like Catie-beast through the kitchen.

Okay.

Okay . . .

Gone are all the knives Ophelia chucked at Rosalyn.

So I rip open every random drawer to find a sharp enough tool. I find . . . a pancake turner, a can opener . . . ooh, a dusty ol' knife! It's right next to a spatula, and both have seen better days. Never more driven nor focused, I get to work, slicing open my palm with the ugly, serrated knife.

Blood dribbles to the floor like syrup.

It bubbles, dangerous, and yes. Yes! Ophelia's floor rumbles in delight as my blood continues foaming. "I swear to become the house!" I tell every last opponent in the house. I guess there's that older ghost woman I saw upstairs, but there's no point in yada-yada-ing about it. Not sure what role she plays.

The floor rumbles in earnest, and it feels good to know that I can do *something* to save Rosalyn.

Bitter pollen pours over the room while a vine-shaped hand sneaks between the wood in the floor and scurries up my leg.

It prods my skin, tentative at first. Then, it sinks its teeth into my muscles, like it owns my calf.

"So glad you have decided to join us," Ophelia says.

The air twists and fills with a dark haze. It clogs my lungs —a big smoke with a heavy, bitter aftertaste. I want nothing more than to reach for my sister, but I can't risk anything happening to her. Plus . . . the vines.

"Lower my sister," I tell Ophelia, refusing to sound one bit weak.

Ophelia slips a feeler-like vine beneath my nose, giving me a figurative clap on the shoulder. *"You have my word."* Another purple flower dips from the ceiling, whips around, and retrieves all the knives surrounding Rosalyn.

Ooh, I can breathe easy as additional vines cushion my sister's back and feet. It's like they never meant her any harm as they pillow her landing.

Rosalyn's laid to rest—er, she's laid *unconscious*—on the hardwood floor, thankfully.

Okay . . . I have to believe she will be okay. Rosalyn *will* be okay! It's time to do this.

Slowly, I turn, evening out my rickety breathing. If I'm goin' to save *both* Luther and Rosie, I need to be more pliable and obedient than I have ever been in my life. With any luck, I'll destroy Ophelia's heart, but *that* is a second priority. Both Rosalyn and the boy matter more than anything.

"Come along," Ophelia says from the mirrored wall.

Fragments of broken glass flit together, jagged edges meeting up in perfect, stark lines. It's a puzzle, a puzzle just like the rest of my life.

When it's finished, instead of one reflection, *two* girls with long, dark hair stare back into my eyes.

Two girls with semi-ironic smiles. *Two* with long, slender faces . . .

Only my chin is scraped.

How in the Samwise Gamgee?

How . . . does Ophelia look exactly like me?

While my face is solid and more scraped, Ophelia's is transparent and shimmery. Dark circles rim her eyes, and her complexion's so ashen, she makes Luther look like a rosy-cheeked Prince Harry.

The diva tilts her head to the side. We have the same face, but I don't even have time to guess why.

The kaleidoscope table suddenly scoots across the floor

and digs into my thighs as I back up. I half-expect Ophelia's translucent spirit to float up to me, but she winks before placing her left foot on the wall . . . and climbs.

Her footholds are Bastian's cards.

Those stupid, glowy cards he's always throwing.

When Ophelia nods at me to follow, I know there's no way I'm climbin' that way. If I'm going to do anything to free my sister, it'll be climbing that stairway.

Ophelia's gauzy, tea-stained dress bleeds into the walls, and, 'cause I know I need to listen to her, I tromp up the stairs, my dress dragging along the hardwood and carpet.

She scales the pea-green wallpaper, and, like a drone, I ascend the steps.

Things sure can't get any weirder than this.

The stairs rattle, becoming less opaque—more and more translucent. Like Luther said, it looks like Ophelia's choice to become *both* a human and the house is certainly a strain.

Grabbing hold of the banister, I look down one more time at Rosalyn and Luther while a vine wraps around my ankle. Pricking my skin, it leeches onto me for more blood. Ah, this must be how Ophelia gains her power. Feasting on those people is why, even after I pulled Bastian's eye out, she and he aren't weak.

"Do not fight the gift I give you," Ophelia purrs, passing the mirror, which crackles below her as she glides higher. Nodding at the top of the stairs, she adds, *"I have something I should very much like for you to see."*

The house rumbles. Reminds me of my stomach, and as I move up, I grip the banister, hand squealing. We wouldn't be in this predicament if I'd been a better sister and didn't let my hormones rule my every choice. Then, I wouldn't have wanted to get to know Luther. Then, I wouldn't be fixin' to be a Dutch Colonial with flared eaves and dormers.

At the top of the stairs, I end up in front of the portrait of

Mama Dvorak. Henrietta Pearl, so they say. Now, though, the image of is sharper, clearer, showcasing her hair set in a high bun. The image isn't kaleidoscope-fashioned this time. Or foggy . . .

Yep, the woman certainly is a female version of Bastian, with her cruel, long face and dimpled chin. She looks like a first-rate Nazi.

Flickering in transparency, Ophelia coyly sidles up to me. *"Even then, you could tell she was not a nice lady."* She coasts to the ghostly portrait of Bastian and raises her hand to cover her milky throat before looking away.

"What did they do to you?" I fight the urge to tuck tail and run—right into Granny's room to do a little slice and dice to Ophelia's heart, but I've made my commitment. Must stay the course for Rosalyn.

Floating even further down the hallway, Ophelia turns her girlish head unnaturally far to face me. *"Come along, darling . . ."*

We pass Granny's room. I can hardly believe I'm not doing *anything* while we pass it. While more vines scuttle up from the floorboards, part of me wonders if I can survive permanently joining Ophelia.

"You needn't bother with my heart." Little Miss Perfect appears to have the ability to read my mind. *"Trifling with that will result in . . . well. We wouldn't want your sister to be blind and deaf."*

She'd steal Rosalyn's hearing? I'll stab her in the face. Experiment a little more with those knives. She and Bastian deserve each other far more than I realized.

Gliding by a mostly closed linen closet, Ophelia lifts her translucent hand and mentally tugs little stems from the baseboards, looping them into pretty Monkshood flowers as she sashays past. She crochets them into elaborate loops and designs, and I hate to admit it, but they're *really* pretty.

Ophelia means for me to follow her—follow her is what I'm doing—but am I being flagrantly stupid by not sprinting off for Granny's room?

Part of the floor loops up—*I'm* about to be crocheted—so I slip down her hilly, carpeted slide and allow myself to be dumped before a door's threshold.

This door's smaller than the others. Houses a low, dipped ceiling.

"*I was an affable girl.*" Ophelia drifts up somberly next to me. "*It is why Bastian was so drawn to my nature. But he wasn't the beau for me . . .*"

Without being nudged, the door suddenly swings open. It tousles my hair, and Ophelia's invisible wind grabs my arms and wrenches me sideways.

I don't wanna go in, so out of reflex, I grab onto the dusty walls.

I don't wanna go in!

Something tells me, I *really* don't wanna see what's inside.

A black spirit in a gray, diagonally striped dress whooshes past me as my hand knocks into an empty portrait while another set of Monkshood flowers lobs me to the doorway.

That black spirit's the same one I saw earlier.

The older woman with the high bun. Henrietta Pearl?

Ophelia crooks a misty finger while the wind flings me inside the room.

CHAPTER THIRTY-SEVEN

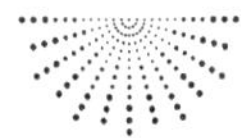

M OLD GREASES my grip as I cling to the doorframe. Wind shrieks and whistles through my ears as the floor rumbles in tidal waves.

With another fanfare-ish shove, Ophelia flips me, head over toe, inside.

I land, hard, at the foot of a tiny bed. At least this blanket's not crocheted.

Ducking her head, Ophelia shyly steps forward and leads me to a brown and white rocking horse with a red leather saddle. Wheels expertly strap to hooves, and a pair of porcelain dolls lie in the buggy.

We're . . . in the Dvorak nursery.

But this house didn't exist during the Dvoraks' natural lives. Ophelia wouldn't want this room. So why does it exist in the first place?

More rosy-cheeked dolls lie in strollers with wicker baskets and wheels as wide as bicycle tires. Another doll lies in a brass-barred crib alongside a stuffed, brown bear.

A sideways-laying clown with a green hat and bowtie

reminds me of Uncle Jimmy. The clown's fallen from its perch—a spring-led crash landing.

An old tea set with dainty, beige cups meets a rocking chair with a floral cushion and shawl draped over the side.

The rocking chair moves—*creak, creak, creak . . .*

Where did the newbie ghost lady go?

I grip the knobby legs of the bedframe, forcing myself to face whatever Ophelia plans on showing me. As the door slams shut, though, a gust of baby powder flies into my face.

I cough for what feels like eons while the impatient wind rifles through a childhood book with a dueling police officer and villain, entitled *Brownie.*

Blocks chaotically spill across the floor.

The thick, metal bars on the stained glass window tell me no Dvorak children are ever getting outside, and why oh why, again, is Ophelia showing me this nursery? "I thought you didn't want kids."

"Do not worry about your sister," Ophelia primly ignores me. *"Sebastian knows that if he lays a finger on that child, he shall have to answer to me."*

"Hey, you strung her up to the ceiling!"

"To get your attention." She inclines her head, her lips perking up in a teasing smile. *"Now that I have secured it . . ."* She turns her glassy eyes to the toys on the floor and on the shelving. *"I tried getting rid of them."* With her foot, she dismissively shoves aside a teacup. *"But they simply will not be destroyed."*

Ohhh, so *she* didn't make this room.

I'm not sure if that's a good or bad thing . . .

Other ghost lady did? Henrietta Pearl? Where'd she go, anyway?

Footsteps dash and scurry over the room like someone's chasing or being chased. From my peripheral vision, I make out the thin, black outline of a woman.

Tall.

Dressed in that old-school, black and gray dress with diagonal stripes.

I can barely blink three times before the woman flickers out of vision—a dying strobe light.

Casually extending a hand toward the table with a dollhouse, Ophelia sends a burst of flames between a miniature, wooden bed and . . . an armoire, I think.

The miniature furniture won't burn.

It's cast in an icy, blue blaze.

But, again, none of this makes sense. "That was Henrietta Pearl, right? And don't you have control over your own, er, body?"

With the flick of her hand, Ophelia telekinetically slams the lid to the jack in the box, nearly giving the clown a solid beheading.

"This room is the exception." Ophelia focuses to spin another top on a sewing table. *"She tried* everything *to have me wed Sebastian."*

She.

Henrietta Pearl. Mama D.

"Balls. Dinner parties. Tea. Little did I know that the Dvoraks were penniless after their father spent everything. They put up a great façade, pretending their inadequate living circumstances were temporary . . ."

The tin-made house round back. Yeah, upper and lower classes didn't mix back in the day.

"I could not love Sebastian, you see. It did not take me long to ascertain his temperamental ways." Turning, Ophelia settles twin somber eyes on me. *"Actually, it was your sweet Luther who originally caught my eye."*

My back smacks into the dollhouse where a set of a miniature table and chairs shake. "You don't like Luther. You hurt him all the time!"

Ophelia glowers. *"It took me decades to learn that we are not suited for one another. Luther was always far too interested in tending to his dearest* papa *to pay any attention to me."*

"How could you even kill his father like that?" I'll never forget the burnt look of his charred remains.

"He was as good as dead, anyway . . ." In the mirror, Ophelia gazes at her hollowed-out cheeks. Running her hands over the slim, cylindrical body of a nearby sewing machine, she explains, *"When Noah Dvorak did not hear from his son for months, he returned home to his family. He had a serious falling out with Henrietta Pearl, you see. Something about him spending their living on trinkets and her . . . 'questionable' methods for finding her sons brides."*

Ophelia pauses like she wants me to say something. I don't know what to offer, so I say, "Every marriage has issues, right?"

"Because Luther and his father were close, Noah planned to whisk his favorite son away. Sadly, when Noah returned home, he was greeted by yours truly. I ensured that Noah Dvorak would never take my Luther away. I kept those rocks he loved so much hidden from daylight. Kept Luther's father barely alive just in case. Of course, when Luther decided to pull up my flowers, I knew I had to end things with his father. Luther requires a great deal of discipline."

"You are cruel to him. You boss him around like a slave!"

"Of course, when Luther failed to live up to my expectations, I eventually gave into Sebastian's advances . . . for a time. It didn't take long, though, for me to see that Bastian could never truly make me happy. He wants a simpleminded, contented wife, while I am no longer either of those things."

From the dollhouse, I pluck up a miniature couch, absorbing what she's telling me. "You like being the house."

"I am fond of making my own rules, yes. I enjoy inviting guests

and tying up the loose ends by sucking out the marrow of their bones once they're finished with their tea."

How very refined. "So then . . . why do you want me?"

Shimmery Ophelia examines the shawl on the rocking chair with tender eyes. *"I have long known that both brothers have been obsessed with finding someone to take my place—in an effort to buy their freedom, supposedly. And I quite enjoy my boys having ambitions and dreams. They become rather dull, otherwise. Since I have all the time in the world, I agreed."*

"Finding me was *their* idea?"

In her threadbare dress, Ophelia paces through the strollers, settling her gaze on me. *"Your presence is a different matter, entirely."*

I'm not sure what to make of that. I imagine it has something to do with us having the same face, so I take the direct approach. Maybe ol' Henrietta Pearl will take my side. "Not sure if you've heard, but twins live separate lives all the time."

Ophelia's dark voice hardens. *"We are far more than twins, Ophelia Cate. You and I both know, because of what you have done, you do not deserve to leave."*

My heart rate takes off as the rocking chair rocks back and forth, picking up in speed.

"As I am sure you have observed, I tend to grow very tired as of late. The years have been a strain. But you, dear, will supply the additional energy I need."

"You . . . want me to be your battery?"

Ophelia leans forward and, concentrating slightly, causes the forehead of the doll in the nearest stroller to fold in and cave.

A forehead that could just as easily be Rosie's.

Holding out her hand, she demurely says, *"Your time has come to serve a different purpose. Now you must rejoin me."*

Rejoin?

It's like I'm being pushed through a trap door, and there's nothing to grab onto. No bargaining chips lay around, besides my own life.

Is it worth it?

To succumb my will to hers even though I have no bloody clue what this room is or why Ophelia's showing it to me?

"You'll leave them alone." I really don't know what I can say otherwise. "Luther and Rosie."

Ophelia giggles, twirling a colorful, toy Ferris wheel nearby. *"Certainly, my sweet."*

To my left, the rocking horse on wheels rolls of its own volition straight toward me, and the top of the jack-in-the-box suddenly springs open. Bells and whistles blow from who knows where, and, for all I know, chupacabras are gonna jump out and do some ballroom dancing.

When the rocking horse bumps into a brown, wooden chest, about two feet by three feet in size, though, I know something is wrong.

Wrong.

'Cause all the toys fall silent as church mice.

A tricksy grin contorts the features of Ophelia's pasty face. *"And now to show you how and where I died."*

Reaching out, she suddenly wraps her stony fingers round my neck like it's a Gogurt and forces me to my knees.

What happened to Henrietta Pearl? Maybe she'll help me.

In another gust of wind, the chest flies open as my esophagus burns.

Won't stop burning.

"Do not fight it," Ophelia says brightly. She's superhumanly strong, and I doubt she eats her spinach, so none of this is fair in any way. *"To be sure, it is pointless. All along, I have been infusing you with far better tinctures than what you would obtain from an apothecary."* What in the heck is she saying? She taps

the skin below her nose—the spot where she's strung the vine beneath my nostrils so I can breathe.

Ooh, I'd forgotten the breathing tube was even there. Not liking the sound of being drugged at this time, I reach up to rip it off, but Ophelia's nearly invisible thumb crudely clamps the cool vine in place.

"I told you. You are part of me . . ."

I make the mistake of looking down at the wooden chest —at the hair that's stuck in its hinges like floss between teeth.

I swat at Ophelia's fingers.

Must rip the breathing tube away, but my foot collides with the rocking horse, and rusted hinges squeal as the toy jerks side to side.

No way'm I climbin' into that tomb.

I'd rather be one of the gargoyles, honestly.

A vine slithers round and strangles my leg. Another creeps higher, higher . . . nearly skittering to my belly, and as I grab hold of one of the toy shelves, part of me wonders if the reason why Mom and Dad knew I was disposable was 'cause they knew that I couldn't truly sacrifice myself for Rosie. The desire to live is strong, and I hate that I feel so torn about this all the time.

Shelf half-wrenches from the wall.

I grip harder, knuckles burning white, and with another gust of the wind, the shelf slips from the plaster the rest of the way.

I let it go and tumble to the floor, rattling and rolling.

Henrietta Pearl hovers nearer with a baby doll in her arms—the doll with the skull that's half-caved.

I don't wanna look—I don't wanna look into the ghost lady's eyes—but I do succeed in finding the gall to do it, and the woman's skin's like sandpaper covering her face.

She thrusts one free hand into Ophelia's back, and Ophelia does this high-pitched eagle scream. The woman's eyes are marble white, and *her* yowl is the sound of ravens croaking.

The woman grabs my arms—sandpaper's chaffing—and like I'm made of linen, she lifts me high above the wooden chest.

Just before the lid closes, she drops me inside.

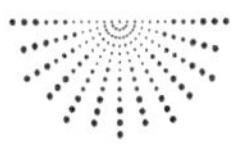

CHAPTER THIRTY-EIGHT

At least there aren't any bright lights.

The woman . . . Henrietta Pearl sure didn't seem friendly. I mean, she stuck her hands into Ophelia's back. Guess, on the more generous end, they're frenemies.

No wonder Ophelia hates this room. This toy chest is where she died. Did she suffocate?

Everything's gone quiet.

Quieter than a sow that's delivered a litter of stillborn piggies.

Honestly, I expected Henrietta Pearl to cast a spell or for Ophelia to tell me to never *go* in this room, 'cause it seems to have quite the negative vibe.

Are the two of them chatting in the other room? Having a little heart-to-heart on ghost hierarchy?

Pressing my palms into the rough cedar lid, I try to push my way to escape, but the lid will not budge nor creak.

Thick, rough slivers embed in my palms, and I force my mouth to work. "Hey!"

I pound the lid.

"HEY!"

I pound it again and again, wondering if I really am going to suffocate.

If Luther can free himself from Bastian, maybe he can run up here and try to rescue me. Not exactly a "macho female" scenario, but it's okay to let others pitch in a little half the time.

My throat's so clogged I swear I've been gagged with cotton candy.

As I move my hands to free my airway, my knuckles smack wood, and a host of new slivers embed in my knuckles.

Takes *everything* I have not to scream.

Something in the box sizzles near my head, and it's my blood I just scraped from my skin.

Guess Ophelia needs it to be her battery. After she's successfully betrayed Bastian.

Almost makes me feel bad for the guy.

When all's said and done—when the fiddler comes, and the credits are rolling—*this* is how it's going to be?

Ophelia and Henrietta Pearl are going to show up every now and then to stab me for my juices, à la straws in a juice box. Yummy.

If only I'd been given *any* other name.

My wind pipe's stopping up—lack of oxygen, CF, everything.

Time to sleep with the fishies . . .

TAP. TAP.

I gasp for breath. Who in the gas-hat is that?

HP?

My arms sag, and I have no bloody strength. My entire body lays prostrate like a block of cement, and I'm not real sure I can withstand seeing Henrietta Pearl's creepy face. I mean, she forced Bastian into submission, and he is no easy-peasy boy.

Dust rains in buckets as someone slaps the lid from the outside.

I don't know how I'm able to move, but I slap back real fast.

Something metal and pointy slides beneath the lip of the lid.

Oh, mercy!

I flinch back so hard, the back of my skull has to be flattening. The wooden chest groans as someone pries off the lid, and with his dark, messy hair and layers of ripped clothes, I could kiss Luthy.

The biggest smile I've ever seen ripples across his face as oxygen swims over mine. I . . . didn't know he could look so alive and happy.

I tear outta the box, throw my arms around his neck, and scream, "YOU'RE SO HOT WHEN YOU'RE SMILING!"

And I cough a lot. 'Cause, you know. It's me.

Luther's arms feel like Nova Scotia—the coast, by the beach. His hair is Mexico, and his lips, connected to mine, are the bloody Ukraine with gold domed cathedral and unforgettable Black Sea coastlines.

I don't want to, but when we part, we pant, and I want to kiss him again. But that makes zero sense, 'cause I gotta find Rosie.

I do find the willpower to let go, though finding the right words sure ain't easy.

"Are you all right?" Luther cups the side of my face. He gazes at me with the softest expression, and I might be willing to go back in that box if it meant I'd always receive a reception like this on the other side.

Fighting back the tears that threaten to fall from my eyes, I gulp. "Where is she?"

Luther opens his mouth to answer, but he probably wants

to know if I mean Ophelia or Rosie. Shoot, for all he knows, I could mean HP.

"Where's Rosalyn?" I lower his hand from my face.

Luther grimaces, emphasizing one of the many scratches on his cheek. "My brother hid her . . . before I could get free."

And that would be my heart, dive-bombing from a plane. "But we can find her, right?"

Luther becomes Mr. Shifty Eyes. "Both he and Ophelia are temporarily weak."

"But they were eating all those people! Replenished their strength!"

He rubs the back of his neck. "She does not have the strength to sustain a projection of herself, support him, *and* be Monkshood for any stretch of time."

Question is, is Henrietta Pearl on Ophelia's or her own side? If Ophelia tried destroying this room, and Henrietta Pearl *murdered* Ophy, I would say, yeah, they're prolly not exactly on the same side. I can use that to my advantage, right?

The rocking chair's become still as a statue, and that shawl on the chair's arm has nearly slipped to the floor.

Think, think, think.

Lowering his hands to my shoulders, Luther seems to need to comfort me, but I have to play this just right.

"We have to find my sister." I take his hand as I pull him to the hallway.

Luther nods in agreement, avoiding my eyes. "What did she say?"

An awful pang cramps my heart. Why's he asking about my conversation with Ophelia and HP? "Ophelia wants me to be an additional power source . . ." Something prevents me from bringing up his mommy.

Squeezing my hand, Luther seems to understand my meaning. "And your sister?"

I pause. Why's he fishing for so many answers? ". . . She promised she would let Rosie go if I stay . . ."

Luther flinches almost imperceptibly whilst taking another stride. His eyes skirt sideways before returning forward. "What else did she say?"

What is up with him wanting a play-by-play? Rosalyn's down there, probably scared out of her mind, and he's . . . "*You* don't get to play Twenty Questions." I raise both my hands. "We are way, way past that point!"

Luther's ears turn so red I feel kinda terrible for belittling the boy, but now's not the time to drill me.

Leaning over, I give him a small peck on the cheek. "Sorry. I'm sorry. Let's just go find Rosie."

CHAPTER THIRTY-NINE

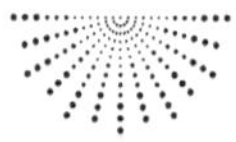

HOLDING ONTO LUTHER'S ARM, I can't help wondering if he's ever joined in on his mother's dream—where the Dvoraks find their cute, little perfect wives, and they have their cute, little chubby-cheeked babies. Surely, Luther's not into all that. The boy wants to travel, play pickle ball. Loves gardening, poetry . . .

When we make it to the bottom of the stairs, though, and I look all around the coffered ceiling, I find that Luther's right—Rosalyn's not anywhere in sight.

"I thought you said the living room would be safe . . ." I falter.

"Usually, Ophelia prefers to make her activities more clandestine." He ducks his head.

"Usually?!"

"Guess she's growing desperate," he's mumbling.

Rosalyn's vine dangles like a sea bass bit off the hook of a fishing line. And the others . . . I don't see any other bodies.

Grabbing my hand, Luther tugs it and says, "Let us search the hallway."

Bastian—the human Bastian—comes a strollin' in like he

owns the place, eyepatch covering his missing eye. Extending a long, fingernailed hand, he juts out his chest.

"Luther is the one who hid your sister," he says. He must be lying. "I wouldn't dare trust him." He stands *way* too close when he looks down on me. "The boy *lies*."

But aren't lies why I came over here in the first place?

I lied about my CF. I still haven't told Luther about my other thing. Shoot, Luther's mysterious aura is the very thing that drew me to him in the first place.

We have both been very adept at spinning our own tales. It's a gift! A talent, see! And the mocking, transparent way Bastian talks is a reminder that I'd rather work with Luther over him any ol' day.

Regardless, I turn to Luther, checking that everything's going to be hunky-dory. "Tell me you're not working with Bastian."

Luther's eyebrows shoot up defensively. "I am *helping* you find Rosalyn."

"Sure, my brother has a bleeding heart." Bastian tsks his tongue. "But if we're going cards up, even *he* has a desire for children. A family."

"I DIDN'T HIDE HER!" Luther shouts, throwing out his arms and accidentally knocking the Scrabble off the table. This fantastical clatter has my stomach twisting. *Please* don't tell me all of this is what Luther was hoping for since the beginning.

Bastian smiles, surveying the spilled, square tiles. "The truth is, we *both* hid her while Ophelia took you upstairs to the nursery."

My heart rate backflips—goes topsy-turvy.

I try not to look at Luther, but it's kind of impossible since all the color's draining from his face.

Holding up his hands, Luther, in this speedy-Gonzalez,

voice says, "That *was* the plan. Way, way back. Originally. But it is no longer. You don't deserve any of this, Cate!"

And that, my friends, is what a broken heart feels like. Beaten. Pulverized. It's what I've feared all along.

Luther really bought into the Dvorak agenda? He wanted me . . . to have his babies?

Staring into Luther's beautiful, olive-toned face, I can't help thinking about how we were stupendous texters and more than excellent make-out buddies. He made me feel beautiful and wanted and desired and . . . *clearly,* I'm not old enough to get married.

"You could tend your sister here," Luther says, flipping my heart over sideways. "Or, that is what I thought when I originally learned Rosalyn had been captured and we were getting along as well as we have."

Tears automatically burn in my eyes. "But you tried to get me to go! You wanted me to leave!"

Luther grips his hair. "AARGHH!" He spins away from me to pace. "I have struggled with what to do since the very moment you arrived. I wanted you to go; I wanted you to leave. I poisoned you, then *threw out* the poison when I saw you were about to ingest the Monkshood leaves." Throwing out his hands again, he yells, "I deserve to be punished for all of it! But you *do not* deserve to be trapped here, Cate."

I can feel the truth of his words. They hit me in the center of my chest—dead center, sharpshooter, bullseye.

Gah, I have no idea how to react or how to behave.

Am I supposed to thank him?

Box him up some candy-striped fudge with other Christmas candy?

What happened to the other people hanging from the ceiling?

Ohhh, whoa. Whoa, whoa, whoa. That bone bag has

maybe, definitely, quite possibly tripled in size . . . Arms, legs lay stacked in a cocoon of blood and vines.

Seizing my hands, Luther meets my eyes, and his smooth, calloused fingers are *way* too warm and reassuring. "You deserve to live a long, happy, and *free* life!"

Bastian gives his brother the most exaggerated roll of his eyes. "This has all been very profound, but can we go to her sister now, please?" He raises his hand and waggles his fingers. "Pretty please?"

Visions of Bastian leading Rosalyn up the stairs and showing her the toy room suddenly pop into my mind. He said he would . . . I can't tell what he's really up to, but there's *no way* he's taking Rosalyn from me.

"Cate." Luther takes a tentative step toward me as he pleads. "I am not working with them . . ."

"You already admitted that you are!" I throw his hand off mine while more tears burn in my eyes. And, against my better judgment, I join Bastian at the head of the hallways. Not sure what to do with Luther—I *hate* that this is the crucible for one of his lies—but I gotta make a deal with a demon to save Rosalyn.

Seizing the kaleidoscope from the table, Bastian straightens his shoulders to lead the way, when Luther throws himself between his brother and me.

"Did Ophelia tell you if she plans to let Bastian live?" He stretches his arms wide.

Spinning, Bastian rears back and head-butts Luther straight in the face.

Blood pours from Luther's nose as airy whispers swiftly reverberate through the hallways. Ophelia's coming. She's coming. And I'm not even one step closer to finding my sister.

"Where'd you put her?!" I yell at both boys.

The whispering grows louder—chanting, echoey. A foreboding squall, causing the hairs on the back of my neck to stand on end for the hundredth time.

"*Cate . . .*" Ophelia whispers so loud from the window that it's like I'm being splashed by the sea. "*You promised you would take my place . . .*"

A broken vase rattles from the confines of the fireplace. Curtains billow, slugs line the fabric, and the dead plants on the walls stretch like zombie arms, ready to eat me alive.

I stagger, semi-wishing I could simply disappear, and all of this would go away. "I NEED TO FIND ROSIE!"

"*SEBASTIAN.*" Ophelia's low growl turns feral. "*Where did you put the child?*"

Smugly, Bastian sweeps part of his robe behind his shoulder. "You are not the only one who needed insurance, *darling.*"

An invisible hand rips Bastian from the floor and throws him to the wall of plants, which absorb him like intestines attacking a slab of meat.

"*I have things under control!*" Ophelia wails, causing the newly put together glass in the mirror to crackle and break. The pollen from the flowers still floats in the air, but it's not as thick as before. Maybe Ophelia's weakening . . .

Running a shaky hand through his hair, Luther whispers, "There's a passage in the room with all the aquariums. You just have to come with me."

More visions of Luther and Bastian convincing Rosalyn to climb inside that toy box barrage my mind, and I shake my head.

"I want to help you!" Luther cries. "I have *always* wanted to help you." He drops his voice again to a whisper. "Ever since you came."

"But not at the library?"

"Yes, at the library!"

"Then why did you invite me over?"

His voice is a double-edged sword. "I DID NOT HAVE A CHOICE!"

Bastian makes this nasty, choking sound as he flops and fights against Ophelia's vines. I could get used to that. One vine has him round the neck, and another slips beneath his eyepatch, digging into every orifice on his face.

Holding out my palms, I try to get Luther to see reason. "How do I know you're not trying to take me to the aquarium room to trap me?"

"Because." His tender eyes throb inside mine. "I really, truly have fallen for you, Cate." He reaches into his pocket. "I fixed your phone . . ."

I reach out, hungry to call everyone from Mom to the US army when another vine slaps my phone out of Luther's hand and absorbs it even before it hits the ground.

Where'd it go?

The muffled sound of crunching glass comes from the mound of vines and *nooo*. That was my lifeline.

Bastian's teeth and claws begin to elongate; he's going to escape the vines. Though the vines snatch at his hair and his hood's fancy purple lining. One snakes into his robe's wide-mouthed sleeve, and, reaching into his pocket, snatches the kaleidoscope, and drops it to the hardwood with a masterful clank.

"*I will show you your sister*," Ophelia says as the bejeweled kaleidoscope rolls with precision to my feet. "*All you need to do is look inside.*"

CHAPTER FORTY

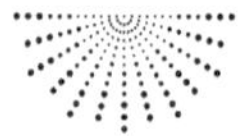

FOR ALL I KNOW, Henrietta Pearl's going to show up and rip the kaleidoscope away from me. She prolly doesn't want me to see Rosie.

I'm not sure how it works, and we certainly don't have an abundance of time, so I scoop up the jeweled cylinder. Like I'm Cap'n Jack Sparrow, I place it over my eye.

Swirls and ribbons of color—red, blue, and gold—loop in fancy ringlets. They whirl in an endless collision of bright lights.

Diamonds glitter. I'm staring directly into the sun, but a shaman is spelling me; I can't look away. In refracted gold, all the geometric shapes spin and pause, and, in angry studs, they multiply. My iris is tugged nearer by conical shapes. As the patchwork pieces rear-end into each other, all I know is I couldn't pull off the kaleidoscope if I tried.

Something grabs hold of my consciousness. An obnoxious sucking sound pulls my every thought and presence inside.

Shelves of lotion, a broken ceiling fan, and a high-waisted counter tell me I'm . . . in a tanning salon.

The tanning salon.

Oh, take me back. Let me go back outside!

I grip the handle of the door, trying to run back to the street, but the door becomes an electric prism of interconnected, spinning shapes.

With my fist, I pound the door harder. The vinyl and glass convert into gobbledygook. It's not a real surface. Angles and colors spin, spin, won't stop turning.

With a sob, I try to lay into the prism—do *everything* in my power to avoid staying in this place.

Mom asked me to stay home while she went tanning. "Keep an eye on your sister," she insisted, just like she did every time. *I* selfishly didn't think it was fair that I should have to sit around, pastier than an albino, while Mom got to do whatever she liked.

So . . . I waited—'til mom hopped in her car and drove away.

Following her on foot, I made sure Rosalyn didn't lock us out before we tread to the tanning salon, only a few blocks away.

I couldn't leave Rosalyn home alone, so I had to bring her with me, naturally.

She was a fast walker. In her pink little rain boots, she did whatever she could to keep up, and when it began to drizzle, I became even more excited to lie in one of those cozy, fluorescent tanning beds. I'd only done it one other time.

Ten or so minutes later, Rosalyn and I made it to *Bronzed and Beautiful*—the business sign's purple letters offset by fluorescent green. The front flowerbed flouted a bronze Buddha, and Rosalyn giggled at his belly.

"Sit in the waiting room," I told her once we got inside. She was only eight at the time, but I pretended leaving her was a normal enough thing to do in a sketchy part of town in an establishment with wadded-up magazines.

When I handed my money to the cashier behind the counter, he didn't even bat an eye that I was too young to tan and my sister was unsupervised. He was busy listening to something on his phone and waved for me to go ahead and take any room I liked.

I can *still* smell the cheery orange air freshener that only slightly smelled like chemicals, and as I purposely strode forward, I spotted a light emanating from the bottom of the first closed door. A light from Mom's tanning bed, probably.

The second room appeared empty, but, not wanting to be too close to Mama Hellstrom, I hurried to the third room.

Which was entirely open, and, feeling very Lex Luthor, I slipped inside.

Not much was in the room. A framed Chihuahua with sunglasses hung from the wall above a rickety table for personal items, and another air freshener was plugged into the wall. Coconut this time.

Knowing there was no time to lose, I pulled off my clothes and lathered on the bottle of tanning lotion Mom left behind. Only when I donned the goggles and climbed into the bed did I feel the teensiest pang of guilt that I abandoned my sister. But she would be fine, right?

Honestly, I could have laid there for hours. I forgot to set my timer, and the tanning bed was so warm, it was like falling asleep, socks off, in a cumulonimbus cloud in summertime . . .

I don't know how long I laid.

I do remember my leg falling asleep, and thinking that salt and pepper sensation was just me in the clouds, floating.

Ahh, but, eventually, guilt pricked me with its sharp-edged face.

I reached out to read the clock on my phone, and, clumsily, I grabbed it from the table.

The fluorescent numbers taunted me. *Holy haystacks*, it was already twelve-thirty!

Pretty sure I'd been lying there for over half an hour, I just knew that Mom would find Rosalyn if I didn't hurry.

Scrambling outta the bed, I threw on my clothes. Swiped a little at my hair to make sure I looked cute for headphone boy. And, outside the room, I scampered down the hall, only to find the chair in the waiting room empty . . .

"Rosalyn?" I automatically searched beneath a magazine.

Headphone boy barely looked up from his phone. "Hmm?"

Maybe . . . Mom found Rosalyn already?

But Rosalyn would have told her I was there, and Mom woulda tore down every single door until she found me and grounded me for the rest of my life.

Unless . . .

Spinning around, I tore back down the hall.

First room—Mom's room—was no longer occupied.

Second room still stood empty.

The third room—my room—also stood dangerously, horrifically vacant. *Where* could she be?

By the time I hit the fourth room, though, I *knew* Rosalyn had to be inside. I could hear her lil' voice humming her favorite YouTube song for the week.

Luckily, she didn't lock the door. I was able to knock it open and march inside.

Feeling the fear rise in my throat, I looked down to find Rosalyn, lying on the phosphorescent bed, still fully clothed in her polka-dot shirt and jeans, eyes open wide.

I'll never forget the look on her face—how blank it was when Rosalyn was always smiling.

Part of me thought she might be asleep. She could sleep with her eyes open, right?

I sprinted to my little sister. Heaved the top of the

tanning bed the rest of the way open so that I could reach inside. Leaning in, I extended my arm to pull her out, but . . . she didn't reach back to me.

Her arms were lank sausages as she continued lying there, staring, blankly.

Desperate for any kind of response, I patted my little sister's smooth cheek. "Rosalyn, I'm here!" Tears charred my vision. "Sissie, talk to me!"

Face slack, my sister's eyes stretched wide with panic. "Catie?" She rarely used that whispery voice. "Why is it so dark? I'm opening my eyes."

CHAPTER FORTY-ONE

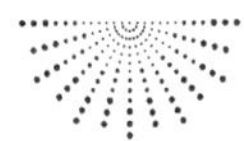

WHEN I DROP THE KALEIDOSCOPE, I'm not in the living room.

Bat-skeleton sconces, frayed scarves . . . I'm in the hall maze.

Actually, I'm in Luther's arms.

Oh, holy hell, no. Holy, holy.

I deck him in the jaw since he admitted a part of him wanted to make me his lil' wifey—and scramble past a few smashed-up urns at my feet.

Sure wish Ophelia didn't know about my past. There's a reason why I locked away that memory. I'm not ready to face it. She can't just do whatever she wants and dangle it in front of me.

What, does she revel in my shame?

Does it make her feel all-powerful to know that I screwed up in the *worst* way imaginable and that I'll feel horrible about it for the rest of my life?

What Ophelia doesn't know is that I pushed away my friends.

I stopped going to class.

I failed algebra and English, 'cause, when it happened, I couldn't focus on *anything*.

Well, guess what. I can't sink any lower than I already have. She wants me to be the house? I'm willing to be the bloody house! Or be her battery-pack. Whatever she needs! She just needs to come through on her part of the deal and help me free Rosalyn.

Luther finishes straightening his jaw, 'cause I dislocated it, apparently. We're at the screaming statues, and they both look *way* more weathered than before. Even crusty.

"I was only trying to help," Luther says as he works his jaw back and forth again. "I was carrying you to escape . . ."

I don't wanna hear any of his explanations or excuses. Nothing. "Let's just find Rosie." I take a decisive step toward the front door when way more petals flitter in the air. There's a heap of more meaty sconces lining the floor, blocking my way.

Everything's so mixed up.

I can't believe Ophelia can just make things appear or rearrange any way she likes.

"Whatever Ophelia showed you in that kaleidoscope . . ." Luther casts a nervous glance at a broken urn. "It was a lie."

"She showed me my past!"

"That's what she does. She twists the truth, Cate."

"SHE DIDN'T HAVE TO TWIST ANYTHING!" I didn't realize I'm sobbing. "I blinded my sister. I deserve *anything* Ophelia does to me."

Luther's eyes soften at my revelation. I *hate* it when I cry. I lose control and sound so broken, and *this* is why I locked every bit of the memory away. His round eyes make him look like he's about to give me a giant hug, but I don't know if I can accept that right now from the boy. He's always so conscientious, but secretive, and we probably bring the worst of out each other, if I'm honest with myself tonight.

A robed figure comes outta nowhere, grabs Luther by the collar, and tackles him to the ground. Pedestal urns crackle beneath both figures as they roll, punch, and run into everything.

An arm breaks off—from a statue, I mean—and Luther's a crumpled mess of emotions as Bastian stretches his arms and stands, clearly the winner of their little charade.

Cracking his neck from side to side, Bastian drawls, "Are we ready for the final show of the night?"

Truly, I'm not fully aware of everything around me as we stumble past the second broken, screaming statue, and a bare-bellied Buddha statue I'm *sure* Ophelia put there to taunt me. Mostly, though, I do everything in my power to avoid Luther's eyes.

After a few more zigs and zags, Bastian marches us into the land of aquariums with its super bright lights. While I don't know that Rosalyn's here, I'll go ahead and believe that Bastian will show me where she's hiding.

Also, I can't tell if Bastian's working on his own or with Ophy . . . She tangled him up in those vines, so I'd say he has his own agenda. We all do, actually.

Bastian's throaty laugh has me pausing. 'Cause the first aquarium? It's chock full of those bright yellow tiger moths and . . . something else, but I can't tell what it is. I can't see.

The second's been smashed to bits, and it isn't until we've reached the fifth, sixth aquarium that I-Spy a suspicious-looking figure, ripped apart in segments, lying inside. He or she's covered by the canary yellow butterflies.

"What did you do?" Luther's voice drops low as he asks his brother, and I shouldn't be freaked or surprised that Luther's worried.

The aquarium reeks of black mold, and Imma gonna murder someone if Rosalyn's inside.

I hold a shaky hand up to my mouth. I'm too terrified to

look. The smell truly is of decomposing bodies. A light shines directly into my eyes before it turns and showcases the aquarium housing the body.

The glass reflects part of the light. Reminds me of that mobster quote about death—how, when one kicks the bucket, they wear a pine overcoat—but this isn't pine.

Glass crackles beneath my boots.

I have to pull off the lid.

Please, please, please don't be Rosie.

I secure my fingers round the thick, moldy casing. Part of me wonders why the boys aren't helping. But there's no time to worry or whine. Ms. Muscles is who I am, and I pry up the thin ledge with ease.

After I push the glass top back far enough that it's able to stay in place, the decomposing smell's enough to flatten an army.

Holding one hand over my nose, I use my other to wave the pretty little moths away. Little brown, squirmy things greet me from inside.

Maggots.

Pale, ridged, wormy.

The maggots cling to the side of a rather tall man's face. A tall man's! *Not* Rosie's.

His nose is sunken in, and the squished Monkshood flower marks the hole where his lips used to be.

A trio of maggots slink from the poor man's eyes, and Bastian chuckles, prolly never more jovial in his life. He claps a comforting hand on my shoulder. "Robert, here, was at the wrong place at the wrong time. He saw you escaping from the mailman—well, yours truly—and thought he would run over to try and help. He was my inspiration for that form, actually. I always saw him lurking around our house, sticking his nose where it didn't belong. The fogged-up glasses were a nice touch, don't you think?"

But the "glasses" on poor Robert's face have been reduced to a pile of glass next to a dismembered arm.

I'm going to lose it. Oh my gosh, it's so disgusting.

"We kept him upstairs for a while," Bastian's saying. "I do believe you heard him while you were sleeping. He made quite the to-do, claiming that he was on the historical society and would bulldoze the place—though I knew where to put our guest to keep our sweetling happy." He playfully pats Robert's cheek, which moves way too easily, since his head is no longer attached to his body.

Aquarium after aquarium suddenly flickers on with bright lights.

Yellow and black, yellow and black, yellow and black. Luther said the moths are here just because they're attracted to the plants. So why are the aquariums here in the first place?

Every single doggone aquarium appears to be full, and I know the reason. I wasn't far off with the coffin analogy. Guess that bag o' bones? It's not housing everybody.

"What is wrong with you?" I bump into another aquarium's filthy glass . . . filled with the pieces of a middle-aged lady in a hairnet and a thick cobweb stretched over her face.

Bastian clucks his tongue, eyes flaring fiery. "My love has very eclectic tastes. We lure people here—or they come of their own idea—and we plug them in." He gestures to the aquarium with hairnet lady. Stringing them up in the living room earlier was just us improvising."

"And the bag o' bones?" I don't know how I'm able to ask while my throat's so dry.

Luther knocks on hairnet lady's aquarium. "That's a sampling of where Ophelia sticks them after she's sucked up everything. Bones are hard to digest, you see."

"You are sick!" So sick. "*Why* are you serving her?" My back knocks into another aquarium with I don't want to know what inside, and I wipe the sweat that's beaded up on my forehead and started dripping. "Ophelia doesn't even like your sorry face!"

Bastian grabs another fistful of cards and flings them into another pair of aquariums—full aquariums—causing them to shatter and explode on my left and right.

Luther comes scrambling outta nowhere and grabs his brother by the scruff of his robe so that they're face to face. "Where did you put her sister?" Luther's eyes look wild and dangerous, yes, but still handsome while he's panting.

Bastian growls this awful noise whilst tossing Luther at another aquarium.

Luther hits his head so hard I can feel the movement in my teeth. He looks so dazed and confused while Bastian struts like a freaking peacock in a zoo parade.

Straightening his robe, Bastian proudly presents a murder of crows, which shoot from the back of his hood's lining.

I have to duck to avoid the birds' wings. They screech and flutter—before disappearing into the shadows and cobwebbed ceiling.

Dude's parlor tricks are getting really old. Snore. Sleep through the alarm, peeps.

"When Ophelia told me of your fear of bright lights," Bastian splays his hands, gloating, "I just knew you would love our final resting place. As of now, she *may believe* that she wants to use you for her energy, but she will come to terms with what she needs." His eyes flit to Luther, who's rolling and finding his feet. "My darling *always* grows tired of her playthings. But me? I have been constant. For her, I have *always* been self-sacrificing. She likes a distraction or two, but she also needs—*requires*—constancy in her life. When my fiancé's ready to settle down, I shall be ready."

It's all I can do not to laugh straight in his face. Does he really believe that Ophelia will ever truly want to "settle down?" She enjoys sucking on severed kneecaps and playing skeleton bowling.

Clamping his fingers round my wrists, Bastian drags me to where "Robert" is lying.

I dig in my heels, 'cause I don't really wanna spoon the dead guy.

"No!" I try prying his ironclad hands off me. "I know we never really hit it off, but I made a deal with Ophelia—I *will* stay. I just need to make sure Rosalyn's okay!"

Luther limps toward us from across the room, glass crackling beneath his boots, and Bastian digs his nails . . . er, claws, into my waist. "You and I both know Ophelia can be stubborn at times. But once she realizes she wants to be with me, *you* will be our home. Doing so may even cure your insufferable disease."

"Why don't you just live in another place?!" I ask, desperate to shoot down his ideas.

He guffaws. "You can't honestly believe that we could survive anywhere else. We are over a hundred and thirty years old. Ophelia is tied to this place. Remember, when we killed her, she deposited her essence *here*. There is no leaving."

Shadows and nightmares seem to haunt Luther's eyes. He wants to get out. More than anything. It's why he has those maps, but maybe he got them before he realized he couldn't leave. He met me at the library, true, but "day pass," he had claimed. If he had stayed out there for longer than a few hours, he would have died.

Gruffly, Bastian lifts me up by the arms, his muscles like galvanized steel as he holds me above Robert-laddie. "Really, thank you, Catherine, for dropping by."

My name's not even Catherine, and, like a disgusting piece of trash, Dog Boy dumps me inside.

Luther screams, "No!" while the maggots inside Robert's aquarium become elongated cocoa puffs, some of them crunching along with Robert's fleshy bones beneath me.

This is the finale of the boys' magic show—their twisted, macabre Halloween prank. I thought the ending would be more fun somehow. Where we all jam to Monster Mash and pull out the scary costumes and things.

"Rosalyn!" I scream for my sister, praying she can hear me as Bastian lifts the glass lid to seal me inside.

Luther tears across the floor like a mad cheetah and dives for his brother's knees. He actually succeeds in toppling Bastian like a linebacker. But that well-intentioned move is what causes the brunt of the lid to fall directly in place.

CHAPTER FORTY-TWO

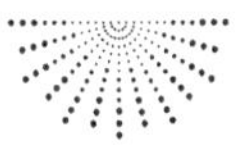

To understand just how cruel it was of me to make my sister blind, one has to know what she could do when she had her sight.

Some people are unusually gifted in visual arts. Some people have "it," or "the gift" as Mom used to say.

Of course, one of those people who was that gifted happened to be Rosie.

"Tell me what you think of this one," Rosalyn had said a few weeks before following me over to *Bronzed and Beautiful*. She'd drawn a pair of skinny, pale girls in fashion clothing, and it was pretty good. The girls looked exactly like her and me.

The lines were straight and professional. She'd drawn the pair in skirts with matching patterns that looked an *awful* lot like the fabric on a dress we'd gotten at a garage sale the prior week.

"Dadgum . . ." I marveled aloud. The drawing actually looked like it'd been drawn by a fashion designer from New York City. "That is *really*, really good, Rosalyn." I wrapped my arm around her thin, eight-year-old shoulder. I could barely draw stick figures, and Rosalyn was only in second grade.

"I can draw the outfits, then we can sew them together!" she squealed. "Ooh, and then Mom won't have to spend so much of her money!"

Her last comment was a punch to the gut. Rosalyn was far too aware of our money issues; she was a perceptive little thing. It wasn't like Mom or I ever spoke about making rent in front of my sister, or the fact that we never seemed to have enough for fresh fruits or veggies.

Still, it was like I was speaking to an aged woman of forty-five. Rosalyn was far too aware of our stress over money.

To top things off, my baby sister hung her head, her pink headband slipping slightly out of place. "I heard Mom crying last night . . ."

Ah, that would give things away. Emotions . . . they can be a beast.

Never more grateful that my sister could be so in-tune to our money problems, but definitely not wanting her to worry, I hugged her petite frame. "All right. I'll get the sewing machine."

And, after eating a few breadsticks and string cheese, we sewed.

All day.

Rosalyn drew, and while the first skirts we sewed needed to be taken in at the waist, by the third project, it was clear that Rosalyn had found her calling in life.

We created an apron, a maxi skirt, a beret.

Girl could open her own boutique store.

Land in New York. Do anything.

In the meantime, I borrowed every single book on sewing and fashion design I could get my hands on from the library. We spent a stint learning punk fashion just so that we could wear those plaid schoolgirl skirts (one of Rosalyn's friends started wearing them when she began private school). We used men's old shirts, and they turned out perfectly.

One of my favorite weeks was when Rosalyn sketched funky outfits with fur cuffs and neon leggings. No one could ever understand why we wanted these random items at the garage sales we stopped by, but we knew the fabric wouldn't go to waste.

That was the nice thing about Rosalyn's age. Her imagination knew no bounds, and half the fun was grabbing weird fabrics and supplies.

Now, of course, Rosalyn no longer draws.

We wear whatever Mom buys.

CHAPTER FORTY-THREE

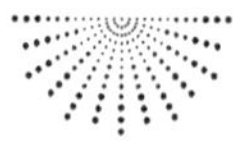

One can be sealed in an aquarium for a very long time.

Betchya didn't know that.

Especially despite having a condition that makes it very difficult to breathe.

Ophelia's got her vines sneaking through a tiny hole a little down and to my right—behind ol' Robbie's arm—and I guess that's Ophelia's plan to keep me alive. I'm her juice box. She kills all the others, but I get to stay alive. Yay.

She's stealing my blood, my energy, whatever she needs as long as I breathe.

What makes me so special?

It's gotta be connected to the fact that we have the same name and face.

Beyond that, who knew that this is the way I'd beat my disease? This whole scenario sure would be a lot cooler if I had elf ears, daggers, and a fancy wardrobe with enchanted gold chains.

Guess I never knew I'd prove this useful.

Wonder if Ophelia and I are doppelgängers.

You know, that's such a cool word. "Doppelgänger." I'd move my lips, but don't want any larvae slipping inside . . .

Remember, "Hellström" is a berserker, a Scandinavian name.

Maybe Ophelia's the descendant of a berserker, and so am I.

Though that still doesn't explain how we have the same face.

"Cate," a husky, low voice says—like it's right in the aquarium-slash-coffin with me. At first, I think it's Robert, but, of course, he's not able to talk anymore, poor Robbie. Plus, I'm pretty out of it. Been passing in and outta consciousness for hours now, ever since Bastian shipped Robert and me.

"Cate!" The low, husky voice grumbles again, and, ah, yes. It must be Luther. I very much want it to be the boy. But should I want it to be him? Really? He admitted that he had ulterior motives the whole time.

Wonder what I would've done if I were in his place.

Hmm . . . problem is, my neck muscles are freakin' weak. I can't really lift my head to look around, and instead of an Elvin princess sorceress, I've become a newborn baby.

The bright lights would pretty much burn off my retinas if I opened my eyes.

BANG!

Ooh, that was a really loud bang.

Bang. Bang!

I shift, Robert and ze maggots squishing beneath me.

Oh, maybe Luther's in another aquarium. He's trapped, just like me.

Trapped and alone. Sorry, Luthy . . .

I'd say it out loud, but these here maggots are formin' a mustache above my lip-line.

"Mustachio" a question, I might say.

"Listen," Luther says through the breathing tube that's apparently connected to mine. "Cate . . ." His voice is much like a security blanket. I like it, even if he had more hidden agendas than I had foreseen.

Is it weird that Ophelia made it so we can talk to each other? I feel like it's weird. Maybe that's her way of saying she doesn't mind making a love triangle outta Robert, Luther, and me.

I still can't believe Bastian thinks he has a shot with Ophelia after *murdering* her, for Pete's sake. What's so special about her, anyway? Bastian finds me repulsive, and Ophelia and I have the same face. Of course, once he thought I had "the tuberculosis," he backed way off.

Hmm. Gotta say I'm a fan of his germaphobe tendencies.

Feelin' brave, and wanting to look at Luther, I try *really* hard not to look directly at the bright lights. Grateful that none of the maggots have dripped into my eyes, Imma able to turn my head just a teensy-tiny bit to look in his direction.

Well, whaddaya know. Light's not nearly as bright on Luther's side.

The boy's bloody. Beige shirt sure is lookin' skimpy, though his red and cream scarf manages to cover up anything and everything that would be a sight for sore eyes.

"You . . . *need* to not give up," Luther says, pounding on the side of his own cage. "You don't need to stay here, Cate." A few tiger moths flutter against the inside of his glass. When they settle back down, I see that he's got his old blanket.

The blanket.

The one he freaked out over when I first arrived.

Kicking it so that it falls a little lower on his feet, Luther grumbles something I can't quite make out. Prolly cursing. Well, at least the maggot that was above my lips slips off, and now it's finally safe to speak.

"Hey, Luther." My voice comes out coarse. "What's up with you and your blankey?"

Luther grunts something else untoward as another maggot crawls across my hairline. I become uber still; a ceramic, or something else just as frilly.

Thumping his coffin, Luther rattles whatever's alongside —or beneath—him in the cage. "It's not a blanket," he says, voice muffled. "It's what's left of my mother . . ."

My breathing comes out ragged. "You mean, Little Miss Ophelia . . . made your mother into her own Ophy trophy?"

"We poisoned her." Luther's voice saddens. "Poisoned Ophelia, never suspecting that we triggered an ancient Berserker curse that allows shifters to come back to life."

Well, huh! Looks like ol' Grams' tale was much more than another scary story.

"We buried Ophelia—you saw her grave." Luther places the palm of his hand on the glass facing me. "She began to change forms at first light. First, she connected with the roots of the plants surrounding the house. Then, thinking it poetic, she decided to become the plant my family was named for *and* the house my mother, brother, and I had always dreamed of."

"She trapped you." I don't know why, but I feel like I can, kinda sorta, see the day. I picture lightning and thunder, and more of a purple sky.

"First thing Ophelia did was force Monkshood down my mother's throat since that's how Bastian and Mother poisoned *her* before sticking her in that chest. Then, Ophelia *literally* hung my mother out to dry on the clothesline."

"Oh, wow! That's not a very happy ending!"

"It didn't take long for the vultures to make quick work of her," Luther adds quietly. "This 'blanket'—" he scoots away from it "—is what is left of my mother's body. Her skin. Her . . . hide. Ophelia keeps it about the house to bother me."

"Man." I can't come up with any comforting words, so I mumble, "Scorned women sure can be tough at times."

Luther quiets for a long ten seconds as my breath comes out a little rockier, but steadier, if you ask me. "It has not been a smooth road, but . . . eventually, Ophelia accepted the fact that my feelings were fleeting."

I gasp. "So, you *did* like her!"

". . . For maybe three days."

"I don't really have the tuberculosis." I roll around a little to try to get comfortable on Robbie. "Sorry I lied."

When a handful of maggots find my belly button, though, I really do feel like I've reached my limit for crazy stuff happening to me. I do everything I can to hold still. Even if I do have to pee. "The truth is . . . I have something called cystic fibrosis. It's a genetic disorder. It affects my lungs, my digestive tract. My breathing . . ."

Luther knocks once, real soft, on his glass. He's either startled or, what feels even more likely, he wishes to comfort me. "I am sorry . . ."

"Good thing is, I'm not contagious!" I laugh as traitor-y tears spring to the fronts of my eyes. "I still can't believe you were willing to be infected by me."

His voice softens. "You are worth it, Cate."

Even with the separation of our glass, I can feel the hope and woeful smile in his voice.

Ah, how precious they are—his smiles. I wish the lights weren't so weird so I could really see his face.

Itching to press my fingers to my glass, I fight back the remnant of his admission that he had *other* plans for when I came. "Did you really woo me to have your babies?"

"It sounds rather barbaric when you say it like that."

"You don't deny it. Color me worried."

"You were a much-needed torch in a black season of my life. I have lived in a dark, dark world for a very long time."

"And now?"

"Your optimism is . . . spellbinding."

I try not to get all mushy at that. The boy's pretty, pretty words . . . they get me every dang time!

I could drill him with questions. Demand that he tell me *exactly* what he's *now* thinking, but, for now, all I can come up with is one question. "Are you one of those guys who's really good with his words but doesn't pull through in the end?"

He's quiet for one—two heartbeats.

As he presses his fingers into the glass, the skin on his fingers stretches white. "I really hope not, Cate."

CHAPTER FORTY-FOUR

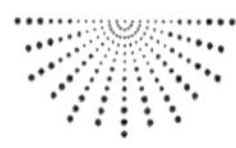

I DON'T KNOW how long we've been in here.

One . . . three days?

I hope Rosalyn's found a way to leave. Maybe Ophelia's a girl of her word and let her out now that she has me?

I'm not holding my breath . . .

Ba-dum, ching!

If I saw my baby sister, I know exactly what I would say. *I am so, so sorry for taking your vision. I am sorry for taking your talent and your joy.*

Sure, Rosalyn's the type of person who will always find other things to do, but *nothing* else brings her joy like drawing.

The truth is, I stole that from her, so I deserve *everything* Ophelia can dish out on me.

Maybe dying in a star-crossed love triangle in this here coffin will help me atone for what I did in some small way.

Only other thing I can think to do is pay for Rosalyn's surgery. But, frankly, I'm outta cash. Spent the last of it on a popsicle last week.

Ya know, if I open my eyes—stare straight at the bright lights—I'll get exactly what I did to Rosie . . .

That would be a simple form of poetic justice.

If I receive just *one* more soft word from Luther, maybe I'll find the gall to do that very thing.

I begin the painful process of parting my lips to talk to him, but they're cemented shut. Rubber cement, feels like. Sweat stretches like Saran wrap over my chest, arms, and legs, and it rightly feels like I'm in a tanning bed again.

Whispers curl from the curtains—no, the halls. The type of whispers that sounds like it's beckoning. I don't know what's happening, but suddenly, a child-like voice shouts, "Catie?"

Rosalyn?

That sounds an awful lot like Rosalyn's voice . . .

Barely even conscious, and feeling a whole lot like King Tut's twin sister, all lain out and mummified, I shift my gaze, far as I can to the right.

More whispers echo in the halls while I take in the sight of an aquarium, smashed to smithereens, body parts spread out like odds and ends at a dummy factory.

Another aquarium's still intact, but mold's got it so covered, it almost looks furry.

Child-sized footfalls draw closer as the whispers urge my sister nearer.

Nearer!

Ophelia *could* be working with Bastian, holding my baby sister at knife-point.

Step-step.

Step-step.

Crunch.

I'm pretty sure that's only two feet walking . . .

My voice doesn't work. Prolly 'cause there's gorilla glue

in Ophelia's "bond-with-the-house" CF cure recipe. Glancing round—gosh, even my eyeballs feel like marbles rolling round in socket wrenches, so dry!—I do spot a few new lightbulbs. I accidentally look a little too directly, and now I'm seein' extra spots on a polka-dot shirt I've seen a million times.

Rosalyn grabs and shakes the lid to my coffin. "Cate!"

She's really here?

Totally, one hundred and ninety percent, really, and truly?

I try to move my hand to block out the glare from the light but seems as though my hand's heavy as a semi. Rosalyn's thin arms try to lift the top of the aquarium, but why would Ophelia help her help me escape? Unless she's a woman of her word and simply wants to see that I'm satisfied with Rosalyn leaving.

The lid doesn't budge. Bastian did a mighty fine job of sealing that, it seems.

Mostly, since I'm so far gone, I'm just glad I get to see Rosalyn one last time . . .

I'm just able to lift my fingers enough to touch the glass' side. If Rosalyn could see, she'd know I was praying for her. Praying that she gets out safely.

Two solid knocks suddenly come from the direction wherein Luther is lying.

Startled, Rosalyn says something, but my ears won't work. They're too stuffed up. She darts over to Luther, but I can't make out what the pair's saying.

Time goes on and on. Lasts *forrrever*. Lasts longer than *Lord of the Rings*.

Maybe Luther did the right thing and convinced my baby sister to leave.

BOOM! Something's just hit my aquarium. Itty-bitty glass shards fly in a monsoon over my eyes.

I brace myself—glad I can be a shield for ol' Robbie—but, oh me, oh my. The aquarium's open, and oxygen suddenly spreads and wriggles its delicious fingers through my chest cavity.

I suck up air.

Air!

Nothing's ever felt more outstanding.

Shovel in hand, my sister stands a solid five inches from my face. She smiles the goofiest, crooked-lipped smile and says, "She helped me find you. And he—Luther—told me you were three glass boxes past his. He said I could do it. And the lady told me this is where you'd be and that I could say goodbye to you one last time."

"*Goodbyes are important,*" Ophelia's voice says from a scarf that's rustling in the hallway. "*I never got to say goodbye.*"

Rosalyn wails, "But I don't want to say goodbye to you, Cate!"

I choke back a sob. I don't know how I'm able to move through the mummification and cement, but I do manage to push through everything tying me down. Throwing my arms around my sister, I give her the best hug of my life.

Her thin frame sags hungrily into me. Luckily, she seems completely oblivious to the maggots and Robbie.

I keep her clear. Just this once, I am selfish and breathe in her little kid, bubble gum-scented hair, and her clothes that smell like whatever laundry detergent Mom was able to buy.

"Did I hit you?" Rosalyn asks as I finally pull away.

I swipe at her hair. It's *so* smooth and pretty. "Nope!" And I have to hug her again, 'cause I can't believe Ophelia values such things as goodbyes.

Rosalyn giggles as I accidentally whack her polka-dot headband sideways.

"And Luther?" I breathe into her baby-soft hair. How much time will Ophelia give us for this goodbye?

Rosalyn tentatively nods to the back of the room to where he's lying. It's a wonder she has any sense of direction at all, but then I realize she's been holding onto the bottom lip of my aquarium the entire time.

Sense of touch. She's learned to memorize directions that way for a very long time.

Hobbling in Luther's general direction, she stoically takes the lead. But I seize her arm. "You don't have to do that. I'll get him, Rosie."

Accepting my hand, she sags into me in relief. I'm happy not to let go. With all the random bright lights shining down on aquariums, part of me still thinks we're still in that kaleidoscope memory.

Moths flutter in gorgeous, yellow waves.

With my one free hand, I run my fingers through my hair, making sure it's maggot-free, and pat away any undesirables from my face. Luther may have thrown me for a loop, but a girl's gotta do her best not to look like a zombie.

Patting down the lace and tulle tea-stained dress I'm *still* wearing, I promise myself to barter with Ophelia to let me get in one more shower before I stay in this place.

Taking a deep and final breath, I ready myself to face the boy. Hopefully, Ophelia doesn't mind that I free him, too. Bastian must have put him there, and, considering their loversl quarrels, seems like Ophelia and Bastian don't always see eye to eye.

Gently, I take the shovel from my sister's hands, which are shaking. I don't want her to be scared, so I give her whatever comfort I can. "I can do this." I *will* free the boy. Rosalyn begins to nod when the sound of breaking glass prematurely steals over the gallery.

Er . . . that wasn't me.

Another aquarium bursts—this time, a little to the right—

and Ophelia's face emerges from the curtain where I originally called up my granny voice.

Her powers rustle and twirl the fabric in fanciful ringlets and strings. *"I cannot hold off Sebastian for long,"* she simpers. *"We are running out of time."*

CHAPTER FORTY-FIVE

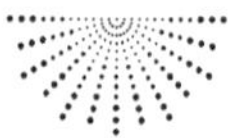

I HAVE no idea where Bastian is, but I imagine Ophelia's done with him pretty much like she did to him in the living room with the vines.

Ooh, maybe she added him to her doily collection? But she said she couldn't hold him back for long. Why doesn't she just finish him off for good, already?

Not sure if I'm ready to face what's next, I grab my sister's hand like we're a pair of Teletubbies.

Gosh dang it, I wish we'd freed Luther already.

If I broke him out real quick, would Ophelia get impatient and hurt Rosie?

A splattering of cards on the wall tells me Bastian's already rejoined us for the millionth time, and his robe jostles as he moves, the yeasty smell from the mailman roiling off him in waves.

Lowering the shovel in my hands, I say, "No one invited you. And no one's impressed by your magic tricks anymore, by the way."

Drink in hand—where'd Dog Boy get that?—he smiles this wolfish smile that sends a chill up my spine. "Looks like we're all in the same room." He sneers at the cloth imprint of Ophelia's face. "You thought you could keep me down with that silly dog crate?"

"It's worked before," Ophelia speaks like there's a shrug in her voice.

Getting down to business, Bastian throws back another drink. "I said I would be more mindful of you. I trimmed the flowers out front. Polished the tea set . . . you don't even like tea!"

"Sebastian, I had been onto you to accomplish those tasks for weeks."

"I'll go fix up your bedroom. Repair all the frames. You can't string me along forever." He chokes up with tears actually shining in his eyes. "You promised, you belong with me."

Ophelia's curtain flaps while she mutely takes in Bastian's groveling. *"Are you done? I cannot abide this sniveling."*

Bastian snivels again before wiping his eyes with the back of his robe's sleeve, and I had no idea he could be vulnerable and weak. Not that love, itself, is a weakness, and we've definitely seen his feelings for Ophelia are real.

"Why do you love her anyway?" I discretely put Rosalyn behind me.

In a fit of anger, Bastian spins and chucks his empty liquor glass at me. He's a full foot wide, and Ophelia tsks before vanishing from the curtain completely. Bastian's outstretched arm, though, tells me he wasn't ready for her to disappear, but her face flickers in and out of the fabric. She doesn't have much strength.

"Aren't there any other doppelgängers you can harangue?" I ask the pair of them in case they really don't need me.

Bastian snarls, and hmm. Extemporaneous freedom prolly isn't happening . . .

"What I mean is, I know you want me to be your battery

pack, but why do you even *want* to be a house? I know, Ophelia, you like bones and things, but houses—man, they grow mold. Foundations break. Shingles get loose." I wave my hands with emphasis. "The air conditioner goes out, and don't even get me started on the plumbing!"

An aquarium explodes—right next to Rosalyn—and I drop the shovel and, since she's shaking, I hold her tight. "All right, all right!" Ophelia doesn't want me to try talking my way out of this a second time. "You prefer to be a house. For the time being. But don't come cryin' to me when you have issues with your HOA."

I'm tempted to point out that they don't seem like they'll *ever* be happy, but I clamp my mouth shut. Don't need them sending me to an early grave.

Every single curtain in the room ripples as Ophelia moves from one to the next to the next—she's a ballroom dancer enjoying her grand finale. Looks like she got a burst of energy.

Giggling in this ghoulish, sing-song way, Ophelia purrs, "*It is time.*"

I'm just opening my mouth to tell the witch I'm ready when Rosalyn screams. "NO!" She blocks me with her twiggy arms, doing her best to protect me.

I . . . totally didn't take into account that Rosalyn might fight us at this point. But I'm doing this for *her*. Nothing else matters besides getting her to safety.

Bastian fluidly runs his hand across his slicked-back hair, showcasing his gaunt face. Winking at me once, he reaches over and tugs Rosalyn from my hands faster than I can react.

It's a cold snap, the feeling of Rosalyn's fingers breaking from mine.

My sister bats for me in the dark while Bastian not-so gently grabs her arms, restraining her like she's a wild animal or something. His mouth is way too close to her ear as he whispers, which has Rosalyn paling.

"Don't touch her!" I snarl. What happened to the fire poker? Oh, shovel! Yesss. I pluck it up from the glass-riddled floor and hold it like a baseball bat, ready to hit this dude's head to Mercury. "You hurt her, and I *will* find a way to convince Ophelia to put you in the ground next to her grave."

Rosalyn whimpers. Not sure if she does or doesn't like my idea.

Regardless, I grip the shovel harder, ready to play ball. "Rosalyn, it will be okay."

My sister sniffles, clearly trying to find the words to convince me that I don't have to stay, but we both know that I do. Even if it means we'll never make hot cocoa together or taste test chips until midnight.

"Go home," I tell my sister, voice cracking. "Sneak up on Mom and fill her hand with whipping cream." It's a joke I played on Rosalyn once when she was asleep. "Insist that Mom buy you new music *every* week, and don't let her get away with that eighties stuff. Insist that she buy you songs that top the music charts. Okay?"

Rosalyn's voice makes this strangling noise as Ophelia's curtain swishes. *"Bolt the door shut once she's outside."* Looks like time's running out for Rosalyn's and my goodbye.

"But how can I trust Bastian to deliver Rosie safely?" He's the cruelest person I've ever met, and I've met a lot of douchebags in my life. And at this moment, slowly, ever so slowly, my heart feels like it's being nicked by a bowie knife. "Ophelia, you know he already threatened to . . ."

The aquariums around the room wobble as Ophelia's anger boils, just beneath the surface. *"Then he shall regret his choice."*

Okay. I have to hold onto this. Ophelia *won't* stand by idly while Bastian threatens to assault Rosie.

Leaning in, I kiss my baby sister on the forehead with traitory tears stinging my eyes. I'd rather die than see her hurt, and her soft skin's smoother than I expected—every single time.

Doing everything I can to keep the tremor outta my voice, I say, "Go with him, Rosie." I blink three more times real fast to make sure my eyes keep dry. "Don't be scared. Mom will take you out for milkshakes."

"I'm not going anywhere without you!" Rosalyn wails, her gaze a full two inches from mine, but *I* blinded her. I deserve this.

"Shh. It'll be okay."

I don't wanna send her off like this. Knots are building up in my stomach, but I need to stop being so gosh darn selfish with my goodbyes and send her off already.

Wrapping my arms, I whisper, "I love you more than fashion design."

It's dumb. No one's going to put that on a mug or T-shirt or jewelry. And I wish I could be clever enough to say something more poignant when Bastian grabs her by the arms and heaves her over his shoulder.

She's so terrified as she sobs, kicking and screaming.

Unable to watch her go, I turn to Luther, still in his aquarium, looking like a very dapper Sleeping Beauty. "You need to free him, too, Ophelia." I swallow the knot in my throat. "If I'm goin' to stay."

Ophelia whooshes and rattles the curtains like that should terrify me. *"I already told you, he's useless to me . . ."*

Not sure if that means she approves or doesn't approve of Luther's release.

Banking on the latter, I stumble over the broken glass and a slew of dead yellow moths to where the boy's lying.

Grabbing hold of the lid, I find that it's cemented shut. "Hey," I grunt. "Sleeping Beauty . . ." Tears burn in my eyes, but Luther's form lays lifeless, his ripped clothes covered in so many larvae.

Using arm muscles I didn't know I had, I secure the lip of the lid between my fingers—and *lift*.

Imma Black Canary.

Hmm. Stupid thing's a million pounds.

Still not budging.

Looks like I've gotta use the shovel Rosalyn used on me.

Spotting the salsa-stained tool a few paces behind me, I hobble over to it, grateful I don't have to deal with Bastian, but feeling even worse that I approved of him taking Rosie.

"If Bastian lays *one* hand on my sister . . ." I glance up at that stupid imprint in the curtain of Ophelia's face.

"I would never condone that," she says solemnly. *"He fell in love with me because he likes my subtle use of authority."*

Subtle?

"He knows very well that I would hang him out like his mother if he crossed me."

Still, it doesn't make sense. Why is he *still* obsessed with Ophelia after all this time? "What, you were head of the knitting committee or something?"

"To be sure, I had a title, Cate. I was to be the heiress of a great fortune. Of course, I only got in the position after poisoning my sisters. It was all very clandestine. I was the youngest, you see, and Sebastian helped me. I was only using him to get what I needed at the time. I had no idea that, after I refused Sebastian's proposal, Henrietta Pearl would use my same method and poison me."

"You people seriously need to find more intriguing murder weapons," I mutter. "Switch things up with every other kill in the very least . . ."

A few of the aquariums rattle, and last thing I need is body parts flowing through the air, so I put aside my judgment. "Okay! Okay. I guess, if you say that he'll honor what you say, I'm good. I believe you. I think. Just lemme free Luthy."

Not really seeing any other options, I seize the shovel and bring it down on Luther's glass case. I'm actually successful at sending the glass as far as Venus and Neptune the other way.

Soon as I'm able to gauge my handiwork, I find that, fortunately, no glass has embedded in Luthy's face.

"Hey!" I pat the beautiful boy's cheek. I don't like any of this, but here we are. "Wakey, wakey!"

Luther's eyes roll a little, but something tells me Ophelia won't be patient for any extended amount of time. So, I grab Luther's mama's blanket—and toss it at the guy.

Takes only a split second before Luther's sorrowful eyes bulge wide.

He swats at what's left of his mother before I'm able to pull the blanket away.

"Sorry." I can't help the laugh from my voice. "But we're on kind of a tight deadline . . ."

Luther sits up as little pieces of glass crumble beneath his hands and legs. He winces at what appears to be a collection of larvae on his left elbow that seem to be setting up The Day of the Dead festivities.

"What happened?" He glances at the curtain where, whaddaya know, Ophelia's face is currently missing.

The shovel in my left hand suddenly feels unnecessary. So I drop it. "I bartered. Bastian's runnin' Rosalyn to safety . . ."

Luther's eyes stretch wide—with a sheen of understanding, then . . . panic as he grabs hold of what remains of the aquarium and climbs out. The boy's moving relatively well, considering. "We need to find them." He glances round the war-zone of body parts, glass, and all the pretty yellow moths—some of them dead, some of them fluttering with torn wings.

Uh, I do not like the knot that's settling over my stomach, and I don't exactly like Luther's tone, either. "Why?"

Grabbing my hand, Luther pulls me to his chest, his body heat automatically a comfort to me. "Bastian's not the only thing out there who wants your sister, Cate."

"Who—wha—whaddaya mean?"

"My mother." Luther attempts to scrub the tired lines outta his face. "She wants Rosalyn for her nursery."

CHAPTER FORTY-SIX

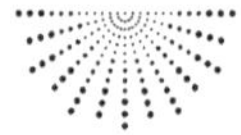

After Luther and I climb through a tunnel in the back, shadowy corner of the aquarium room—kinda cool, yay!— we end up in one of those montages in the movies.

The camera pans out.

The director showcases Arkansas' lush, green forests and hills that are rather roly-poly. You can't even get in the car without getting carsick round here. Just ask Rosie.

There's also the other matter of the bruised, smudged sky. Sure, the architecture looks electric, dynamic . . . though, in our case, the sandstone of Monkshood is visibly corroding.

To think that Ophelia chose to become a porous hunk of rock when she coulda been a wolf or lion . . . or moved onto a better place.

The black-winged moths fluttering before us tell me she's sicker, weaker than she's been the entire time. She's tried to do too much, between controlling Bastian, doing who knows what with Henrietta Pearl, and sustaining the entire house.

True, Ophelia's feasted on and torn apart I don't know

how many bodies, but it's like her power is hollow. It *will* erode, I pray.

Spotting the lonely garden spade we once used next to the greenhouse, I stoop down and grab it, just in case.

Gone are the days when I come to a fight empty-handed.

Feels good in my hands.

Lighter than the shovel, but still substantial in a way.

I still don't know if I should attempt to get outta here, but it sure feels nice to find a weapon. It's something I can do to take charge, anyway.

Luther grabs the pair of pruning shears I'd thrown at Bastian at one point, and, mmm, mmm, the boy's sexy when he turns into the "take charge" kind of Luthy.

Wonder what the boy's been thinking. Wonder if he's contemplated what it'll be like if I truly am permanently stuck here as Ophelia's battery.

Though that whole aquarium arrangement certainly isn't comfy. Wonder if there's any way we could pull a fast one on Ophelia and all three of us could escape . . . No, no, no. I can't. I won't even think it. There's too much at stake. I *can't* risk anything else happening to Rosalyn.

The east side of the house is the only part of the Estate I haven't seen. Wild pumpkins and squash line a weather-worn path, and I don't like the tautness of Luther's shoulders and arms. Even the wind lingers and hovers as if in stage fright.

No birds, no sun . . .

Just a drab, dull, expressionless sky.

We're so high up in relation to the other homes in the neighborhood I could *almost* see my house's chimney . . . if it weren't for the thick layer of mist and pollen still coating everything.

At the back corner of the house, we round a set of broken pillars, and a stone gazebo overgrown with leafless vines.

The old, stone path loops round a diseased oak with warts swelling from its leaves.

Suddenly, a dark, silvery shadow darts down our path.

Henrietta Pearl. Has to be.

As the air drifts and sours—smells like those stinky cherry trees—some movement down the path reveals two figures . . . struggling.

Through the jagged branches of the cedars, I can make out Rosalyn's pink and white polka-dot shirt, and she's flailing against Bastian's robed, muscular frame.

She's only about half his height, and she launches herself into his gut with a ferocity that pricks tears in my eyes. "TAKE ME BACK TO CATIE!"

Henrietta Pearl hovers above the pair—a wolf spider, hungry. She raises her black-winged arms, becoming the Grim Reaper, about to claim its prize.

Her arms thicken; elongate. She's like a six-foot-long vulture, swallowing its carrion from the roadside.

"ROSIE!" I scream.

Bastian snarls beneath his mother. No way he wants to give up his chance to be with Ophy. Teeth flashing, still in his human form, he nips at his mommy. And Luther stands there, pruning shears in hand, jabbing them where his mom scatters and dissipates.

Disgusted, Bastian kicks my sister in the ribs as Luther pales.

"She is IMPOSSIBLE!" Bastian screams.

Boy, he did not just do that. I'll sharp shoot him in the brain.

Robe billowing out, Bastian stalks toward the house while Henrietta Pearl reforms and descends upon Rosie. It's as if Bastian's hoping Ophelia will say he can leave my sister there and not bother with delivering her to safety.

Beneath Henrietta Pearl, my sister goes lifeless with stone

dead eyes. Luther feels her forehand with the back of his hand.

"Rosie?!" I scramble to be near them while Bastian throws his shoe at the house, yelling, "Forget about the brat! Just BE WITH ME!"

Rosalyn's fingers twitch, and Luther and I exchange frantic looks. Okay. She'll be okay. Dodging Henrietta Pearl, I lean down and scoop Rosalyn into my arms, cradling her head like she's a baby. But by doing so, Henrietta Pearl, above us, looms larger and that raven's croak contorts her uneven face.

Luther raises his shears to protect us, to bat her away, and, all the while, Ophelia doesn't so much as flicker her lights.

Stalking back to where I'm holding Rosie, Bastian riles back to kick her in the ribs or something easily as nasty. Luther cocks his shears, ready to swing, and while Bastian growls, I lean over to grab the garden spade.

Settling my baby sister on the ground, I grip the handle of the tool even harder. "Hey, Bastian." I ready to swing. "I found your queen of spades."

And with a strength I didn't know I had, I smack him upside the head.

Dude flies backward, flipping horizontally one-and-a-half times.

Ooh, musta had the wind working in my favor. Luther half laughs, half gasps, and his reaction is glorious, all right.

A little worse for wear, Bastian dusts off his robe and rolls to his feet. Fire flares in his cruel eyes and his fangs twist into long, sharp ropes. Black hair prickles along his neck and face, and he's becoming the Doberman.

The Doberman.

One more time.

I can stand by and wait for Dog Boy to *really* hurt Rosalyn, or I can handle him much more permanently.

Chuckling mid-shift, Bastian growls and his voice is deadly as strychnine. "You *really* think you can hurt me?"

"Well." I wriggle my left thumb, then, while Luther chuckles, jut the same thumb pointedly at my left eye. "That's what history says."

"You can forget about your sister being safe," Bastian spits. He opens his mouth to tear her apart, so I sprint toward him, spade like a spear in my hand. While I highly doubt there's *any* way I'll succeed, something about the wind shifts. My grit combines with Ophelia's power, giving us some pretty fantastic aim.

The metal tip of the spade severs the top half of Bastian's skull. His watermelon noggin gets a little slicey-slice as Luther gasps again, and Bastian tips over like a hollowed-out cedar.

Poor thang.

Everything falls still and silent while the top part of his head comes to a stop in the grass and leaves.

"Uh," I mutter to Ophelia, not sure if I should feel guilty about taking a page from her battle strategies. "Thanks?"

Her icy voice is like a cold shower. *"He was no longer compliant. It was his time . . ."* Stealthy wind flickers through the cedar branches, and I shiver as she combs through the other nearby wisps of greenery.

"But aren't you . . . like, weakened now?" You know, since she and Bastian were tied.

The garden tool spasmodically twitches in my hands. *"Sebastian is not the only one I can hurt with this spade . . ."* She points the tip at me, and then at Rosie, who's lying, catatonic, beneath Henrietta Pearl's elongated wings.

"What is your mom doing to her?" I ask Luther as he kneels down next to me.

"She's trying to keep her," Luther assesses the black translucence of his mother with guarded eyes.

"Well, she can't!"

He nods in ready agreement. "Nice one with the spade."

"You don't hate me for killing your brother?"

"I . . ." He grips the side of his hair. "Didn't see how far gone he was. He would never change."

Rosalyn's lips stretch wider and wider, almost rubbery, and, ohmygosh, *what* is happening? Luther's willow-wisp of a mother spreads into a dark streak of fog before barreling right between Rosalyn's teeth.

My sister's usually calm and easygoing eyes flit unnaturally wide.

Whaaat is Luther's mom doing inside her?

Henrietta Pearl utilizes Rosalyn's skinny arms by seizing me by the scruff of my dress and throwing me into one of the columns next to the house.

My head slams into sandstone painfully.

"She isn't for you!" Luther screams. But ol' Henrietta Pearl doesn't so much as look in his direction or blink. Luther grabs Rosalyn by the shoulders that I'm still putting together are now his mama's shoulders. "Go *back* to your nursery!"

But Henrietta Pearl hums her dissonant tune—the one Luther played earlier—and my sister's lips aren't her own— they aren't her own!—as Henrietta Pearl twists them into a smile that means she intends to inflict pain.

I tug on the ripped shirt on Luther's arm. "How do we make her stop? How do we get her to leave Rosie?"

It takes three full seconds before Luther's able to take a deep breath and clear his head. He scrubs his palm over his forehead. "We have to remind her of what she loves more than anything."

"The babies?"

He's nodding. "All she cares about is her 'grandchildren.'" Standing, he twists the pruning shears in his hands while he finds steady feet. "Those stupid dolls are real to her. And Rosalyn's young enough that she thinks she needs her, too."

"Okay." Wishing more than anything that all this was over, I look down to Henrietta Pearl inside Rosie. She's gone on to swaying back and forth. It's as if she's sitting in her rocking chair, humming her creepy melody.

I'll get to the "babies" and hopefully convince Henrietta Pearl to jump outta Rosalyn and back into the nursery. That should work, right?

Luther's hair's a beautiful disaster as his teeth clamp in anxiety. "I'll stay with your sister," he promises me. But can I trust him, really and truly?

"Maybe *you* should go!" I don't know if we have time for arguing.

He throws out an arm. "I can, if you want."

"No." My reply on the fly. "It has to be me."

Ophelia can't think that I'm even thinking about going back on my word. She would want me inside.

Everything hinges on me saving Rosie.

CHAPTER FORTY-SEVEN

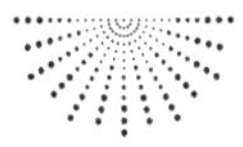

HERE I THOUGHT I was coming over to make out with a boy. Instead, I've scalped Bastian, watched my sister get stuffed by a ghost, and pretty much made a deal with a house to be a frankenbattery.

Really, I'd love nothing more than to grab my sister and head to Chuck-E-Cheese. We'd stuff our faces with pizza and listen to the video games at the arcades, but I can't trust that I'd be faster than Ophelia's witchery and vines.

Gosh golly, whose idea was it for me to climb this tree?

The leaves are multi-lobed, like a red oak's, but these thorns? They're like a honey locust's, about three inches long, the whole shebang.

My elbows and hands are getting pretty scraped.

Hey, if I'm able to free Rosalyn and stay with Ophy, maybe I could work alongside Luther as his master gardener of the east . . .

Though, I'm pretty darn sure I'll be as mobile as ol' Robert once Ophelia has me.

Do I really have to be stuffed in that aquarium again?

That would suck in a lot of ways.

Wonder if she'll keep me in one piece . . .

By the time I'm able to make it to the window on the second floor, I'm feelin' all sorts of dweeby. I totally forgot about Granny's window being covered by vines. I could see if this branch—or another tree—could take me to the nursery, but that window had bars.

I try tugging on the closest vine, but it doesn't budge. It's nearly the size of my arm, but not nearly half as pretty.

As I pull on another branch, the bark comes off all brittle.

"How do I get through?" I shout down to Luther, but he's so far down and focused on Rosalyn and his mother, I don't think he can hear me.

Chainsaw. I need a chainsaw.

Ooh, the branches are suddenly parting. Ophelia's stretching apart her sneaky tentacles to let me inside. Guess, in terms of containing Henrietta Pearl, we're on the same side.

Every second that passes, I am not so sure that I like seeing how Ophelia and I are getting to be a stronger team. I mean, we both like taking off body parts. There's something seriously wrong with people who have our name.

Once Ophelia's vines are neatly folded and stacked outta the way, I stretch out a foot and my arms . . . and dive-bomb inside.

I sorta land on my head, but it ain't anything I haven't felt already.

Grandma's room . . . well, it doesn't look exactly the same. The big black hole's still there, but it's shrunk to more of a gourd's size. And the inside looks more like a peanut buttery membrane. The walls have little droplets of moisture covering them as if Ophelia's sweating. Shuddery breaths emanate from the plaster, and the few crocheted doilies still hanging on the walls tremor—in fear or exhaustion. Low blood sugar or something.

Actually, this could be good. If her severed connection to Bastian truly has weakened her, maybe there's hope for me to escape.

Though she helped me sever that connection, so maybe I better not entertain such an idea.

Inside the room, Ophelia's turnip-sized heart still pumps, a dying lamp in a monster's twilight. I'd go ahead and stab it right here, right now, but I *can't* risk Henrietta Pearl not vacating Rosie.

Hmm. Gotta grab a doll. Threaten to hurt it . . .

This better be the way to get Henrietta Pearl back inside.

So . . . not willing to think of the dangers and risks I'm taking, I hightail it back to the nursery.

The carpet's kinda rollin' in hills, and I happen upon a few new gnarled vines.

They twist in ropes, beetles scuttling over stems and in and around larvae.

Luckily, the nursery door's open wide. The trickiest part is knowing which doll to grab and threaten to lure HP.

Between the two in the crib—and the three others in various buggies—I go with the one with the sunken skull, still on the floor, since Henrietta cradled that one and seemed to like her—him—anyway.

Scooping it up, I tuck it in my arm like a football and hightail it back to Granny's.

Vines in the hall have grown bigger—clunkier. Is Ophelia showing off or something? But they break with every step I take.

When I make it back to Granny's room, only thing I can think to do is hold the doll over the hole. "Got your baby doll, HP!"

Turning the baby with its cute suspenders and hair combed to the side, I shimmy it back and forth, simultaneously praying that no one's videotaping me.

I do the shimmy-doll thing for a full thirty seconds, but Henrietta doesn't so much as coast to the window to watch my charade.

"Oops!" I dip the doll's toe in the "peanut butter," which churns and broils, hungry. The membrane darkens the doll's toe a little, but still no HP . . .

I could destroy Ophelia's very open and available heart —'tis practically begging me—but I *can't* risk her hurting Rosie. The second Henrietta Pearl comes through, I'll work with Ophelia to shut the window, and hopefully, Luther can get my sister to safety.

Once she's through, Henrietta can't float *back* through the window to get us, right?

Er, but she's a ghost . . .

I am definitely seein' a flaw in every single plan I make.

Worrying my lip, I make the doll do a cartwheel over the lava pit. A backflip. Barani. All the fancy, gymnasticky things.

Seeing as no freaky ghost lady comes sailing through the window, I toss the doll aside.

Rosalyn's down there, having supernatural seizures, and I'm up here doing doll routines.

Ophelia's bright, brown, demented heart pulses not unlike a strobe light. I could destroy it. Ophelia and Henrietta Pearl could be linked. But if they're not . . . I don't even wanna think about what Ophelia would do to Rosie.

A *tap-tap* sounds on the window. Worry lines mark Luther's eyes while he climbs inside.

My heart seizes to see him abandoning his post. "Why aren't you down there with my sister?"

Luther frowns down at the doll I just tossed to a leg of the desk where I was nearly blood sacrificed. "Isn't it working?"

I grab the stupid doll and dip its other foot in the gobbledygook. "Nope. See?"

"You need to *really* hurt it." Luther jumps from the window to join me.

"He said non-creeptastically . . ."

Sighing, the boy looks more tired and worn-out than even Mom is after an eighty-hour workweek. I don't think he'll ever be fully awake and healthy. I suppose it's because he's over a hundred and thirty years old and Ophelia's the only thing keepin' him alive.

"A true injury is the only thing that will garner Ophelia and my mother's attention." Luther's thigh comfortably brushes mine as he crouches beside me. "They are too far gone to understand anything else."

"What, you mean, like body part removal? 'Cause that happens to be my specialty."

Luther nods sagely, hinting that every second of my damaged yet well-intentioned life comes down to this moment.

To truly hurt a doll baby.

Not wanting to waste another second, I drop the doll into the hole, cementing my not-so future serial killer days.

CHAPTER FORTY-EIGHT

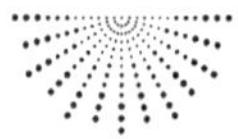

A MIX of high and low tones rip through the air as Henrietta Pearl comes barreling through the window like a geyser shootin' through tectonic plates.

She's much less of a mother than a demonic bird with her spidery eyes and skin that's so thin it actually reminds me of moonscape.

Diving through my stomach, Henrietta sends ice buckets roiling through me. She plummets through my hips, icy fingers leaving an imprint on my tailbone.

She drops to the hole beneath.

Aw, she's plunging for her baby.

At the window, Luther waves all urgent-like for me to escape. "Come on, Cate!"

But that wasn't mine and Ophelia's deal. I can't slip through the window now. I swore to be her battery . . .

Luther's brave and somber eyes wind their way through mine. "You *need* to get your sister to safety."

But there's no telling how soon Ophelia would deafen or do anything else horrible to Rosie if I went back on my word at this point. "I've already accepted that I have to stay . . ."

Marching over to me, Luther gruffly grabs both my shoulders and leans right up to my face. "She's at her weakest point. You *have* to go. Now!"

"You *know* she'll hurt Rosie!"

Luther bites back a curse I'd love to hear actually. "I'll distract her."

I arch an eyebrow. "How?" But then I shake my head. "I can't risk it. I deserve to stay."

Luther's grip tightens round my shoulders, and he gives me a firm shake. "You *deserve* to get out of here, Cate."

"You don't know anything about me!"

It's not true, but I say it, 'cause self-punishment, consequences, and karma are a thing. I may have admitted that I blinded my sister, but he doesn't know about my other faults. How I lick the salt off my chips before eating them. How, sometimes, I use my illness to get out of having to wait in the lunch line. There's worse stuff, but it's not currently coming to mind.

Luther not-so-gently grabs hold of my cheeks. "You have deserved to get out all along." His voice is a hush, but his eyes blaze in a riptide. "*Stop* punishing yourself for what happened to your sister. We all make mistakes."

But all I can do is look down the hole, all my words running away from me. Luther's hit the mark—how'd he hit it so easily?—but if I *don't* sacrifice myself, how'm I goin' to prove to Rosalyn that I'm sorry?

Besides, I can't risk her getting hurt.

Henrietta Pearl spins round and round in that peanut butter membrane as I suggest my final idea.

"Maybe we should stab the heart." I boost a shoulder, not wanting to be greedy.

But Luther firmly shakes his head. "We can't. You and Ophelia are tied."

Wha—? We are?

Well . . . after the last hundred-some-odd hours, it makes sense, actually.

I'm outta options. I don't know what to do, and the turnipy root keeps pulsing from brown to gray. If I stab her and Ophelia gets mad, I risk hurting Rosie. Also, if I stab her, it seems that I could *also* actually die . . .

God, Maker-Man from upstairs, will you help me make the right choice?

"Caaaaaate." From a gas lamp on the table, Ophelia flickers her weak light. *"I wouldn't disappoint me . . ."*

Henrietta Pearl continues to swim in that hole as crows emerge from her dress, molting. Good thing she's not in the mood to be hasty.

How exactly, though, are Ophelia and I are tied?

"I know Ophelia used her medicine on me," I suggest helpfully.

"No . . ." Luther shakes his head as the floor rumbles so hard another one of the framed doilies slips from its hook and crashes to the ground, shattering.

Eyes darting round in panic, Luther takes a super hasty step toward me. "Remember my earlier to plan? To make her permanently go to sleep? That's the only thing that will work, Cate. If she dies, you die . . ."

Ophelia's walls rumble louder, and he has to be making this up.

We aren't *that* tied.

Taking my hand, Luther promises, "I'll wear her out."

Everything's been so tense I can't help gasping in a tease. "Luther Dvorak, how do you propose doing that?"

Luther rolls his eyes. "Not in *that* way." Rubbing his hands along the backs of my arms, he sends me another wave of glorious heat. "I shall . . . slow her down. I won't let up. I *need* you to trust me."

But the boy's been so ambivalent the entire time. He said

he wanted me to go, only to woo the heck outta me. He poisoned me with the tea, then he threw it out when he thought I was about to do the exact same thing.

Tears burning in my eyes for the millionth time, I reach down and grab hold of one of the porcelain figurines. "I don't care if we're tied. I can't risk my sister getting hurt. All that matters is she's safe."

Luther gruffly grabs my arm and snatches the figurine from my hand. "That is *not* all that matters!" Eyes simmering in a volcano, he steps up so close, he's either going to bite my head off . . . or kiss me.

Reaching out with his manly fingers, Luther caresses the side of my face. After only three seconds, he leans in and presses his lips to *my* lips, giving me hot flashes, and I'm only sixteen. "You deserve to be safe."

Tears threaten to tear down the floodgates in my eyes, but he can't mean that. He can't mean that! Like he said—I am semi-evil and obviously tied to the ripper of this place.

Brushing his tender lips along my ear, Luther causes a friggin monsoon to rush through me. "*You.*" He runs his thumb along my jawline. "Should be admired and protected and cherished and taken on that bloody cross-country train ride."

My throat cracks. "Mom would never say okay." I clear my throat, refusing to cough. "Plus, it would be too complicated with Rosalyn and me."

"She doesn't even know where you are."

"She came over!" Tears lurch from my eyes.

Luther gives me a sympathetic look that melts every square inch of my heart. I only wanted a tête-à-tête with the boy, so that's saying something.

I could deck him right now; he's not supposed to make me *feel* such things, but he did, and he does, and I'm bloody well going insane!

Wait . . .

"Bastian . . . he pretended to be Mom, right?" I close my hand over my lips, thinking through earlier things.

"No one robbed your house." Luther nods, holding my hands firmly. Ah, his hold is so surefire and steady. "Cate." The boy's never sounded more self-assured my entire visit. "You have been missing for seven days."

Mom's new coat.

She didn't want to see inside the house.

That terrible, horrible way she refused to hug me . . .

None of that was real?

She doesn't hate me?

I stagger—nearly stagger into the peanut butter hole of mysteries.

Looking to Ophelia's heart one more time, all I can think of is Rosalyn, lying, all alone, on that cold, hard ground outside.

I can't risk losing her.

I can't risk losing her!

"You'll hold Ophelia back?" As I accept his final offer to stay, my eyes sting at the thought of abandoning him in this place.

Luther nods, and I bite my bottom lip.

Okay. Gosh, boy, I love you. Okay!

Round up the horses and chariots, 'cause it's time to save Rosie!

Scampering toward the window, I suddenly run back to give the boy the fiercest, most grateful kiss of my life. Kissing doesn't really give him justice, but I do my best to maul him long and hard before running back to the window and lifting a leg.

"You're glad you met me?" It's a selfish question, but I ask it anyway.

Luther nods twice, real quick, eyes shining, but Henrietta

Pearl's thick molasses frame is slinking outta yonder hole with the charred baby doll clutched to her breast tightly. And her breathing's a garbage disposal, yeesh.

Spinning, but not before locking eyes with me one more time, Luther grabs one of the porcelain figurines—and drives it straight through his beautiful, salted caramel-colored neck.

"Nooo!" My jaw unhinges, and my tongue falls lame.

Luther didn't—he couldn't—

"I am ready to earn back the privilege of shifting," he tells Ophelia, his eyes zoning in on her heart's faint pulsing. "Please. I beg you to reconnect with me."

His hands ball into fists, proving that this request is the last thing he truly wants, but he's doing it—the big, stupid lump is doing it for me.

Luther's blood dribbles round the porcelain figurine, and the ceramic absorbs it, proof that Ophelia's drinking up his life force thirstily.

"*Yyyessss!*" Ophelia hisses from the pea-green wallpaper—and the lilac side.

The hardwood rumbles, and the bed looks like it's about to sink through the floor, there's so much quaking. I don't want to leave him—Luther's finally the man I knew he could be—but he's already being swallowed up as Ophelia wraps him up in a cocoon with her sketchy vines.

No arms are poppin' off. It's almost like a hug, the way she brings him to her heart.

There's nothing to do but climb back outside.

CHAPTER FORTY-NINE

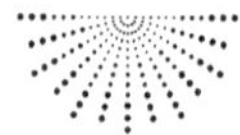

ONCE UPON A TIME, there was a girl who was blind. She was wildly creative, talented, insightful—and she had an older sister.

That older sister was me.

The problem with being the older sister, though, is sometimes you lie.

You lie about your cystic fibrosis.

You lie or hide the truth about how you unintentionally caused your sister to be blind.

Chances are, though, if you're as good of a liar as me, you also don't fess up about a slew of other things.

Like, how Mom, despite being obsessed with houses, really is pretty patient and loving. She doesn't go to band concerts? Yeah, 'cause I begged her not to go and gave her the wrong date on purpose last time.

And you lie about how there are times—just like any other kid—Rosalyn can be tricky. Not anything out of the normal, mind you, but hard. Stubborn. We can *all* be hard and stubborn at times, right?

While I lift Rosalyn into my arms and step over the brittle, leaning fence that stood so tall before Ophelia stretched herself too far and got too greedy, I have to allow myself to think of a final moment. My finishing memory . . .

About a month ago, Rosalyn wasn't too thrilled about leaving the house or going to the library. Deciding to pull a fast one, the lil' trickster decided to up and leave her cane at home.

She seemed to think that I wouldn't make her go in for her books if she didn't have her cane.

Not willing to let her off the hook and despite her protests, once we got to the parking lot, I grabbed Rosalyn's arm and guided her inside.

'Course, the devil grumbled on and on about not wanting to read in braille—"It's too hard, Catie!"—so I promised we'd get frozen yogurt afterward, just like the last time.

When Rosalyn grumbled about the weather, I told her it was the perfect temperature for a light sweater—which she was wearing. And when she tried claiming that she needed to go to the bathroom, I told her I knew she didn't, 'cause we went *right* before we came.

After we made it through the double library doors, visiting the information desk didn't prove easy.

I asked the librarian for the book I'd reserved for Rosie, and learning it hadn't arrived quite yet, Rosalyn, along with her already overwhelmed emotions, sprung a leak.

She raised her arm, struck the pencil jar, and it flew to the tile, shattering.

Pencils and pens skipped and rolled across the tile while a few onlookers watched, faces blank.

The kindly librarian jumped up to help us and gather everything, but I assured the gentle soul that we—I—could handle it.

Except Rosalyn wouldn't stop making a scene.

She kept stamping her foot, grumbling about the fact that

I *made* her come, and they didn't even have her book on puppies.

"Seuss!" she wailed on the top of her lungs. "I want to read Seuss!"

I already knew they didn't have any Dr. Seuss books in braille at this library, and I didn't know if I should break this to her then—or later.

Desperate, and in tears, Rosalyn grabbed a pencil and jabbed it into her leg.

I couldn't believe she did it. Luckily, no one saw what she did but me, and upon further inspection, I found that the tip of the pencil didn't actually go in further than Rosalyn's pant leg. Whew, that really got my pulse going.

Rosalyn still didn't know how to live in the dark. She was still learning, and I *hated* that I'd been the one that caused her misery in the first place.

Wrapping her in my arms, along with her crusty Pinocchio sweater she wouldn't take off that entire week, I told her that it was okay.

It was okay to be angry.

It was okay to feel that things weren't fair because they weren't most of the time.

I told her that once, I cut the cord on Mom's cell phone charger when *I* was angry, and if the library didn't get any Seuss books in braille soon, I'd TP the entire place.

Rosalyn laughed a little at that, but I didn't know if I could keep the good mood going.

Slipping the pencils back into the broken jar, I handed the entire ordeal back to the librarian who didn't mention that the jar needed to be thrown away. I took Rosalyn by the hand and whispered, "Let's do some puzzles, Rosie."

And just like that, my little sister stopped screaming.

I didn't think of myself as a miracle worker. Again, Rosalyn wouldn't have been in this predicament if it hadn't been for me, but we did those fatty raised puzzles with the obvious edges for hours. She did grow upset when one of the pieces came up missing, but I stayed with her. 'Cause that's what big sisters do. We help our younger sisters traverse the scariest parts of the forest, 'cause we're often the ones who put them there in the first place.

It wasn't until Rosalyn and I made our way back up to the front desk—with three different puzzles in tow, and a stuffed animal I'd beg the librarian to let us borrow—that I got to meet Luther Dvorak for the very first time.

I was fumbling with the puzzles and ended up dropping my card when this cute boy with leather patches on the elbows of his jacket scooped it up with this foreign grace.

Cate comma Ophelia, Luther's soulful eyes scanned the first line.

Embarrassed that he already knew about my old-fashioned name, I casually pretended I didn't care. I boosted a shoulder. "Weird, right?"

Luther's lips twitched in amusement, his dark, somber eyes dancing beneath the library's stark lights. "On the contrary..."

That right there is the first time I met the Dvorak who would change me. The one who helped me see that I could stop punishing myself all the time.

The truth is, I'm not so sure why it took me so long to accept that I don't need to throw myself in front of a train for blinding Rosie. Running head-first into danger won't make her better. Laughing about it certainly won't turn me into a martyr or a saint.

Still, I do know that as I carry Rosalyn down the dark street, a teensy part of me finally accepts that I *do* deserve to be safe.

Part of me knew it all along. I just refused to believe that the courtesy should be afforded to someone like me.

I may have been the sole person responsible for causing Rosalyn's blindness. But, even at home, I have been atoning for my mistake.

I play with her instead of spending time with my friends.

I feed her breakfast when she's not a breakfast gal and can be *impossible* to please.

Actually, I don't know if I have to earn the privilege of being safe. Aren't we born with it? I must have squandered that privilege, right?

Regardless, Rosalyn *is* my sister, and I love her more than *anything*. Just 'cause she got hurt, doesn't mean that I deserve to be drawn and quartered 'til I go to the big place.

Raindrops ping gutters and slanted roofs. The sky's a tortured combination of roiling purple and green, but Rosalyn and I are getting closer and closer to home.

To a cornflower, baby blue sky.

CHAPTER FIFTY

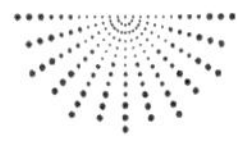

MAIL CALL!

No one writes letters nowadays.

Except, apparently, they do, 'cause a Washington-era piece of paper's in my mailbox, and, whaddaya know? It's addressed to me.

Linen paper and . . . calligraphy?

No. Freaking. Way.

I thought Luther's whole stabby trick and getting wrapped up in Ophelia's vines would mean he isn't still alive, but . . . he or Ophelia must've had another trick up his or her sleeve.

Tucking the letter in the crook of my arm, I slam the mailbox lid shut—gotta shove it real hard or it falls open, Hungry Hippo style—and tear off for the house.

I'll need to read this one in privacy.

Of course, ever since I left Monkshood, there *have* been a few questions rattling around in this head o' mine.

For one, why *did* Ophelia look just like me? Was she born with my face, or . . . did she simply choose to look like I do to make me freak?

It's the question I've been asking myself for several weeks.

Once Rosalyn and I came home that day, Mom wrapped us in her arms and immediately called the police. She'd been scouring the neighborhood for days. She filed a missing person's report the moment she realized I wasn't home that first morning. She thought she'd lost me.

What's really crazy is Mom actually *knew* about my dream to go on a cross-country train ride. Once Dad left, my three-year-old self became obsessed with trains. I believed that if we got on one, we'd find Daddy.

While Mom always felt that kind of trip was too expensive—not to mention complicated with Rosalyn's and my health issues—after getting us home and settled, she and I sat down and picked a day next year to go on the train.

We'll finally feel the glaciers in Montana's Glacier National Park. Absorb the wind on our faces on the Space Needle. Hear the hubbub and bustle in Times Square. Sometimes I have to pinch myself, 'cause the mere idea feels like another lie.

It won't be what anyone would consider a perfect trip—we'll have to hire a personal nurse to tend to my medications and get special permission to bring my equipment and everything, but Mom promises she *will* make it happen. She said, ever since she thought she lost us girls, she decided to do more with us. Even the hard things.

We've picked out new patterns to sew, Rosalyn and me. She's asked that I sew twin dresses in aquamarine. Actually, I detest the color, but . . . anything for Rosie.

Once upstairs in my room, I finally feel brave enough to smell the letter I *know*, the boy somehow sent me.

Smells like his licorice breath, and the exact scent isn't one I've been able to find.

The thin outline of a Monkshood flower is faintly water-marked on the other side . . .

Closing my bedroom door, I-Spy Rosalyn currently tucked in, knees folded up, and reading in my window seat.

She's got her headphones on. The girl doesn't even notice me.

"Hey, girlie," I say.

"Hey," she says, in a zone. She's in her own world. Perfect timing.

Carefully unfolding the letter, I perch on the side of my bed, heart thwapping. Looking to the door once more to make sure Mom isn't going to interrupt, I open the letter.

Cate Ophelia, the first line reads.

You asked me why Ophelia could not be killed. I said it was because you and Ophelia are tied, but I did not have a chance to explain how or why. I may get some of the details wrong, but it is how I remember them. Ophelia told me the night after you left, and ever since then, I have endeavored to write you the truth in privacy.

Nervous she might interrupt, I glance up at Rosalyn once again to make sure she's settled. She's got such a deep look of concentration on her face, she's got that little wrinkle on her forehead. Girl's fine.

A long, long time ago, a beautiful girl who looked <u>exactly</u> like you died. The girl's shock and sorrow were so intense that her emotions took root amongst the Monkshood flowers, grew, and splintered from her grave. While Bastian and I believed only the family grounds were impacted by Ophelia's reawakening, her influence stretched much farther than any of us thought—she burrowed beneath the soil, passing house after house until she ran out of grief.

It was on the front yard of a little house with an open mailbox that Ophelia laid her influence in a single seed.

That seed grew to be a Monkshood flower. And your mother,

believing it to be a bluebonnet, plucked it, and sniffed the bloom. According to Ophelia, that simple gesture imbued her with the child you would be.

Uh . . . That makes sense. Totally.

I know what you are thinking. This is complete and utter madness, right?

Ophelia claims you were born nine months later, and her influence was so powerful, she was able to convince your mother to give you her name. Your grandmother's name may truly have been Ophelia . . . or Ophelia may have convinced your mother to believe that lie. Do you happen to know which it might be? Search your family's books. This is a mystery I believe is worth solving.

Regardless of the outcome, Ophelia claims you *are* her. *A part of her, anyway. Though I must tell you, I could not more strongly disagree.*

You are most amiable while she is not. You are not liberal with the truth while Ophelia adores parading and twisting the truth into any version she likes. Simply put, Ophelia lives *to destroy lives.*

You protect your sister. Ophelia only cares about herself, and she has always *been this way.*

While she may have begun as an amiable person—when she was in boarding school, anyway—she was murdered by my family. I may not have taken any part in it, but I should never have invited you to Monkshood in the first place. I wanted to, I adore that I had the privilege of spending time in your company, but I should not *have placed you in such grave danger. It was selfish, and, for that, you have my deepest of apologies.*

You met my father. Rather, you saw his remains. My goal was to nurse him back to health, but when I betrayed Ophelia in my attempts to free you and Rosalyn, she murdered him while, I believe, he clung on for dear life. I had hoped that perhaps his *spirit would visit us once she killed him so mercilessly, but she must not have wanted him to stay. She only keeps those she likes. And for* *that, I shall never forgive her. I am doing everything in my power to keep her in a deep sleep. While my father spent my family's fortune, thus leaving us penniless, he was <u>always</u> a loving father to me.*

He wanted no part in my mother's methods.

Neither do I.

Cate, I need you to know that you are the most selfless and bravest girl I have ever had the privilege of knowing. I started falling in love with you from the moment you aided your sister at that library. Even more so when you stood up to Bastian, Ophelia, and me.

While it was originally my brother's and my idea to find a replacement for Ophelia back when we foolishly thought we could leave, she bided her time for you to become of age. Then, when she saw you and Rosalyn driving to the library, she sent me to retrieve you, her power only strong enough to support me outside Monkshood for a single day.

The truth is, when I met you, I foolishly believed that you were worth trapping so that my father and I might go free. When I saw you and Ophelia had identical faces, I assumed your personalities must be the same.

It wasn't until you were in our clutches, giving that speech about salsa and my future tomato babies that I knew you were truly selfless and kind. Someone who made me laugh, which I had long believed to be an impossible feat.

It is for these reasons that I put my selfish ambitions aside. My father and I are from another era. We do not belong in this world—especially when it comes at the expense of you and your sister's lives.

I am <u>so</u> sorry for how my brother behaved.

Cate, you must promise me to look in the mirror—an unblemished mirror—and tell yourself <u>every</u> single day, "I am worthy of being safe."

You don't didn't believe that at first, did you? Oh, how your habit of constantly placing yourself in danger irked me. I suppose that is how I fell in love with you in the first place.

Though I believe you know it deep down, each of us has an innate value that we were given by our Maker even before we were born. Nothing can diminish that reality.

I do plan on getting out. When I do, imagine me resting with my father in our mountains of black glass in the Armenian countryside.

Truly, I am better for knowing you. You are a beautiful, harrowing hallucination that shall haunt me the rest of my days.

Always and forever yours,

Luther Dvorak

I close the letter and tuck it in my back pocket, fingers tremoring slightly. I'll wait to hide his note when I know there's no chance that Rosalyn's peeking.

Aww, Luther! You make me want to go to Regency-era balls and sip nontoxic tea. I miss your beautiful hands that caressed the piano keys, and I miss your layers. I miss your lips that brushed along my ear, sending me delicious, skittery shimmers of heat.

Mostly, I miss his ability to help me see the good in myself. Always. That's the hardest part for a lot of us, isn't it? We can see the good in everybody else, but when it comes to ourselves . . . zip! It disappears completely.

We all need encouraging, selfless people like Luther in our lives.

Sighing, and putting all fanciful thoughts aside, I decide that I'm ready to leave my daydream. Glancing at Rosalyn, I realize she's started to hum a different melody.

I do my best not to make a sound while I perch next to her. I lay my head on her shoulder, 'cause I know that song. We learned it from the same place.

Do I believe Luther and Ophelia's story?

Am I "part" of her?

Pffft. I'm my own person. Always will be.

Though . . . I suppose we're *all* tied to evil or tragedy in some way. Bastian's innate goals weren't bad—he simply wanted to marry a girl and raise a family. Henrietta Pearl wanted what most future grandparents want—grandbabies. Luther's father wanted to go back to his homeland. But these conflicting desires came to a dramatic clash when a young woman from the eighteen hundreds was murdered for not going along with someone else's dreams.

Our job is to rise above the drama. Believe in and never forget our innate worth *that came from our Maker*, Luther reminded me.

Dude, we all get to be our own people—despite the naysayers who wanna stick us in bags of bones or aquariums or crochet us into little skin doilies.

Plus, we've always got music, which can work wonders for changing our moods and bettering things.

My music—Rosalyn's music—is the song Luther played on the piano, that same song Henrietta Pearl hummed when she overtook Rosie.

It might be macabre, I know some would consider it haunting, but it's a reminder of what we've learned, and it's the song Rosalyn's currently humming.

So I up and decide to hum it, too.

'Cause it's the new soundtrack of our lives.

ACKNOWLEDGMENTS

All along while writing this book, I knew two people would see this book. Cammie and Janet, THANK YOU for editing my crazy haunted house book. I knew my story would be in crazy capable hands, and knowing this gave me the gumption to put in all the time.

Cammie, thanks for helping me level up the title *and* for the amazing cover. Remember our awesome work sessions in those matching recliners? It was my favorite. Really, I know that I couldn't have delivered this work without you.

My beautiful family, I love you, I love you! You are so understanding and patient when I disappear in my room. B, A, and L, I hope, even though I tend to get a little obsessive with all of this that you'll continue to develop your love of reading. You're often an inspiration to me when you read your books!

Toni, Karin, and Linda, remember when we went to the McFarland house and Thistle Hill? See! I added all the details, from Henrietta Pearl's dress to the nursery.

Tamara and Hillary, our little trip to the Crescent Hotel sure did give me some stellar ideas, including the bumpy floors and the shawl on the rocking chair. Thank you for taking me there! Vanessa, thanks for telling me that you're excited to read this book!

Also, a huge thanks to all those who trust me enough to spend a few hours in my morbid little worlds. You are my people. I couldn't imagine doing this without you.

ABOUT THE AUTHOR

Mary Gray balances dark and twisty plots with faith-based messages. Some of her best ideas come when she's lurking in the woods, experimenting with frightening foods, or pushing her kids on the tire swing. She is the author of several fiction and nonfiction titles and the co-owner of Monster Ivy Publishing. Please find her by following her on social media and becoming a Monster Ivy Insider at monsterivy.com/contact.

HUSH, NOW FORGET - two sisters team up with a pair of hottie hunters to unveil the truth about the Blurred Ones and what they really are.

SLEEP, DON'T FRET - The Abram sisters head out to New Orleans to contend with some witch doctors and Raylan's ruthless sister.

RISE, TAKE FLIGHT - Unwilling to stand around and wait while Eva's been taken over by one of the Despairity, Frost works tirelessly with Beau and Leo to figure out how to free her sister.

OUR SWEET GUILLOTINE - a young executioner falls for the daughter of a woman he had to kill…

HER DARK FANTASY: A PREQUEL TO OUR SWEET GUILLOTINE - A short story prequel to French Revolution-era novel, OUR SWEET GUILLOTINE. Young Tempeste witnesses an executioner break apart her mother's feet in an attempt to extract a confession.

THE DOLLHOUSE ASYLUM - a group of teenagers are granted asylum from the apocalypse, only to be forced to reenact some of the most famous, tragic literary couples… or die.

THE DEVILS YOU MEET ON CHRISTMAS DAY - a short story anthology about the outliers, the murderers, the misunderstood, and the forgotten.

HOW TO WRITE FAITH-BASED MESSAGES FOR A SECULAR MARKET - for secular writers who hope to incorporate messages of hope and faith.

HOW TO WRITE CLEAN YET SCINTILLATING ROMANCE - bodice rippers are some of the most lucrative books in the industry. So what if you write books that aren't as steamy?

HOW TO WRITE DARK AND TWISTY BOOKS TO SHOWCASE THE LIGHT - in this brief nonfiction booklet, Mary discusses a psychological and scriptural basis for tackling darker books, some

of her favorite techniques for mastering the craft, and how to show
the strength of God's light.

OUR SWEET GUILLOTINE

CHAPTER 1

Only the nobles have the luxury of losing their heads.

That's the way it used to be, anyway. Now, the crowd twists and turns like maggots packed inside a dead mule's body. And I cannot help but smile, for at last we have our weapon that offers death with the softest of caresses for rich and poor alike.

Our sweet Killing Machine.

The sun's rays splash against the high blade suspended between twin red posts, and I lick the sweat from my upper lip, greedily. *He is going to die. A stranger, true enough, but he is set to die the way you should have, Maman. We've done it. We have our painless Killing Machine.*

Because I've no doubt stolen from, cut, or maimed at least a dozen townspeople in this square, I duck my head, careful not to make eye contact with a single soul in the Place de Greve. The last thing I need is another squabble with a fish wife or cobbler over a mangy trout or shoe they didn't need anyway.

I wind past boys tossing buttons and black-robed clergy clutching rosary beads. It isn't until I've veered around a cart full of potatoes and a slew of toy soldiers scattered on the ground that a pit rises in my stomach. *It's supposed to be* you *enjoying this tender mercy. Where you never writhe and sway and gasp for breath—please, God, make it stop. Stop stop stop, I am screaming for mercy.*

"Tempeste?"

Unwittingly, I spin at the sound of my name. Before I can hide my stringy hair and dirt-stained face, I lock eyes with a girl I've known for half a decade.

Charlotte, my friend. *My enemy.*

I could muse over the time we spent together transcribing scrolls at the convent, or the fact that we swapped secrets in the dead of night when we should have been sleeping, but the heat of what she did crawls like a hungry parasite through my body. She tattled—tattled like a rat—which only ended up hurting the kindest of souls I have ever known and my one true ally.

Choosing to be as stoic as Charlotte, I lift my chin, taking in her carefully manicured curls. Curls, I might add, which I had managed with a fine pair of scissors to obliterate while she was sleeping.

"I see your hair grew back well enough," I say almost sweetly.

Charlotte doesn't bat an eyelash. "And I see you've taken a fall since the convent."

So I haven't bathed except for the icy cold fingers of a stream, and my dress has become so thin and torn that one can see my skin through the sleeves. Well, with Charlotte's lavender gown and matching feather bonnet, she might as well be a peacock strutting about during mating season.

Regardless, I cannot help wondering why she is in Paris at all. She always planned on returning home to rectify a harm done to her family. But to ask why she's here instead of there would denote that I actually care, that I haven't forgotten her painful past which has been seared like a brand into my memory.

I dig into the folds of my dress to rub my thumb over the cool paring knife I stole from an apple vendor earlier this week. Not because I feel the need to defend myself against Charlotte, but because finding a weapon is what one should do when one feels uneasy.

A group of children scamper past, their dark shoes *click-click-clacking* against the cobblestones, and an old woman crows as she plants a black soldier's hat on her own head. These laughs, these drums, each and every out-of-tune drunkard singing is enough to make me want to run from the lot of them, shrieking. Where are my corners, my dark alleyways, my tunnels far, far below ground? Oh, to enjoy the savory sound of nothing but a furry little rat gnawing on a bone ever so quietly.

"Who might this be?" a young man asks, stepping up to Charlotte in her purple travesty.

To be clear, I had not realized that Charlotte was in fact with a gentleman. But of course she is. She's always on the hunt for the male species. His long, narrow nose and face mirrors the shape of *mon papa*'s, but his dark, wind-swept hair and splash of blue energy in his gaze suggest that he might be somewhat interesting. The red cravat dangling from his neck implies he's a commoner, but the way he holds himself and the careful articulation of his words means he's enjoyed a higher schooling.

A member of the bourgeois, just like *mon papa*. Just like I'm supposed to be.

The young man quirks a brow as he studies my clothing, so I level him with my gaze. "I've decided to save a few *sous* in lieu of my outfitting."

He laughs, carefree and throaty. "So I see," he says far too cheerily, like he believes there's a God, but I've long decided that if there is, he doesn't reside in this city.

I expect Charlotte to assign me an insult before pulling the young man away, but instead she cordially extends a ring-clad hand, which mystifies me. "Tempeste, meet my— meet Louis."

Before I have time to dissect why my former friend is actually being civil, Louis thrusts out his hand.

"It's Saint-Just." He winks, correcting Charlotte. "No one actually calls me Louis."

Tentatively, I accept Saint-Just's hand, my chapped fingers betraying what the elements have done to me. It's only the briefest of moments that I enjoy the smooth feel of the ruffles of his sleeve before I remember what "gentlemen" tend to do to girls like me, and I jerk my hand away.

"Tempeste," Charlotte says, laughing at my blunder, "is from another lifetime. If my memory serves me, I would say she's in the throes of rebelling."

I spread my teeth to arrange my lips into a smile but find myself grimacing instead. Who is she to say that she still knows me? It's been a year since I left the convent for the second time. People change, and daily. Am I still disenfranchised with *mon papa*? True. *Do I want to stick a pitchfork in his eye? Oui.* But that doesn't mean—

"Did someone say something about rebelling?" Saint-Just's olive-toned skin contrasts with his blinding white teeth. Only his dark blue eyes are not on Charlotte's. They're on me. Scouring. Like he, too, can unfold my darkest secrets, my carefully tucked away memories. "And whom might you be rebelling from, mademoiselle? If you don't mind my asking."

Automatically, I look to Charlotte, remembering the long nights we discussed my falling out with *mon papa*. How he had the power to stop Maman's execution, but Papa claimed that admitting our connection to Maman would, heaven forbid, soil our name.

Who am I rebelling from? I take a deep breath, burying my partial madness the way I always do when I speak. I offer Charlotte's friend the most sincere answer I can. "Someone close to me."

Saint-Just frowns, transforming his otherwise pleasant face. "You hate him?"

I fight the urge to shout a few obscenities. "If we weren't related, I'd shove an apple in his trap and pig-roast him already."

Saint-Just lifts his face to the sky, shaking. At first I think he might be suffering from convulsions, but then I see the smile tearing open his oval face. He's laughing at me. "You have suffered," he says, calming his breathing, "but to make a point. Tell me, Tempeste, do you miss your mama, *ta maman*, so terribly?"

Heat flares like a wildfire inside me. How—how could Charlotte tell him about Maman? Can no one see that she needed our protection, that her life was *far* more important than Papa's need to ensure whom I would marry?

"You are a prodigy," Saint-Just is saying, but I could drop-kick him in the knees. "I believe in a proactive people, and you are the very essence of what many of us are trying to be. You choose to abandon the comforts of home to honor her life. To put it quite simply, Tempeste, you inspire me."

Anger? It deflates like one of those silly hot air balloons I sometimes see flying over the city. How long has it been since someone has understood why I left in the first place? Has anyone ever understood?

All I can do is stare at him, stupidly.

Training one wary eye on me, Saint-Just gingerly takes my hand in his own, and feeling the cool material of his bone-made ring against my fingers, I force myself not to dash away like a spooked rabbit.

"Before you return to your papa," Saint-Just says softly, "think of what difference you can make." He squeezes my fingers, which buzz like a colony of bees. "Settle a score. Fulfill a debt." My heart ricochets against my rib cage. "Make a difference."

As soon as he releases my hand, everything spins wildly. A fountain a few paces off and the blur of blue, red, and white flags flutter in my periphery. My, if Charlotte hasn't met a young man with a little more substance than knee breeches and cuff-links.

But he is right. He speaks so clearly. What improvements in the world have I made these past few years? I've stood up for my convictions and refused *mon papa's* expensive gowns and jewelry, but beyond that—nothing. Might I live in such a way that my words, my actions might reflect who Maman, if she were still alive, would be?

Cheers break out from the crowd, and the final tumbrel is just now approaching. In the back of my mind, I know that it's him—the young executioner who caused Maman so much pain that day—and as quick as a flash, I can see her red dress falling so low that her breasts are fully exposed, and how he tried to snap her neck so that her hanging was quick and painless but *he misses time and again and she cannot breathe and my chest is screaming for oxygen because she's lifting her shoulders like it might help! help! she isn't breathing.*

His dark hooded eyes survey the square, like a hawk sniffing out a foundling. It's been months since I've watched him from the shadows, imagining ways to help him "slip" and fall prey to the Killing Machine. But a score of soldiers already flank the bottom of the stairs, guarding against overzealous onlookers, muskets ready.

Is it possible? To "settle a score, fulfill a debt, make a

difference"? What about now? I'm licking my lips. I itch to act quickly.

The ghoul jumps from the front of the cart to tie the horse's reins to a lamppost in the square. He's actually close enough for me to spot a dimple working in his cheek, which—how can he be smiling? Doesn't he consider the life he will soon take? My teeth are grinding so hard that a tendon in my neck pops loudly. I'll grab him by the hair, lay out the times I've watched him force a prisoner to drink an entire bucketful of water as the poor wretch sputtered, drowning. *Maybe I'll do that to you,* I'll say, *only with your* maman *watching.* I'll remind him of the time he took a club to a brittle old man tied to a wheel and smashed apart his bones like they were bits of glass in need of pulverizing. *What if I smash apart* your *bones, bourreau? Make a necklace out of the most fetching pieces for your grandparents?*

It's like I've just been launched atop the highest mountain overlooking the widest valley. The sun is fair; the sky is clear. Even the poppies are in bloom, which always have me sneezing. Now, what is it Saint-Just just said?

Settle a score. Fulfill a debt. Make a difference.

I have found my trajectory.

Gripping my knife, I fly past a braying goat, through a wad of children sticking a rodent's head into a toy Killing Machine, and pause only when the tumbrel is at my feet. *This this is it.* I run my thumb along the edge of the blade, drawing blood just to know the sharp sensation he'll soon be feeling. Should I go for a foot or gouge out an eye so that he resembles a pirate, giving him nothing to work for but treasure and whiskey?

As he nudges the prisoner forward, I tense to plant my knife just below the wrist so that he can never again execute another innocent person, but as I lift my arm a fraction of an inch, the strangest thing happens.

My resolve weakens. Literally, I freeze.

Why is it so hard to hurt this one? I am not one to shy away from enacting justice. He deserves this action far more than the butcher whose nose I helped relocate when he refused me his last scrap of meat.

But the bourreau's already walking past me—his shoulders back, his chin held high, marked off by twin sideburns—and it amazes me that he doesn't notice my indecision, that he doesn't even know my name.

So I gather all the recesses of saliva in my mouth and spit upon the fiend.

It is far less impressive than blood spurting from his hand like a geyser, or crimson droplets running down his nose, peacefully. Even so, my chest swells with pride, for my saliva has found its mark: prime center upon his dimpled cheek.

Slowly, as though he's suffered from a heavy dosage of brain softening, the young executioner bows his head to me. I expect him to growl, *Piss off, hussy.* Instead, he raises two round, sorrowful eyes—doe eyes. I grit my teeth as he says, *"Je suis désolé pour tous vos soucis."* I am sorry for your pain.

He doesn't even bother to wipe the spit with his sleeve, but keeps it there like a damned metal or trophy. These imperious, narcissistic Frenchies. They assume every feminine gesture symbolizes a girl's love for them in some way. His hooded eyes turn downward like he's truly suffering, and his broad shoulders slump like all he wants to do is mock me. Anger twists in my stomach because he's not supposed to feign an apology.

We're supposed to fight, have a brawl, sever a limb or something. But now all I know is my heart is flopped sideways like a dead fish tossed out of the sea. And as I look past the white bonnets, red caps, the black soldiers' hats clogging the square, my eyes snag on a red cravat and a pale lavender gown—Saint-Just and Charlotte beaming at me.

I should be proud that I have finally made my point (albeit, not quite as dramatically as I first dreamed) but the brute pretended to know who I was, pretended to feel guilty! He's one of those crows that pecked and pecked and *wouldn't stop pecking at Maman's eyes—two black holes swallowing.*

The crowd's chatter quickens; a soldier's found his drum and has begun pounding. As I look high at our weapon with its white, flowered wreath, my pulse slams in my neck, strangling me.

Everything is quiet. The hairs on my arms stand up straight like infantry. I should be running to Charlotte and Saint-Just, bracing for the rich sound of metal sliding on metal before the blade severs head from spine. But I do not get to cheer nor gloat nor bray for our new grand weapon; nor do I get to enjoy the speed at which my heart is racing. For all I can hear is the short, candid reproof of my one true ally.

Do not hold onto your anger, Tempeste.

But without my anger, dear friend, I have nothing.

Continue reading at your favorite retailer online.

www.ingramcontent.com/pod-product-compliance
Lightning Source LLC
Chambersburg PA
CBHW071132180726
48291CB00007B/2145